BITTERSWEET

Mishawaka - Penn Public Library
Mishawaka, Indiana

GAYLORD M

*Also by Emily Toll
in Large Print:*

Murder Will Travel

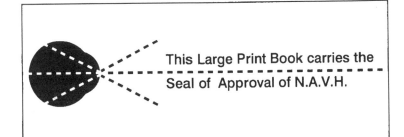

MURDER
Pans Out

Emily Toll

WHEELER
PUBLISHING

Mishawaka-Penn-Harris
Public Library
Mishawaka, Indiana

Published in 2004 by arrangement with The Berkley Publishing
Group, a member of Penguin Group (USA) Inc.

Wheeler Large Print Cozy Mystery.

The text of this Large Print edition is unabridged.
Other aspects of the book may vary from the original edition.

Set in 16 pt. Plantin by Minnie B. Raven.

Printed in the United States on permanent paper.

Library of Congress Cataloging-in-Publication Data

Toll, Emily.
    Murder pans out / Emily Toll.
        p. cm.
    ISBN 1-58724-653-8 (lg. print : sc : alk. paper)
    1. Women detectives — California — San Diego —
Fiction.   2. Tour guides (Persons) — Fiction.   3. San
Diego (Calif.) — Fiction.   4. Heritage tourism — Fiction.
5. Women travelers — Fiction.   6. Large type books.
I. Title.
PS3553.A5295M86 2004
    813'.6—dc22   2004041781

*For Carol Weise Herrera
and for
Peggy Parrish, Marsha Carney,
Jan Wilber, Kelley Ebel,
Larry Ainsworth, Jan Christinson,
Margie Balderrama, and Pam Pritchard
with appreciation and gratitude*

As the Founder/CEO of NAVH, the only national health agency solely devoted to those who, although not totally blind, have an eye disease which could lead to serious visual impairment, I am pleased to recognize Thorndike Press* as one of the leading publishers in the large print field.

Founded in 1954 in San Francisco to prepare large print textbooks for partially seeing children, NAVH became the pioneer and standard setting agency in the preparation of large type.

Today, those publishers who meet our standards carry the prestigious "Seal of Approval" indicating high quality large print. We are delighted that Thorndike Press is one of the publishers whose titles meet these standards. We are also pleased to recognize the significant contribution Thorndike Press is making in this important and growing field.

Lorraine H. Marchi, L.H.D.
Founder/CEO
NAVH

* Thorndike Press encompasses the following imprints: Thorndike, Wheeler, Walker and Large Pr int Press.

Acknowledgments

For providing specific information, often at a moment's notice, I'm grateful to Elizabeth Anderson, Joan Bray, Chris Durnan, Doris Ann Norris, Verna Suit, Brian Swanson, Penny Warner, Egon Weiss, and Elaine Yamaguchi.

Weapons information was supplied by Captain Dale Stockton of the Carlsbad Police Department, Detective Red Songer of the Glendale Police Department Robbery/Homicide Division, retired, and C. J. Songer, girl gunslinger.

The Scary Stories are an amalgam of tales recounted by two special online families and a number of other friends. Thanks to: Letha Albright, Donna Andrews, Beverly Bayer, Wendy Birkhan, Rhys Bowen, MarySue Carl, Dana Carvalho, Chris Durnan, Sally Fellows, Anne Gallagher, Julie Wray Herman, Beth Hulsart, Maria Lima, Sally Lynch, Susan McBride, Betty McBroom, Holly Moyer, Chris Roman, Stephanie Shea, Vivian Sternbridge, Pam Thomsen, Pat Tracy, Theresa Walker, Dina Willner, and Jenn Woolf. While gratitude would probably be inaccurate here, I'd like to acknowledge Chris Cannon, DVM, for her role in the tale of the gerbil.

I'm grateful for the continuing support and

enthusiasm of my editor, Martha Bushko, and my agent, Jane Chelius.

And I couldn't do anything at all without Bill and Melissa Kamenjarin, who understand what I do, know how crazy it makes me, and love and support me anyway.

Gold Country Crossword Clues

Across

1. Country of origin for most 49ers
4. River where first gold was found
9. Dame Shirley's husband's occupation
12. Seeing the __
15. *By the Great Horned Spoon* author, first name
16. __ Pacific Railroad
17. __ Hopkins, merchant turned hotelier
18. What Jenny Wimmer boiled in lye
19. __ Rock, site of first English graffiti
23. At center of vigilante seal
24. Transcontinental one finished 1869
25. Copper bit used in Strauss's canvas pants
26. Assayman in Nevada City
27. Lola's stage makeup
29. Judge who ruled against hydraulic mining, 1884
30. Major strike
32. Tri-branched mining river
34. Bar in cradle, etc. to catch gold
35. First gold found in fish "soup"
39. __ Valley, site of Empire Mine
41. Killer stretch in Nevada on overland route
43. Visitor to Roaring Camp
45. Periodic table name for gold

46. Sixty __, potent liquor
47. Fort and mill owner
48. Rock containing minerals
49. Tom __, doctor turned gambler
    turned robber
50. Loose rough dirt
52. Nickname for goldseekers
54. __ Camp, site of formal battles
55. Mining method using water
56. Long __, 12-foot mining trough
57. Disease on overland trail
58. __ Angeles
60. Business partner to Wells
61. Leland __, grocer
64. Group fighting in 54-Across
66. Dugout canoe used to cross isthmus
68. Hydraulic mining diggins
70. Heavenly camp
72. Town started by Irish brothers
75. Periodic table iron name
77. Dire straits for sailors
80. First miner in Quartz, married
    a Donner
81. Donner __, snowbound site
83. Rich __, Dame Shirley's home
84. Chinese Golden Mountain
87. Gem of the Southern Mines
88. Type of weight for gold
89. Nickname for Jamestown
90. Spider Dance performer
91. Scratches out a living
93. __ Dorado

94. Rock found with gold
96. Most common mining town meat
102. Used to fight bulls
103. Charley Parkhurst's pronoun
104. Odd Fellows abbr.
105. Type of gold
106. Dandy mining camp reporter
107. Inclined water trough
108. Black Bart's specialty

Down
2. Search for
3. Placerville wheelbarrow maker
5. "Nozzle" in hydraulic mining
6. Rare formal pathway
7. Less glamorous mineral
8. Hottest hour for mining
9. Common animal transport
10. Forty-__
11. Bandit Murietta
13. Used to lead 9-Down
14. General mining lifestyle
20. Name for mining town
21. Rock the __, mining tool
22. Original name of North Bloomfield
28. Rough __ Ready
31. Enticement to go west
32. Original name of San Francisco
33. __ Trees Calaveras Park
36. Condition of placer miner
37. Honorific for Louise Clappe

38. Filled Marysville Streets before
    1884 ruling
40. Forty-niners' expectations
41. Typical miner abode
42. Author of first report of finding gold
43. Spread word of gold through
    SF newspaper, *The Star*
44. Revolutionized trousers
48. Tinned ingredient in 74-Down
51. __ Grande
52. SF theater
53. Mining town milk source
55. Lucy Whipple's specialty
57. Shopkeeper turned railroad tycoon
58. __ tom, mining tool
59. Staging town for northern mines
61. Series of attached riffle boxes
    with continuous water flow
62. Shortcut country for sailing Argonauts
63. Yan __, Chinese Camp tong
65. Emigrant __
67. Fellows in IOOF
69. Scourge of mining towns
71. Assent in Sonora
72. Disease contracted crossing 62-Down
73. Jewelry formed from gold
74. Luxury dish cooked in Placerville,
    2 words
75. Avian river
76. Preferred over alcohol by Chinese
78. Ran Placerville meat market
79. __ Toy, Cantonese prostitute in SF

82. Mining town dame
85. Indian tribe
86. First woman hanged in California
92. Mindset of 49ers on arrival
94. Chinese pigtail
95. __ Mountain overlooks Jamestown
97. Formerly Spanish Corral
98. Turns ore into coins
99. Unit of gold measurement, abbr.
100. __ Hill, site of Chilean and
    French wars
101. Mother __

Gold Country Crossword Puzzle

created by Susi Braun
with some help from Emily Toll

Prologue

The intruder froze at an unexpected sound coming from the next room. A minor crash of some sort, accompanied by a kind of rustle.

Nobody was supposed to be here now. That was the whole point.

What to do?

The tasks weren't finished, but being interrupted in the middle of them would be catastrophic for the plan, even worse than not being able to complete them at all. Had every right to be here, technically, but secrecy was important. And it might not be possible to return in time to conclude the job. Time was a definite factor here.

Listen.

Silence.

Listen some more.

Best to check things out? There was no room for mistakes in this project, no margin of error.

But then a tabby cat sauntered past, coming from the direction of the recent sounds, oblivious to the intruder's presence. The intruder breathed deeply to calm a racing heart and thought for a moment, then swiftly moved through the doorway that the cat had emerged from. A pile of papers and a remote control lay scattered on the floor, knocked off a table.

False alarm.

The intruder returned to the chores at hand, moving with renewed speed and urgency. The most difficult of today's operations had been taken care of first. It usually made more sense to work up to the tougher parts of a project, but this one was a little tricky, and far too important to wait on. The discreet alteration to the equipment had taken longer than expected, but it formed the cornerstone of the plan and was therefore time well spent.

The intruder moved now to another room, opened a cabinet, removed a bottle, and made a speedy substitution. Gloved fingers worked swiftly and methodically.

Only one task remained, and the intruder set about it with patience and enthusiasm. When the job was finished and the final item on the mental checklist ticked off, the intruder checked one last time to be sure nothing had been disturbed that might call attention to these various activities.

All clear.

All safe.

The intruder sighed deeply, feeling the innate satisfaction of a job well done, a task neatly executed.

Executed. That warranted a little chuckle, a recognition of irony.

Bon voyage.

Chapter 1

They'd covered four hundred miles on the road to gold country when the red light on the dashboard began to flash.

It didn't flash, actually, just emitted a steady, persistent glow. It was a glow that definitely wasn't supposed to be there, and ignoring it for a couple of minutes didn't make it go away. What's more, the little needle that monitored engine heat was hovering dangerously near the red zone.

Lynne Montgomery, driving the Booked for Travel van, switched off the air-conditioning and the tape player, stranding Linda Ronstandt somewhere between Tucson and Tucamcari.

"Something's going on with the engine," she announced. "I've got a warning light and I'm pulling off at the next exit." She'd seen a sign for Midvale not long ago, and with luck they could limp along till they reached it.

Beside her, Betsy Danforth craned her neck to view the dashboard. "Overheating? Guess that's not too much of a surprise." Betsy was generally pretty unflappable, as befit somebody who'd taught grade school for nearly three decades, currently at Pettigrew Elementary in Floritas, California. But she'd also been imperturbable as an adolescent, when

Lynne had first known her. Betsy was her oldest friend on earth. She wore her silver-blond hair short and sleek and did daily yoga to maintain a trim, limber body.

"The last temperature sign I saw, on some bank in Stockton, said it was a hundred and seven," Lynne noted. "The San Joaquin Valley's a real killer in summer."

"Not much fun any time of year, actually," Betsy said.

Even on Highway 99, the older and more historic route north through California's Central Valley, everything was hot and flat and dusty. Major cities passed in a blur of car dealerships filled with SUVs and pickup trucks, and rural areas offered only the occasional grain elevator or pallet company. Everything was on a vast scale, however. This bleak landscape produced much of California's agricultural bounty, and California led the nation in agridollars, top producer of just about everything but cotton and tobacco. The only scenic relief came from hundreds of miles of graceful oleanders in a full palate of pinks and whites, lining the Highway 99 median and hiding opposing traffic.

As the needle continued to creep into the red, Lynne slowed to 55. "I hate car trouble," she said. "It always makes me feel so spectacularly incompetent."

Betsy nodded sympathetically. "It's the part where they call me 'little lady' that always gets my blood boiling."

"I guess I was lucky that I didn't have to deal with it at all for so long." Lynne knew Betsy understood her reference. Her husband, Monty, had always taken care of their cars, and since his death she'd become totally reliant on the kindness of strangers. The local Floritas mechanics patronized and overcharged her, but at least they kept the van and her bright blue VW Beetle alive and running. "But it's always worse when you're on the road. It's like automotive potluck."

Betsy laughed. "Yeah. And every dish is tuna casserole."

The welcome green-and-white sign announcing the Midvale exit appeared and up ahead Lynne could see the towering logo of a major chain gas station. She could not remember ever hearing of Midvale before, unless maybe that was the town Janet Leigh had been trying to reach in *Psycho*. She crossed her fingers that the station would provide, along with pork rinds and cheese puffs and eighty-three kinds of carbonated beverage, at least minimal auto service.

"What kind of light is it?" Betsy asked.

"Red," Lynne answered dryly. "I think it's the all-purpose your-engine's-screwed-up light. But we'll soon find out." As she drove down the exit ramp, she scanned the horizon for a town, but Midvale was either well off Highway 99 or a figment of the signmaker's imagination. The gas station had two cars at the pumps, a couple of trailers parked behind it, and a pair of frame buildings tucked off to the side in a lonely-looking grove of shade trees. Other than that, there was nothing on the horizon but the freeway, fields of tomatoes, and a distant orchard.

Lynne coasted into the gas station and parked outside a service bay that actually had a man working inside. Beyond the open door, he was bent over the engine compartment of a dusty black pickup truck. She closed her eyes for a moment, took a deep breath, and then switched off the ignition.

In the few minutes since she'd turned off the air-conditioning, the interior of the van had warmed up significantly. Still it was a shock to step out into the afternoon sun, rather like walking into a blast furnace.

Betsy hurried inside in search of a bathroom and Lynne approached the mechanic, who looked up and lifted the front of a grease-streaked gray T-shirt to wipe a sheet of sweat off his forehead.

"Help you?" he asked. He was lean and sunbaked, maybe forty, with a workingman's tan that didn't include his pale belly. Nobody was ever going to get his jeans clean again.

Lynne described the problem and the mechanic frowned, with that annoying air of automotive superiority that so often accompanies the Y chromosome. "I can look, sure.

But it'll be too hot to work on right away, even if it's something easy. And if it isn't, you'll need to get towed over to Lodi, or maybe even down to Stockton."

A long-forgotten song lyric danced through Lynne's mind, something about being stuck outside of Lodi, again. She'd never before appreciated the desolation that lyric suggested, but if the experience in any way resembled this one, once would be more than enough.

The mechanic followed her outside and popped the hood, still wearing the frown. He used a rag to open the radiator, which gushed and spat. As he poked around the engine compartment, Lynne fought a feeling of helplessness. They were supposed to meet up with two other carloads of teachers in the next few hours in Nevada City, in the northern part of California's Gold Rush country. Thus would officially begin the Highway 49 Revisited tour that Lynne had developed for the group.

This was a much more flexible and casual tour than the ones Lynne usually led, consisting entirely of Floritas schoolteachers, several of whom were her old friends. It was, in fact, the travel agency equivalent of pro bono legal work. Still, they were counting on her, and she was carrying all of the communal food and drink in the van. It would be an enormous complication if she had to stay over to deal with a major engine problem.

And in Lodi, at that.

The mechanic looked up and for the first time he offered a smile. His teeth were dazzlingly white against his deep mahogany tan. Obviously nobody's ever told this guy about melanomas. "Just a broken fan belt, ma'am."

As Lynne exhaled, she realized for the first time how upset she had been. It was one thing to be *able* to deal with most of the difficulties life dealt you, and another altogether to *have* to deal with them.

"Can you fix it?"

He nodded. "I've got the right-sized belt, but first I need to finish up what I'm doing here. Your engine's gonna have to cool down anyway." He waved a hand to the right. "There's a little restaurant and antique shop over there, if you want to wait someplace cool. It's a bit warm out here."

A bit warm indeed. A thermometer on the shaded wall of the garage read 111 degrees. Betsy emerged from the minimart, holding two water bottles frosted by sudden exposure to the heat. She handed one to Lynne, who uncapped it and took a long swig. The icy water poured down her gullet with a jolt she could feel down to her toes.

"It's a broken fan belt," Lynne explained, "and this nice young man says he can fix it as soon as the engine cools down. But we've got a bit of a wait, I'm afraid."

The mechanic nodded at Betsy. "Probably an hour, anyways. I was telling your friend you might want to grab a bite or something." He pointed to the two frame buildings huddled beneath the shade trees. The sign in front of one announced PIZZA AND TACOS and the other read LEDBETTER ANTIQUES — FINE COLLECTIBLES.

"I know where I'll be," Betsy said with a grin. During the years when she followed her husband's naval career around the globe, Betsy's possessions had been limited. Now that he was retired and they'd settled in Floritas, she had unexpectedly become a collector of almost everything. Her house was a cluttered mélange of oddball curiosities, fifties and sixties retro kitchen appliances, and the occasional genuinely attractive piece of old furniture. She held two garage sales of her own each year, just to keep pace with the constant influx.

Lynne sighed. "Might as well join you. Nothing I can do here other than sweat."

Ledbetter Antiques, beneath the canopy of native oaks, was cool and inviting, and when Lynne and Betsy first entered, appeared empty. Then a woman in her early twenties rose out of a tapestry-upholstered chair with atrocious carved griffin feet. She wore a perky little pink-and-white polka dot mini-dress and chunky pink sandals, with a lot of long tanned leg in between. Her sun-bleached hair was gathered in two pigtails over her ears, and the overall effect brought to mind Minnie Mouse.

"Hi," she chirped. The voice was Minnie, too. "Can I help you?"

"We're waiting while our car's being fixed," Lynne explained.

Betsy began a systematic inspection of the shop, in an exploratory pattern Lynne had witnessed countless times. First she stood absolutely still just inside the doorway, her eyes scanning the layout and identifying areas of particular interest. Then she began a leisurely and nonchalant circuit, careful not to reveal too quickly which items interested her.

Apart from the chair the girl had been sitting in, there weren't many large pieces of furniture in the shop. Ledbetter Antiques seemed to specialize in china and glassware, with an excellent assortment of Depression glass and an enormous collection of ceramic plates featuring painted views of Yosemite. The store's aisles were formed by breakfronts and hutches and bookshelves, all loaded down with collectibles. Lynne examined three shelves of salt and pepper shakers, shook her head over a hutch filled with rather unattractive porcelain birds, then began flipping through a bin of overpriced old *Life* magazines. An hour was going to be a very long time in this place.

"Oh, wow!" Betsy's voice came from a back corner. "Look at this!"

Betsy stood gazing reverently at a Victorian table lamp with a large bronze base and a spectacularly fringed shade. Lynne's first reaction was that she'd never seen Betsy tip her hand so quickly in an antique shop. Her second was that it was the ugliest lamp she'd ever seen.

"How . . . interesting." Lynne kept her tone polite and guarded. "Very nice."

"No, it isn't *nice*," Betsy told her with a cheerful grin. "It's ugly as sin. But it's exactly like the one that my grandmother had in her house in Ohio that burned down. I remember playing with the fringe on the shade and getting yelled at for turning the bulbs on and off." She pulled a little chain. Nothing happened. "Oops, it's unplugged."

Lynne looked around, then pointed. "There's a socket here, Bets."

Betsy picked the lamp up and carried it over. "Heavy sucker." She plugged it in and pulled the chain again. Still nothing. She shrugged. "Guess I'll have to rewire it."

"You're going to *buy* that?" Lynne heard her incredulous tone too late.

Betsy offered an incandescent smile. "I sure am. Even though it costs more than the monthly mortgage payment on our first house. But hey, what's the point of being a grown-up if you can't do something irrespon-

27

sible now and then?"

Lynne chuckled, glad that her friend hadn't taken offense. "You want to grab a slice of pizza after you pay for that? We probably have another half hour at least before the van is ready."

Judith Limone knew they'd made excellent time, leaving Floritas promptly at seven, sailing through Los Angeles on deserted Sunday morning freeways, gliding up Interstate 5 at precisely the speed limit. Punctuality and rules both mattered enormously to Judith, and the fact that this was a vacation was entirely irrelevant.

As principal of Pettigrew Elementary, she had learned that if she expected the best possible performance from her staff, they would invariably deliver. Those who couldn't deliver didn't last, and those who could knew that Judith would back them up against anyone. She had once suspended the son of a state senator for foul language. When the senator stormed into Judith's office, she listened calmly and then, in her best Bryn Mawr tones, repeated the son's vulgarities to his father, verbatim.

"Are we there yet?" Lisa asked, picking up the AAA map and refolding it.

Judith looked over at her daughter in the front passenger seat and smiled. Lisa was a lovely young woman, everything Judith might have hoped for. That she'd become a teacher and moved back to Floritas after graduating from UC Davis was more than icing on the cake. It was icing and whipped cream and chopped pecans and a boatload of cherries.

"About another hour," Judith told her. Taking I-5, rather than the older, arguably more scenic Highway 99, had saved them some time, and the slowdown she'd feared going through Sacramento hadn't occurred. "It'll be slower once we're off the freeway, of course."

"Isn't that the point?" Lisa asked. She twisted and stretched, arching her bare feet. Lisa was twenty-six, unattached, an avid environmentalist, and an eighth grade history teacher at Floritas Junior High. "Are you sure you don't want me to drive?"

"Positive." Judith glanced over her shoulder into the roomy back seat of the full-sized Buick. "You feeling any better, Mandy?"

In the back seat, Mandy Mosher offered a little moan. "Fine, thanks."

"Did you manage to get any sleep?" Judith was fairly certain that Mandy was pregnant again, and her older boy was only going to be starting kindergarten this fall. Mandy had said many times that she wished she'd taken more time off when her babies were born and Judith hated the idea of losing her even for a few months. Mandy wasn't just a wonderful primary grade teacher. She was also one of Judith's former fourth grade students and the only Pettigrew alumna ever to join the school's faculty. Having Mandy around was a constant reminder of what teaching was all about. It was also a great deal of fun.

Mandy sighed. "Oh yeah. I've slept plenty. I've been pretty much conked out since Bakersfield."

Lisa turned around. "I tried to wake you up when we stopped for lunch and you said you weren't hungry."

"I did?" Mandy giggled and slapped an ample thigh. "I guess missing a meal won't kill me. Hey, this is pretty territory up here. Are we almost there?"

Lisa laughed. "That's *my* line. And I think that we're coming up to the Highway 49 cutoff any minute now."

Chapter 2

Nikki Mason had gotten up at five this morning so she could sneak a five-mile run in before packing the Expedition and picking up Marianne and Susi. A native of East Texas, Nikki had always begun her days with rigorous early morning exercise, timed to avoid the worst of the broiling summer sun. Transplanted to coastal Southern California, she no longer needed to worry about heat prostration, but the habit lingered. There was nothing like a good jolt of endorphins to get a day off to the right start.

Right now, however, that run seemed an eternity ago, and she was starting to feel downright sluggish. Spending an entire day behind the wheel, even in as good a cause as this one, seemed a tremendous waste of time. Back in the planning stages of the trip, she'd argued for driving up at night and been voted down by the others.

Well, maybe they weren't entirely wrong. Nikki was a high-energy woman, but even she required the physical recharge of a couple of good nights of sleep. Classes had officially ended at noon on Thursday, with teachers' meetings all day Friday, and the final weeks of school had been chaotic. Summer vacation hadn't come a moment too soon for Nikki.

"We need to check on when the rivers are running after we get up there," Marianne Gordon said from the front passenger seat. Marianne, who taught U.S. and California history at Floritas High, was the only other genuine outdoorswoman on the tour. She was a tall, strong woman with hazel eyes, an unruly mop of reddish curls, and great legs. Apart from the hair, Marianne had the look that Nikki had always yearned for. "Susi, I think you oughta go white-water rafting with us."

Susi Braun, in the back seat, gave a little squeal of horror. "No way. You two can do all the jolly woodsman stuff you want, but I'm sleeping in real beds and staying on terra firma."

Nikki looked into the rearview mirror. Susi had been reading most of the way, one of those grim Oprah books that made you want to open a vein. "It'll be fun," she coaxed. "At least consider it."

Too late Nikki wondered why she was encouraging Susi to join them. Nikki didn't know her all that well, and what she'd seen so far wasn't terribly exciting. Susi taught English at the high school, was usually overdressed, and was proving to be a bit of a whiner. Well, no matter. There was plenty to do and lots of others to do it with.

"I can't," Susi insisted. "I had that foot

surgery last month and I still have to be careful not to bang my feet or anything. You know, and rebreak the bones. I have very fragile bones."

Nikki glanced sideways and noticed Marianne rolling her eyes up in her head. It had been a real treat to discover that Marianne was the high school history teacher who'd been suggested as a possible group member when they began planning this trip last spring. Nikki religiously attended all Floritas High School football games, and had immediately recognized Marianne, who also held season tickets and cheered with sufficient abandon to give her honorary Texan status. And she'd been tickled beyond all reason to find that Marianne was also an avid outdoorswoman.

"It's okay, Susi," Nikki soothed. "Nobody's going to force you."

Susi sneezed. "Oh, man, my allergies are *really* acting up." She turned around and pulled a small duffle bag out of the rear. "Must be all this agriculture, or pesticides, or something. If I don't take an antihistamine, I'll get so puffed up I'll look like Miss Piggy."

Nikki kept her eyes on the road and tried not to go where that image wanted to take her. While not precisely fat, Susi was probably forty pounds overweight, and they were soft pounds. Her face was almost perfectly round and her brown hair was cut short, limply feathered around her face.

Nikki noticed Marianne, beside her, carefully inspecting her nails. They were beat-up, chewed, and featured several hangnails. This was not a manicure appraisal.

"Hey!" Susi's tone held alarm. "I can't find my meds bag. I know I had it this morning, when I was packing everything up."

"Maybe it's in your other bag," Nikki suggested mildly.

"Huh-uh. I had that one zipped up and by the door last night. I had this morning's pills set out on the counter and I never went into the bag at all this morning. Oh man, what am I going to do? We need to go back."

Susi had unbuckled her seat belt and knelt on the seat, rummaging through the luggage in the wayback. Nikki allowed herself a moment of private pleasure as she considered how Susi might react if she realized one of the locked cases she was banging around back there held Nikki's Winchester double-barrel shotgun.

Nikki glanced at the trip odometer. "We're four hundred seventy-nine miles from home, Susi. We can't go back."

"But what'll I *do?*" Panic laced Susi's voice. She punched up her cell phone, then groaned. "No reception. I can't even call home."

"How much of this is prescription drugs?"

Marianne asked calmly. She seemed to be taking this crisis in stride, and it was Marianne who knew Susi best, who had in fact brought her into the group. Marianne's current equanimity was reassuring, since they had at least another hour on the road and Susi seemed to be teetering on the brink of full-blown hysterics.

"Just for my blood pressure and cholesterol and allergies," Susi said, her voice still high-pitched and anxious. "But then there's all my vitamins and stuff, too. And my herbals. Maybe I can have Rick FedEx it."

Marianne laughed. "Why bother? Call your doctor's office in the morning and have them call in a script for a week's worth of the prescription stuff to a drugstore in Nevada City. And you can borrow the other vitamins from the rest of us." She rubbed her hands together twice in a gesture of finality and dismissal. "Now. What's the first thing everybody's going to do when we get there?"

"Set up camp," Nikki answered immediately, grateful for the change of subject. Nikki came from sturdy Texas German stock, stalwart men and women who often lived into their nineties without ever visiting a doctor. She took a single daily multivitamin when she remembered, which wasn't often. "It sounds like there's plenty of room for us right outside the cabins where the wimps are staying. And then I'm going for a hike in the woods."

"Sounds like a plan," Marianne answered. "It's way too long since I went camping."

Nikki reminded them which exit to watch for. "We're almost at Nevada City, guys. Lynne said that it's kind of confusing once we exit, because they put the freeway right through town and messed things up a bit." The sign she'd been waiting for appeared even as she spoke. "Eureka! We're here!"

Marianne read the directions and Nikki turned as instructed. In just a few minutes they were driving through thick woods toward a sign announcing the Murmuring Pines Cabins. Beyond the final turn, a cluster of frame buildings led off into the woods from a slightly larger frame building labeled OFFICE.

"You see any of the others yet?" Nikki asked. As far as Nikki could tell, neither Lynne's van nor Judith's sedan had arrived yet. In fact, there didn't seem to be any cars around at all, other than a black Toyota pickup parked beside the office. Where were the other customers? Lynne had told them the place had ten cabins, and Nikki could see the rustic buildings along the road winding uphill.

"Nope," said Susi, sounding peeved. "Guess that means we'll have to set things up. I was kind of hoping all the work would be done before we got here."

"Hey, *everybody's* hoping that," Marianne

told her with a grin. "But I think that Betsy and Lynne took care of almost everything that could really be called work. All we need to do is pitch our tents and open a bottle of wine. And you don't even have to pitch a tent, Susi."

"Amen," Susi muttered.

In the office they found a stout gray-haired woman in khaki shorts and a sleeveless blue shirt behind the desk, sitting in a comfortable chair with her bare feet on a big footstool, reading *Newsweek*. The office itself was warmly inviting, paneled in golden pine and featuring well-framed Ansel Adams prints. The woman got up as they walked in and greeted them.

"We're part of a group that has a reservation," Nikki said. "Under Montgomery, I think."

The woman smiled. She wore no makeup and was probably around sixty, one of those timeless, weathered women who seem so utterly at home in the California outback. "The Gold Rush teachers. Welcome to Nevada City. I think what you guys are doing really sounds like fun."

"So do we," Marianne told her. She waved an expansive hand at the open doorway and the woods beyond. "Running this place looks like it'd be pretty nice, too."

"It's a living," the woman said. Then she chuckled. "Well, not really. But it beats what

I was doing before. Once upon a time, I managed a bunch of strip malls in West L.A. I've been here six years now and I've almost forgotten the smell of smog. I'm Connie Caravaci." She extended a hand.

Nikki, Marianne, and Susi introduced themselves as they shook Connie's hand. Then Connie said, "I've got a message for you, as a matter of fact."

"What is it?" Nikki felt her heart race. What could have gone wrong already? The kids? Her sister-in-law had come out from Dallas to stay with nine-year-old Allison and seven-year-old Greg while Nikki was away. Her husband Larry often worked fifteen-hour days at his downtown San Diego law firm.

"Not to worry," Connie said hastily, noticing Nikki's agitation. "Lynne Montgomery called a while ago. Nice lady. She asked me to tell you that they had some car trouble and she'll be later getting in than she planned. That the rest of you should get settled and they'll be here as soon as they can."

Nikki felt relief flood through her. She felt a sudden, overwhelming urge to hear the voices of her children. Just before she'd left, Larry had presented her with a rented, state-of-the-art satellite cell phone hookup, the kind that you take along if you're climbing K2 or trekking across the polar ice caps. As nearly as she could tell, it cost a zillion dollars a minute, and even though Larry made a respectable living, Nikki had grown up poor. Habits of thrift die hard. "Are there phones in the cabins?"

Connie shook her head. "No, but there's a pay phone outside the office here. The old-fashioned kind that closes up, with a seat and a light and everything."

"Did Lynne say what happened?" Marianne asked.

"Nope, just car trouble. But she didn't sound too worried. Anyway, you all have the last four cabins down at the end of this road, and she said to tell you to pick whichever ones you wanted."

"Some of us are planning to camp," Nikki said. "Where's the campground?"

Connie offered a deep chuckle. "I wouldn't go so far as to call it a campground, exactly. It's more like a clearing in the woods, just past the last cabin. I don't normally do this, but I liked the sound of this trip so much I told Lynne I'd make a kind of exception for you all. You can camp in the clearing beyond the last cabin. And you've pretty much got the place to yourselves tonight. There's people in the two cabins over there" — she pointed past Susi at the first cabins on the road up the hill — "a family up for the weekend from San Francisco. But they're leaving in the morning. We do get some drop-in trade, but the next reservations aren't till Tuesday and those folks won't be getting in till late."

Nikki liked the sound of this. She loved to wake up out in the middle of nowhere, looking up through the screen of her tent at the first warmth of morning light, no sounds anywhere except from nature. Alone, ideally, and out in the desert, though she hadn't camped solo for years now. Having a family changed everything. Campground and car camping had crept into their lives once the kids became a factor. There was a lot to be said for running water and toilets.

Connie led them outside and pointed down the road. "Those are your four cabins down at the far end. How many of you all plan to camp?"

Marianne hooked a thumb at Nikki. "Just the two of us. The others are staying in the cabins."

"Sounds fine to me, however you want to do it. When you figure out who's where, could you let me know in case you get any calls and I have to come find you? I don't want to bother everybody else."

"Of course," Marianne told her.

"Now," Connie continued, "if you campers change your minds and decide you want to sleep inside, go ahead. No extra charges or anything." She smiled. "My late sister was a teacher and I know how pathetic your pay is. Anyway, go ahead and pitch your camp. Just be sure not to store any food outside, and I do mean *any*. The raccoons are particularly aggressive this season, and they're raising large families."

Nikki had noticed Susi shifting her weight irritably. Susi looked hot and uncomfortable, and when she brushed her sweaty bangs back off her forehead, they kind of stuck out straight, like a little boy's cowlick. Connie had a strong fan going in here, and the windows open, but no air-conditioning running. It was still mighty warm, even up here in the foothills of the Sierra, several thousand feet above the broiling San Joaquin Valley.

"I'd like my cabin keys now," Susi told Connie in a firm voice that probably cast terror into the hearts of unprepared Floritas high school students.

"Sure thing," Connie told her, unruffled. She pulled the keys for 7, 8, 9, and 10 off a board behind the desk. "Which cabin do you want?"

"Why don't you just give us the keys for all of them?" Susi suggested, holding out her hand. "We can sort out who's where later. Say, do you happen to know if there's a pharmacy in town?"

Connie raised one eyebrow. "Of course."

"Thank heavens." Susi launched into the tale of the mislaid medication bag. "I can't believe I was so stupid," she concluded finally, "but I guess it's not surprising considering how much communal gear each of us was bringing."

Nikki regarded Susi with interest. Not that it mattered, of course, but she'd packed Susi's belongings into the SUV herself, and as far as she was aware, the only communal materials that Susi had brought were photocopies of stories by Mark Twain and Bret Harte. And some kind of Gold Rush crossword puzzle she'd made up as a group contest. Susi was being ridiculously coy about the puzzle, making a big deal out of giving it to everybody at the same time.

As if anybody was going to want to *cheat* on a stupid crossword puzzle.

Half an hour later, Judith and Lisa Limone arrived with Mandy Mosher.

Marianne and Nikki had pitched their tents in a charming little grove and had unpacked most of the athletic equipment, stashing it in the cabin on the far end, closest to the tents. Marianne, finished first, had noticed Nikki surreptitiously stowing what looked like a violin case on a shelf in the unoccupied cabin closet, behind some extra blankets. They'd decided that this cabin, nearest to the fire ring, would serve as the group headquarters, giving everyone a place to eat and hang out without disturbing anybody's sleep or privacy. It would also provide easy bathroom access in the night for Nikki and Marianne.

Judith and Lisa, rooming together, selected the cabin farthest from the campfire, and began unpacking. Mandy settled into the cabin where Susi had already unpacked and chosen the bed closest to the bathroom.

Marianne and Nikki hiked back up into the woods above Murmuring Pines, then took turns at the pay phone by the office to check on their children. Marianne called her ex-husband's house first, not surprised when she got only his machine. At this point in the afternoon, the kids were almost certainly at the Del Mar Fair with Mark. She didn't much feel like talking to Mark, but it probably wouldn't be necessary. Briana had her own Barbie-pink cell phone and she never left home without it. Sure enough, her daughter picked up on the first ring, sounding altogether too sultry for an eighth grader.

"Hi, honey," Marianne said.

"Oh. It's you." Sultry instantly morphed into disappointed.

"Yep, it's me." Marianne might feel guilty about going on vacation for a week without her kids, but she was determined to do it on her own terms, not Briana's. "Are you at the fair?"

Mark's pool and spa business always rented space at the San Diego County Fair, held each June at the Del Mar fairgrounds, and these three weeks were enormously important to the business. He had not been pleased to learn that Marianne would be gone for a solid week of that period, even though he'd recently taken her to court trying to get joint custody. He didn't want to have the kids as much as he wanted not to pay child support, and he wanted not to pay child support so he'd have more money to gamble.

"Well, of course we're at the fair," Briana answered, her voice dripping ennui. "I can't do anything interesting this week, because you're gone."

This was well-trod ground, and Marianne refused to rise to the bait. "This place looks really cool. We're camping in a pine forest."

"Yippee."

Okay. So much for mother-daughter bonding. "Is your brother around?"

"Curt?" Briana's tone suggested that there might be some other, more interesting brother that her parents had neglected to mention.

Marianne had noticed, watching her friends' kids and her own students, that girls tended to have at least one really awful year during puberty. Briana, who had just turned thirteen, seemed to be plunging into hers right now. It had all the earmarks of a real train wreck. It was probably only a matter of weeks before she'd be standing in doorways screaming that she'd never asked to be born.

"Yes, Curt."

"Nope, he's not here. I think he went to the Midway."

"And where are you?" Marianne asked, determined to engage her daughter in some semblance of a conversation.

"Daddy's booth, which just might be the most boring place on earth. I hate the fair."

When the kids were little and Marianne and Mark still married, the whole family had spent days on end at the fair, entering goofy contests, eating corn dogs and cotton candy, lining up for Kiddyland rides. Back then Briana adored the livestock and they'd hung around the barns for hours, watching the 4-H kids shampoo their lambs and apply hairspray to the fluffed-out tails of their heifers.

"Daddy wants to talk to you. Bye."

"Talk to you soon," Marianne said, though she suspected that she wasn't even talking to her now. A moment later Mark picked up.

"Hi, honey," Mark said, with none of the acerbity Marianne had grown accustomed to since the divorce. In fact, now that she thought about it, he'd been exceptionally nice lately. "Are you having fun?"

As if he cared.

"So far everything's terrific," she told him, and she realized it was true.

After Marianne had headed up the hill toward the campground, Nikki called home herself. Larry's sister picked up on the second ring, assuring Nikki that everything was just fine. Her sister-in-law was childless, adored her niece and nephew, and was thrilled to come out from Dallas and stay with Allison and Greg while Nikki was away.

Nikki leaned back on the little seat against the glass wall of the phone booth, while her son announced that the guys were waiting for him outside, said, "Bye, Mom!," and was gone. Allison prattled on about the new Disney movie, which she'd just seen for the seventh time. Nikki had been along on three of those trips to the movie theater, sitting out in the lobby grading papers the last time, wondering how she'd ever get everything done in time to leave Sunday morning. Well, that took care of the Halloween costume question for this year, anyway. Allison was charmingly predictable. She'd been Jasmine and Snow White and Cinderella and Ariel and Belle and Sleeping Beauty and Pocahontas over the years. And Allison would be wonderfully cute as Genevieve, this latest Disney heroine.

"Okay, honey," Nikki told her finally, after the third time Allison explained how Genevieve had saved the day. "I probably ought to get going now."

"Are you using that special phone that Daddy got you?" Allison asked.

Nikki laughed. "Nope. That's only for when we're in places where we can't use a regular phone." Actually this wasn't precisely true, but it covered the situation. "I'm in a phone booth."

46

"What's that?" Allison asked.

Nikki was suddenly struck by how quickly the world had changed in her lifetime, how technology was accelerating even more rapidly in her daughter's. Feeling almost old, she explained what a phone booth was, describing the one where she sat now, but transported in her mind to the one outside Daddy's service station in Hillandale.

After she hung up, Nikki went back into the office to ask Connie which rivers were running when, emerging with maps and phone numbers and suggestions. By the time she returned to the top of the hill, Marianne had gathered kindling, and the two of them assembled a picture-perfect campfire, all ready to set ablaze. The light was angling through the evergreens now, still warm but not as fiercely unrelenting.

"Hey, here they come!" Marianne announced, looking up at the sound of an engine and pointing down the hill where the Booked for Travel van was parked by the office.

Nikki turned and looked down the hill toward the office, where Lynne and Betsy were climbing out of the van. "Cue the sound system," Nikki said.

Five minutes later, as Lynne and Betsy emerged from the van near the group's cabins, Marianne pushed the button on her boombox and the sound of a resonant baritone with an acoustic guitar filled the late afternoon air. He was singing one of the songs from the original gold rush:

> *In a cavern in a canyon, excavating for a mine*
> *Met a miner, forty-niner, and his daughter Clementine.*

Everyone spontaneously joined in the chorus, and the forest rang with the memory of darling Clementine.

This was, Nikki felt suddenly certain, going to be a lot of fun.

Chapter 3

"You did *what?*" Amos Ledbetter stared at Tiffany in stunned horror.

His dimwitted niece, oldest child of a sister who was none too bright herself and the Neanderthal with which she'd mated, flashed him a perky little smile. "I sold that gross lamp, Uncle Amos. You oughta be excited. That lady paid a ridiculous amount of money for it. I about peed my pants when I saw how much the price tag was."

Amos slowly collapsed into a faux-Chippendale chair and dropped his head into his hands. Killing Tiffany was not a solution here, though it was a definite temptation. He could hear her gum snapping all the way across the room.

How could this have gone so spectacularly wrong in such a short period of time? He'd been gone only a few hours, and now. . . . He couldn't think about what this meant. He couldn't strangle Tiffany. And at the moment, he could come up with no other plans. *Think,* you fool!

He raised his head and offered his numbskull niece what he hoped looked like a smile. "It's fine, Tiffany dear. Don't worry. But you see, I'd promised that lamp to a very special customer, and she'll be unbelievably disappointed when she learns you sold it. So the smartest thing we can do is track down the person who bought it and buy it back."

Tiffany put one hand on her hip and cocked her head. She looked like a character Gilda Radner might have played in an old *Saturday Night Live* skit called "The Morons." She snapped the gum a couple more times. "So, uh, does this mean I, like, lose my commission?"

Amos focused on his breathing. In, out, in, out, in, out. This wasn't the end of the world, after all. Though Jed might think otherwise. The very thought of Jed made him shudder.

Better to just think a little longer about strangling Tiffany. That was much more satisfying.

This was not turning out to be a very good day.

Betsy Danforth was having a terrific time.

The only tour member who currently taught fourth grade, with its Gold Rush curriculum, Betsy had come up with the idea for the trip and talked Lynne into coordinating it. She'd willingly assumed much of the advance prep work: making lists, planning menus, silk-screening T-shirts, and sewing cooling, polymer-filled neckbands for everyone.

As she stepped out on the porch of the communal cabin now, the first thing she noticed was that everyone had changed into their T-shirts, which featured a large irregular lump of gold and the legend ARGONAUTS. There was a bit of poetic license in this, of course. The original Argonauts hadn't been San Diego teachers, and hadn't very often been female, either.

They'd been male fortune hunters, sufficiently well heeled to afford passage on ships sailing from the East Coast clear around Cape Horn. Like the overland forty-niners who'd packed covered wagons and set out across the vast prairies and mountains and deserts of the American West, they'd been part of a frantic race to reach the inland rivers of California. There they expected to pluck gold nuggets by the handful from swiftly running streams.

These were guys in a hurry. Betsy, married thirty-three years to a man in such a hurry that the kids had to pee into bottles on road trips, could only imagine the Argonauts' frustration as their sailing ships sometimes sat becalmed for weeks out in the Pacific, waiting for just the right combination of winds to propel them into San Francisco Bay.

After landfall, many of those beautiful clippers had actually been left to rot in San Francisco Harbor, abandoned with the cargo

51

still loaded, as captains and crews raced passengers to the goldfields. The settlers and entrepreneurs who filled in San Francisco Bay worked around these ships, hastily constructing buildings in and around them. One of Betsy's favorite lithographs from that era showed two ships, reconfigured as a store and a hotel, tucked neatly among the more traditional boom-town buildings, along an unpaved thoroughfare.

Group spirits were high now among the latter-day Argonauts. Betsy was particularly pleased to see that Lynne seemed to have forgotten the irritating car trouble that had slowed them down on Highway 99. Once the fan belt was fixed, they'd made excellent time on the home stretch, and hadn't arrived all that far behind the others.

"Is somebody going to start the fire?" Betsy asked.

"Not me," Lynne called cheerfully from a colorful hammock she'd strung between two sturdy trees. She was reading a literary anthology called *Gold Rush* that she'd borrowed from Betsy. "But are you sure you want to do it so soon? Tonight's food is all stuff we can eat cold, or heat up on that little stove in there."

"I know," Betsy said. Lynne had spent much of yesterday cooking. She'd barbecued chicken, made potato salad, deviled eggs, and baked oatmeal-raisin cookies. "But can't we heat the chicken up over a fire? It'll seem all the more authentic."

Susi Braun stepped out of the cabin next door. "You could put some spiders in it to make it more authentic, too, but what's the point? Heat is heat."

"And a fire provides it just as readily as a propane stove," Betsy answered. She'd known Susi slightly over the years, and had never been too taken with the woman. In Susi Braun's world, there was only one starring role and everybody else was a minor walk-on. "Besides, you can't fix s'mores on a stove."

"Of course you can," Marianne said, looking up from a guidebook to gold country. "I made hundreds of s'mores on a stove when I was a kid in Wisconsin. An electric stove at that. Where there's a will, yada yada."

Nikki popped around the corner and snapped a few pictures with a cutting-edge digital camera. "Did somebody say 'fire'? I can start it anytime you want, Betsy."

Betsy stopped to think a minute. They probably still had several hours of good light, given that they'd gone so much farther north *and* that they were only three days from the summer solstice. Also nobody had claimed to be too terribly hungry on arrival. "We can wait," she agreed, "but could somebody clean off the picnic tables? I was going to bring out some chips and salsa."

Nikki — whose energy level would shame a pack of sugar-charged Cub Scouts — sprang to and she dashed inside the cabin and grabbed a wet rag, scrubbing the weathered wooden tables vigorously. Nikki had come to Pettigrew Elementary six years ago from Texas, arriving in a whirlwind of activity that had never once slowed. When Betsy team-taught with Nikki, she usually finished their joint projects with an overwhelming desire to go take a nap. Alas, this was rarely an option in the middle of an elementary school day.

Betsy went back inside the cabin, opened a beer, and poured tortilla chips into a large bowl. She carried them out to the picnic table — now clean and covered with a red-and-white-checked vinyl cloth — along with a Tupperware bowl of Lynne's famous salsa fresca, made from fresh tomatoes, peppers, onions, and cilantro.

In point of fact, Betsy thought as she took Lynne's salsa from the fridge, the group had brought sufficient provisions to stock an entire early Gold Rush town.

Though Judith had been too busy overseeing the end of the Pettigrew school year to do any cooking, she'd insisted on providing an assortment of salads from the grocery store deli. Lisa had bought a small cooler of breakfast pastries from the French bakery in downtown Floritas. Betsy had cut up bags full of raw veggies the night before, to go along with her signature spinach dip. Susi contributed a huge bag of bing cherries and a platter of brownies she'd been given by a grateful parent. Even taking Hardtack Day into account, they'd probably all put on a couple of pounds.

"I've got the crossword puzzles," Susi announced, stepping off the porch and waving a manila folder dramatically. At the first planning meeting back in April, Susi had claimed that she was far too busy to do any kind of advance scut work, which was, she implied, beneath her anyway. She had, however, volunteered to construct an original puzzle based on the historical Gold Rush and modern-day Gold Country.

Now she began moving around the group, passing out sheets. Betsy leaned over the porch railing to get hers and was impressed despite herself. It looked just like a real crossword puzzle, the kind you'd spend way too much time with on Sunday afternoon. Except that most newspaper crossword puzzles probably wouldn't have clues like 86-Down: "First woman hanged in California."

Three hours later, Lynne looked around the campfire, which was starting to collapse into itself. Like her, the others all sprawled contentedly in low-to-the-ground beach chairs. The night was dark, with almost no moon and an inky sky strewn with glittering stars. Cool breezes rustled the pines.

"I love this first week after school gets out," Marianne Gordon said. "It always feels like I have about six months before anything is going to happen again."

Lynne recalled how exhausted she had always felt at the end of any school year, merely as a parent. The teachers involved, she knew, were under enormous pressure to get everything done, and done well. Those who worked for Judith Limone — almost everybody here — had a particularly high standard to meet. Marianne and Nikki both had school-age children of their own, so they were getting hammered both ways.

"Unless you're teaching summer school," Susi said. She possessed a knack for finding the down side of any situation.

"Are you doing that this year?" Betsy asked.

"Well, no," Susi admitted. She speared yet another marshmallow and held it to the dying coals. The woman had a major sweet tooth and had been alternating brownies and s'mores for hours, washed down with Chardonnay. It was a wonder, Lynne thought, that she didn't weigh 400 pounds.

"My fantasy," Judith Limone said, "is to lock my office door on the last day of school and not go in there again until Labor Day."

Everyone laughed. Judith was the first to arrive at Pettigrew Elementary each morning and the last to leave each night. She also worked most of the summer, even the parts she wasn't paid for.

"Uh, Judith," Betsy said, "not to get into shop talk or anything, but I couldn't help being aware that the Tarantino twins are going into fourth grade." Betsy taught fourth grade. "You *are* going to split them up, aren't you?"

Lynne watched with interest as a shiver seemed to pass among the elementary school teachers. She had no idea who the Tarantino twins might be, but she remembered classmates of her own children who'd been academic hot potatoes, kids so disruptive that nobody wanted them.

"If I could figure out how to do it," Judith said, "I'd split them up by sending one up to Carlsbad and the other down to Encinitas."

The laughter this time was even stronger.

Lynne liked the feel of this group, the sense of camaraderie and good nature and gentle irreverence. She knew firsthand what good teachers — and special women — some of them were. Judith, for instance, had been in the classroom, teaching fourth grade (and the Gold Rush) when Lynne's own kids were at Pettigrew. Judith's daughter Lisa had been a classmate of Lynne's son Michael.

And Betsy, of course, was a very special case.

As if reading her mind, Mandy Mosher

spoke up. "Betsy, I want to hear how it is that you and Lynne know each other." Mandy had gone through the Floritas school system between two of Lynne's kids, and Lynne had been vaguely aware of her over the years as a plump, plain young woman with close-cropped black hair, dark eyes, and a huge warm heart. Everyone loved Mandy. Pettigrew Elementary had lucked out when she married a sporadically employed artist who enjoyed his kids and was often available to care for them.

Betsy looked at Lynne. "Do you want to tell it?"

Lynne waved a hand. "Go ahead."

"Well," Betsy began, "we met when we were thirteen, on Guam. We were both Navy brats and our fathers were stationed there at the same time."

"Guam?" Susi sounded astonished, as if they'd mentioned meeting on Uranus, or the *Starship Enterprise*.

Betsy nodded. "Guam. I'm here to tell you there are better places to be a thirteen-year-old girl, though the beaches were incredible. Anyway, we were there together for maybe a year and a half, and then both our fathers got sent elsewhere. We wrote to each other for a while and then we lost track of each other for a good long while. Lynne?"

Lynne took over. "Flash forward many, many years to the workroom by the teachers'

58

lounge at Pettigrew. I was PTA president and I'd been fighting with the Gestetner for about two hours, trying to copy the wretched school newsletter. In walks this new third grade teacher I'd heard about, Mrs. Danforth, who was taking over for somebody on maternity leave. I didn't have a third grader that year, so I hadn't paid much attention. Anyway, I'm grubby and cranky and muttering words that you aren't supposed to say around little kids. I can tell without even really looking that this new teacher is immaculate, and put together, and has this perfect little body."

This brought appreciative chuckles as everyone looked at Betsy, who was still immaculate and put together, with a perfect little body.

Betsy grinned. "I looked at her, and then I looked again, and she looked up. And both of us realized who it was at exactly the same time. It was like magic."

"I remember that day," Judith said fondly. "But you didn't stay that time, Betsy. Seems to me you left pretty quickly. And by the time you came back, I was principal."

"With the power to hire," Betsy noted, her grin widening. "But even the first time, I was ready to settle down and stay in one place for the rest of my life, and I was really jealous that Lynne had gotten to do that. We'd spent hours on Guam talking about how when *we* were grown-ups *we* weren't going to uproot our children all the time, and *we'd* stay in one place and never, ever move. Unfortunately, I'd made the mistake of falling in love with a Navy officer, so I didn't get to do that until after Jim retired."

Lynne smiled. "And we all lived happily ever after. The end."

A companionable silence filled the next couple of minutes. Then Nikki said, "Anybody want to tell scary stories?"

Susi shook her head empathetically. "Not me. Anyway, the only scary story I can ever remember is *The Hook* and everybody knows that one."

"Then what about *true* scary stories?" Betsy suggested. "Stuff that's happened to us in real life."

Lynne frowned. "Like —"

Betsy considered for a moment. "Hmmm, like . . ." She opened her mouth and eyes wide. "Like killing rattlesnakes."

"Killing rattlesnakes? *You've* killed rattlesnakes?" Susi's tone suggested that this was clearly impossible, that Betsy was certainly embroidering the truth for her own glorification.

Lynne suddenly catapulted back into her role as tour guide and group conviviality guarantor. She held her breath as Betsy stared Susi down for what felt like hours, but was probably only a minute.

Susi was turning out to be trouble.

Over the years, Lynne had heard far more than she wanted about Betsy's rattlers, which were unquestionably real. At least they had been until Betsy slaughtered them into extinction in her neighborhood, newly carved from the dry, previously undeveloped hills of inland Floritas.

Betsy vs. the Rattlers was an amazing tale of bravery, though the battle had offered a few lighter moments, too. Lynne wondered if her friend would mention the night she'd tried to kill a baby rattler in a dark corner of the patio. The ferocious little snake continued to wiggle no matter how viciously she attacked it with the rattler-killing hoe she kept just outside the back door. Sometime later, she realized that she was trying to slay her grandson's far-too-authentic rubber souvenir from the Wild Animal Park.

"Dozens," Betsy answered matter-of-factly. "Mostly babies, I'll give you that, but the babies are every bit as dangerous, sometimes even more, because they spook so easily."

"Unlike your more mature rattlesnake," Marianne added, "who's a pretty deliberate dude unless you really get in his way. Not that I'm brave about rattlers in any way, shape, or form. I hate snakes. We had them for a while, too, when we first moved into the Pettigrew Valley development. Of course

61

they did have squatters' rights. They'd been living there for generations, probably for centuries, actually, till we humans came along and built houses on their territory."

"You all have everything you need?" A husky voice came from the darkness at the edge of the campfire area.

Lynne looked up and smiled at Connie Caravaci, the owner and manager of Murmuring Pines. "I think so," Lynne told her. "Thanks. Can we interest you in a s'more?"

"I don't want to intrude," Connie said. "Just my old den mother instincts coming into play, I guess. Gotta be sure the campers are okay."

They all laughed. This was a sentiment everyone could relate to.

"No intrusion whatsoever," Judith Limone assured her, giving administrative approval. "Pull up a piece of ground and grab a marshmallow. There's chocolate and graham crackers over here."

"Thanks," Connie told them, dropping cross-legged beside the fire. Most of the Argonauts sat in beach chairs, but the agile Connie plopped on the dirt without hesitation. She picked up a straightened coat hanger, speared a marshmallow, and leaned in toward the smoldering coals.

Lynne had a theory about how people roasted marshmallows. Gregarious, adventuresome folk were more likely to set their marshmallows on fire and let the flames melt the sugar inside. Her late husband Monty had been a marshmallow burner, and he'd never minded eating the charred outer layer.

Cautious, deliberate folk, on the other hand, took their time with their marshmallows, holding them far enough from the flames so that the outer layer achieved a golden, puffy appearance at the same time the interior melted all the way through.

Lynne herself was somewhere in the middle and over time she'd developed her own personal marshmallow style, a compromise between the two extremes. She'd first brown the outside, then slide the golden crust off, eat it, and return the spear to the fire to brown the next layer. Sometimes she'd go through three roastings, working down to a perfect tiny morsel of browned liquefied sweetness.

Connie Caravaci, she noticed, was a slow roaster.

"So how'd you happen to move up here, anyway?" Lynne asked Connie.

The group had grown quiet after her arrival, but it was a comfortable silence. Even Susi seemed to finally be relaxing. This would be an excellent time to distract everyone by drawing out their hostess. Also, Lynne was nosy by nature.

"Pure luck," Connie answered with a chuckle. "Out and out kismet. I was at one of those crossroads times in your life, though I didn't entirely realize it at the time. There was a real estate boom going on in L.A., and the company that I worked for was expanding, putting in more strip malls out in what used to be the boonies. Places like Palmdale and Hemet. They wanted me to move to Palmdale and it would almost have been a promotion. But I don't like the desert. While I was trying to decide what to do, I looked around and realized that my kids were grown and my ex was gone. I also suddenly realized that the crappy little house I owned in the San Fernando Valley was worth over half a million dollars."

"So you cashed out?" Marianne asked.

Lynne had noticed that Marianne seemed utterly at home in this outdoor environment, and wondered if she might be trying to find a way to apply this appealing scenario to herself. Marianne had the divorce part out of the way, but her kids were still in school, and not of an age to take enthusiastically to relocating in a town on what they'd probably consider the back side of the moon.

It was the real estate that was the wild card, actually, and Lynne had no idea where Marianne stood in the Southern California Real Estate Derby. It all depended on when you started climbing the ladder. People who'd bought tiny starter homes twenty-five years ago or longer were usually in great shape. It was a boom-and-bust cycle, and the trick was trading up while the market was down. Still, even the folks who stayed put and merely refinanced at opportune moments had watched their property values soar. It always seemed that prices couldn't possibly get any higher. Until they did.

"I cashed out," Connie Caravaci said. The fading fire glowed on her weathered face and she looked utterly content. "I didn't know where I wanted to go, so I got a van big enough to sleep in comfortably and I hit the road. I'm a native Californian and I wanted to stay in the state, but beyond that I was wide open. It's a huge state, after all, nearly a thousand miles from the northernmost coast up around Eureka to the southeastern corner down by Yuma. I went clear up to the Oregon border and started working my way down. When I got to Nevada City, it felt like home, and Murmuring Pines was for sale. And that's the way it is."

Connie's intonation was pure Walter Cronkite and the older members of the party laughed appreciatively.

"Do you ever regret it?" Marianne asked.

"Coming here? Or leaving L.A.?" Connie pulled her marshmallow away from the heat, examined it carefully, then popped it in her mouth.

"Either one," Marianne said.

"Coming here I never regret," Connie answered in a moment, after she'd chewed and swallowed. "But now and then I miss L.A. Of course, the L.A. that I miss isn't the one that's there right now. It's the one back when I was in high school and we'd ditch school and go to the beach. Back in the Ride-a-Wild-Bikini era when we all wanted to be Gidget."

Lynne looked at Connie in astonishment. "You're the last person in the world I'd think ever wanted to be Gidget."

Connie laughed. "We all have our dark secrets, don't we now?"

The group grew silent again and Lynne was conscious of the night sounds, of an owl hooting somewhere off down the ridge, of the nearby creek tumbling toward its own little waterfall, of the wind rustling gently through the trees. The murmuring pines, now that she thought about it.

"What about the rest of the scary stories?" Lynne asked. She explained to Connie what they were doing.

"That's easy," Connie said. "The scariest thing that ever happened to me was being in an elevator headed for the twenty-fifth floor of one of the Delta Towers in Century City when a 5.2 earthquake hit. First there was a jolt, and then the car started swaying from side to side — just a little, not enough to activate the antiquake locking mechanism into place. It stopped completely for a moment and I'm pretty sure my heart stopped too. I just knew that cable was going to snap and the car was going to plummet thirty floors, right to the subbasement."

A moment of awkward silence followed.

"But it didn't," Lynne prompted.

Connie nodded. "It didn't. The doors opened on my floor and I kind of dove out, right into a kid pushing a mail cart. Picked myself up, helped him reassemble the cart, and then I walked down twenty-five flights."

Marianne shivered. "That's so . . . so urban. My scariest story was in the wilderness, or anyway on the way to the wilderness. The most terrifying experience I ever had was on my honeymoon."

Laughter erupted around the campfire.

"Is this X-rated?" Betsy asked.

"I wish," Marianne answered. "No, it's purely medical, actually. I got stung by a bee and went into anaphylactic shock. I could feel my throat closing up and I couldn't breathe. Let me tell you, not being able to breathe has got to be the scariest experience in the world."

"What did you *do?*" Lisa Limone asked anxiously. Lisa hadn't been saying much tonight, Lynne had noticed. She seemed to be feeling her way along, trying to determine her position in this gathering of women who were mostly her mother's friends.

"Well, Mark, my husband, realized what was

happening and he sent somebody running for a ranger. We'd just gotten to Yosemite and we were getting ready to backpack up into Tuolumne Meadows. Thank God, we were still down in Yosemite Village when I got stung, in the parking lot, actually. And I got lucky. There was a doctor who'd just gotten to the Visitor Center, and he helped the ranger. The ranger had a bee sting kit and gave me a shot of epinephrine that stopped the anaphylactic reaction long enough for them to get me to a hospital." Marianne shook her head. "It still makes me shiver to think about it."

"As well it might," Betsy said. "I had asthma when I was a kid. Not being able to breathe is an entire category of Scary, as far as I'm concerned. But I just remembered another really scary story, though it's Lynne's story, not mine."

Lynne blinked in confusion. She'd been hoping that the scary stories would end, actually, because whatever she thought of seemed utterly inconsequential. And she wasn't about to bring down everyone's good spirits by telling the group that the most frightening period of her own life had been the weeks after her husband's death, as she got used to the idea that Monty was never coming home again.

"Me?" Lynne asked.

"You," Betsy answered, nodding. "Remember the snakes on Guam?"

And then suddenly Lynne knew exactly what Betsy meant, and that she was right.

"There was a huge problem with brown tree snakes on Guam when we lived there," Lynne said. "Still is, I think. We called them rat snakes and they were all over the island. There's supposed to be something like a million of them, five or six times as many as there are people, and they're totally out of control. Big ugly things, and they were only active at night. Majorly creepy. Anyway, I got up one night to go to the john, which I usually just did in the dark. I don't know what prompted me to turn on the bathroom light that night, but thank God I did. The biggest snake I'd ever seen was coming up out of the toilet. I bet they could hear me screaming in Hawaii."

Susi grimaced. "I'm never going to be able to sleep after that. And I certainly won't be able to get up and go to the bathroom in the middle of the night. Which, being a middle-aged woman, isn't really optional anymore."

The others laughed.

"What's your scariest experience, Susi?" Lynne asked. Best to get her story out of the way promptly. And maybe she'd go to bed then. It was definitely worth a shot.

Susi shook her head, frowning. "I don't really have one. Anything to do with spiders, I guess. I really hate walking into spider webs."

Her tone was almost defensive, suggesting that the others rather enjoyed the experience.

"I have two terrifying experiences," Judith Limone announced.

Everyone turned to her expectantly. Lynne had been relieved to see that in general nobody seemed to be deferring to Judith because she was their boss. Or even worse, sucking up.

But they did definitely snap to at the sound of her voice.

"Both of them involve travel," Judith went on. "The first was when I was hitchhiking with a girlfriend in Europe."

Lisa whipped her head around. "When you were *what?*"

Judith looked at her daughter fondly. "Surely I've told you about this, Lisa."

"Surely you haven't, Mom. And do go on."

Judith laughed. "How nice to know that I still have the power to surprise you, my dear. Anyway, my girlfriend and I were hitchhiking in Switzerland. It was pouring rain and there was *nobody* on the road. Finally, when we were both pretty much soaked to the skin, a car pulled up. It was long, low, and black, and we hopped in, grateful to finally be out of the rain. It wasn't until the car started moving again that we got a good look at the two guys in the front seat. They were wearing homburgs down over their faces. I was just a naïve girl from Trenton, New

Jersey, but these guys really looked like gangsters to me."

"Gangsters?" Susi asked skeptically.

"Gangsters," Judith repeated firmly. "We told them we wanted to go to Lucerne and they didn't say anything. The driver just kind of nodded. Then suddenly he turned off the main road onto some kind of forest track. It was totally desolate. There was nothing but tall, dark pine trees all around us."

She stopped and waved a lazy hand around the surrounding trees. "Now that I think about it, it looked a lot like this. So I very timidly asked, 'Aren't we going the wrong way?' One of them said it was a short cut and they both laughed."

Mandy shivered. "This is getting really creepy, Judith."

"Indeed," Judith said. "Janet and I started rummaging around our backpacks and the only thing we could find that might serve as a weapon was a fruit knife with a three-inch rounded blade. It couldn't have stabbed a plate of Jell-O. But I kept it clenched in my hand, just waiting for the car to stop and the guys to attack us. I figured I'd go down fighting. We kept winding through the woods, and then" — she paused dramatically — "then we suddenly came out of the forest on the other side, and discovered that it actually *was* a short cut."

"Wow!" Lisa spoke into the sudden silence.

"I guess I understand now why you were always so outspokenly opposed to hitchhiking."

"Well," Judith said, "nothing bad happened, so all's well that ends well and all that. Those were very different times, of course. I actually did quite a lot of hitchhiking back then, including one time when I went from San Francisco to Miami, on my own."

"Why, you careless little strumpet!" Lisa chided.

Judith chuckled. "I imagine that most of us look back on some of the things we did as kids and realize how stupid — and incredibly lucky — we were. And what about you, Lisa? What was *your* most frightening experience? Or does a mother not want to know?"

Lisa grinned impishly. "You mean the time that I was with the football fraternity out in the trailer behind . . ."

Judith put her hands over her ears. "Stop! I don't want to hear it, whatever it was."

Lisa reached over and removed Judith's right hand from her ear. "My lips are sealed, Mom. I'm only kidding, anyway. Though I have a feeling I'm probably still in my young and stupid period." She looked around the circle. "Who hasn't gone yet? Mandy, what about you?"

"Also young and stupid," Mandy confessed, "probably forever. I'll have to talk fast, because I'm falling asleep sitting up. I must say, though, that you all have done a pretty thorough job of mentioning a lot of things that I personally find very scary. So maybe it won't be quite as easy to nod off as I'd expected."

Lynne laughed. "You've got a point there, but I'm guessing we'll all sleep pretty soundly tonight. Now, what happened to you, Mandy?"

Lynne wondered, as she asked, if this was going to turn out to be another one of those things that her kids and their friends kept casually 'fessing up to when they were feeling relaxed, or had been drinking. Clandestine trips to Mexico, wild parties with strange drugs, frightening encounters with people who ought not be walking around unchained. Things that by and large Lynne would just as soon not have known about.

"My sister's gerbil got into my bed," Mandy said simply.

Chapter 4

"Ackkk! That sounds awful!" Betsy's voice radiated empathy. "I dislike rodents almost as much as I hate snakes. But how did it happen?"

"I have no idea how the wretched little creature got out," Mandy said. "It used to ride its treadmill all night long and the nasty thing squeaked. The minute the lights went out, it'd start. *Eeee-up, eeee-up, eeee-up* — it just never stopped.

"Anyway, one night I was having a terrible dream. I dreamed that there was a rat in my bed. I woke up sweating with the covers thrown off, and with something furry running up my body toward my head. I kind of flew out of bed and bolted across the room to the light switch, and just before I turned it on" — Mandy paused — "just before I turned it on, I looked back across the room at my bed. Just in time to watch a dark shadow run across my pillow."

Susi emitted a little shriek.

"That one is *really* creepy," Judith said, "and I'm fading fast, too. Lynne, were you going to give us a little run-through on the schedule? And is it too much to hope that breakfast is optional?"

Lynne straightened and pulled herself back

into gear. "Sure thing. And first things first: *Everything* is optional. You guys should all feel free to do as much or as little as you want. If you want to sleep all week, that's fine with me."

"Ooh," Mandy moaned, holding the back of her hand to her forehead, "don't tempt me like that."

Lynne laughed. "Temptation's my job, Mandy. Anyway, here's the deal. We'll be based here at Murmuring Pines for three nights. Nevada City's a great location for exploring the northern mines area, and I think the setup here gives us plenty of flexibility."

Now Mandy rose clumsily to her feet, yawning widely. "I'm going to flex myself into bed," she announced. "I'm up for anything, Lynne. And Susi, don't worry about making noise when you come in. I could sleep through Armageddon."

Mandy shuffled off to her cabin in a chorus of good-nights.

When she was gone, Lynne continued. "Tomorrow morning we'll go into Nevada City and explore the town, visit the museum, and so on."

"And pick up my pills," Susi added, "assuming I can get through managed-care hell to reach my doctor."

"And pick up Susi's pills," Lynne said. "Then we'll head on north and have lunch in

Downieville, which is a cool little town on the Yuba River."

"You'll like Downieville," Connie told them. "If I didn't have this place, I'd be tempted to move up there myself."

"A solid endorsement," Lynne said. "Thanks, Connie. Anyway, Downieville is as far north as we'll probably get on this trip. It's considered a really good example of a surviving northern mountain gold town. As you know, most of the Gold Rush towns came and went pretty quickly."

"Like my first husband," Marianne Gordon muttered, "the one who didn't make it to the first anniversary." Lynne grinned — she was starting to really like Marianne.

"Tomorrow night we'll have Chinese food in Nevada City," Lynne said. "Then on Tuesday, we'll go up to Malakoff Diggins in the morning. I've never been there, but it's supposed to be an amazing, and really depressing, example of hydraulic mining. Lisa knows a lot more about this than I do."

Lisa Limone didn't look the least bit tired, but that was one of the perks of being in your twenties. Perennial exhaustion came later — along with kids of your own, multitasking, and an inexplicable reduction in the number of hours in a day.

"By the time I get done with you all," Lisa said, "you'll know plenty. It's really quite awful, but I don't want to get ahead of myself here. Or spoil anybody's nice evening."

"Fair enough," Lynne said. "Then Tuesday afternoon, there are a couple of different options and we'll probably split into smaller groups. Some of you might want to go over to Grass Valley to the Empire Mine Historic Park. The Empire and North Star mines were huge operations, with hundreds of miles of underground tunnels."

Betsy shuddered. "No thank you," she said. "Tunnels I can do without."

"Tunnels have spiders," Susi noted. "Count me out, too."

"Well, the Lola Montez house is also over in Grass Valley," Lynne went on. "She wasn't all that great a performer, apparently, but she had a real flair for reinventing herself. The perfect Californian."

"I thought about coming as Lola to the Characters Dinner," Judith said, "but I realized I'm a little old to pull off her Spider Dance outfit, and if I couldn't do that, what's the point?"

"Spider Dance?" Nikki asked.

Judith nodded. "It was apparently quite a provocative number. It involved large dangling tarantulas, an imaginary spider web, and minimal clothing. In short, a mining town blockbuster."

"What's the Characters Dinner?" Connie asked.

"Thursday night down in Columbia, we're

77

having a special dinner and everybody's dressing up as favorite characters from the Gold Rush era," Lynne explained.

The Characters Dinner was Lynne's idea and she'd arranged to hold it in a private room at the restored 1856 City Hotel in Columbia. Each woman had chosen her character secretly, with Lynne coordinating to assure no duplications. After long and careful consideration, Lynne herself had decided to attend as Dame Shirley, the spunky doctor's wife whose letters to a sister in Massachusetts offered one of the most compelling accounts of everyday mining camp life.

"What fun!" Connie said. "I'd have to be Charley Parkhurst."

It seemed a logical choice, as Lynne thought about it. Marianne Gordon, who *was* coming to the dinner as Charley, smiled quietly on the other side of the campfire.

Charley had been a fearless and respected Wells Fargo driver, the sort of early Californian who would have been totally forgotten by history had he not happened to be a *she.* Alas, Charley had died without explaining her reasons for the long-term cross-dressing, but it had always seemed obvious to Lynne that she was simply doing what she had to in order to hang out with horses. In another era, she might have read *Black Beauty* and collected Breyer statuettes and begged for riding lessons and her own pony. Back in the mid-nineteenth century, however, horse-struck girls had to be a bit more creative.

"What else is there to do around here?" Judith asked. "I'm sure I should know all this, but I was so focused on the end of the year that I barely managed to pack."

"Well, there's an Old Town and a couple of good museums down in Auburn," Lynne told her, "or you might want to head out and look through some of the out-and-out ruins of gold towns that didn't stand the test of time."

"There's a nice covered bridge not far from here," Connie put in. "Not too many of those in California."

"No shortage of interesting things to see and do," Lynne agreed, "but everybody will want to get back in time for dinner Tuesday night, 'cause that's steak and lobster night at the National Hotel in Nevada City."

A murmur of pleasure passed around the group, punctuated by an exclamation of irritation as Susi lost her marshmallow in the fire. Two marshmallows, actually. She dropped the straightened coat hanger in irritation and reached for another brownie.

"You'll like it," Connie promised. "I go to that now and again myself, not that surf *or* turf is really indigenous here. It's just the notion of high living, I think."

"You're welcome to join us," Lynne told her, and the others nodded and murmured agreement. "Then on Wednesday morning, we'll pack up and head south. Everybody will meet up for lunch at the Sutter's Mill recreation in John Marshall State Park. Wednesday's also Hardtack Day, and Nikki's in charge of that."

A few groans greeted that announcement.

Nikki seemed delighted. With her short hair and elfin expression, she looked a bit like Peter Pan — the Mary Martin version — in the dancing firelight. "It'll be a great experience, y'all. Nothing but authentic food from the Gold Rush Era, really basic. Hardtack, jerky, and so on."

"Are you sure the forty-niners had teriyaki jerky?" asked Betsy, who'd unpacked Nikki's provisions along with the rest of the group food.

"I thought about slaughtering a mountain goat," Nikki answered, "but I ran out of time. I figured it was worth sacrificing a little authenticity to avoid an insurrection. There's also salmon jerky for those of us who don't eat meat."

"What's the 'and so on'?" Judith asked suspiciously.

"Water." Nikki's smile was infectious. "Of course, if you catch something you want me to field-dress for you . . ."

Judith shuddered and the others laughed. One of the things Lynne had always liked about Judith, dating back to when Lynne had helped out with her own kids' Gold Rush Days in Judith's fourth grade class, was that the woman could laugh at herself. She'd always been serious about her work — even before she became principal — but she balanced that with a well-developed appreciation for irreverence. Who'd have thought she was also a reformed hitchhiker?

"There's all kinds of options on the road south," Lynne went on after a moment. "We'll be following Highway 49 all the way, and it goes through a lot of restored Gold Rush towns, including Angels Camp, where they do the Calaveras County frog-jumping competition."

"Is that this week?" Marianne sounded hopeful.

Lynne shook her head. "We missed it by a month. Anyway, there's plenty of diversion on the road. Antique shops" — Betsy immediately perked up — "and museums and historic relics and so on. Some pretty good wineries, too, and at some point I know we're going to lose Nikki and Marianne for a while when they go white-water rafting. Anyway, we'll all meet up again down in Columbia, and then we'll spend the last three nights there, till we head home on Saturday. Everybody's moving indoors in Columbia, including the campers, and it should be a lot of fun. Thursday night's the Gold Rush Characters Dinner. I trust you all brought your costumes."

"Oh yeah," Susi said, sounding more excited than she had for hours. "I plan to *rock* at the Characters Dinner."

An odd image, Susi rocking. But Lynne decided she just might. Susi had signed up to come as Lola Montez's protégée, child performer Lotta Crabtree. A nineteenth-century Shirley Temple.

"Friday we'll go to Moaning Caverns," Lynne went on, "where some of you plan to rappel down into the cave."

"I brought my gear," Marianne noted, "and I know Nikki's up for it. Anybody else?"

"No thank you," Betsy said, shaking her head. "No caves, no tunnels, no below-ground mines. I'm strictly a top-of-the-earth type of gal."

"You'd have to have a gun on me to get me to even consider rappelling down inside a cave." Judith sounded quite appalled at the notion. "And even then I don't know if I'd have the nerve."

"You would, Mom," Lisa told her with a laugh. "You definitely would. And don't think I didn't notice that you never told us your other scary story."

"Something to look forward to," Betsy said. "I want to hear it too, Judith."

"Maybe you could tell us over breakfast," Lynne suggested.

Judith gave a dismissive little laugh. "It's

nothing, really. Certainly not as dramatic as the hitchhiking."

"I'll be the judge of that," Lisa told her.

Connie Caravaci stood and stretched. "I've overstayed my welcome, I think. Night, all, and if I don't see you before you head out in the morning, have a great day."

In the expanding silence as Connie's footfalls receded, Lynne could once again hear the creek tumbling behind the cabins and a sudden shrill cry from some small animal. She had a sense of the vastness of this rugged country, and of the courage it would have taken to be one of the original Argonauts.

Chapter 5

Amos Ledbetter was unable to sleep. He lay in silk pajamas in the silence of his perfectly appointed bedroom and listened to the slumber machine play sounds of waves lapping onto shore. Normally this was a comfort, carrying him back to pleasurable times in Maui and Malibu and Key West.

Tonight it made him think of rising floodwaters filled with alligators, each of them being ridden by someone like Jed.

Amos didn't know if Jed was the fellow's real name, or if he even *had* a real name. Perhaps he had sprung fully formed and utterly evil from a bubbling natural cauldron on some mercifully undiscovered island.

They sent someone different each time, rarely repeating. Amos wasn't even entirely sure who *they* were, only that he had wandered, with the best of intentions, into a personal nightmare that seemed to have no exit.

Jed had come several times, however, including the day after Amos found the dead cat on his doorstep, a response to his stated intention of no longer participating in the program. It hadn't taken any kind of super-intelligence to make the connection.

Jed's dark eyes were as impenetrable as anthracite, and a wide scar running down from the corner of his mouth split his full beard into two uneven sections, either one of which might easily harbor a colony of small, uncharming creatures. He might have been thirty or he might have been forty-five. Whatever the number, they clearly hadn't been easy years.

Jed hadn't been one to waste words. With the memory of his neighbor's poor Fluffy lying strangled on his doormat, Amos hadn't wanted to hear them anyway.

Still, his situation now wasn't entirely hopeless. Tomorrow he'd get the lamp back, and everyone would live happily ever after.

Yeah, right.

Susi Braun awoke with a cramping in her guts so intense that she thought for a moment she'd been stabbed.

Where was she? The room was inky black and her pillow smelled faintly musty. A thick guttural snore came from somewhere nearby. Not Rick. Rick's snoring had a high reedy quality to it, and he snored only when he had a head cold.

The stabbing returned, even more intense this time. She pulled her knees to her abdomen and clasped her arms around them as her mind cleared.

Gold country. She was in some wretched cabin in the woods outside Nevada City and the snoring came from Mandy Mosher, the young woman in the other bed. Susi was five hundred miles away from home with none of her medications, in a cabin that was probably overrun by spiders.

And something was very wrong with her body.

She rocked from side to side, hands clenched together around her legs, then suddenly realized that she had to get to the bathroom fast. She rolled sideways out of bed and stumbled in the darkness across to the bathroom, tripping as she moved and catching her balance at the last minute as she pushed into the bathroom. Suddenly recalling that awful story about the snake rising up out of the toilet, she flipped on the light, scoped out the porcelain bowl, then dropped onto the toilet. Just in time.

When she was finished, she ran cold water on a washcloth, then wiped her face and neck and arms. She looked pale in the mirror, but maybe that was just the dreadfully unflattering light in this all-too-rustic bathroom. She was thoroughly awake now, in any event, and the cramping was milder, though surely she was emptied.

A sharp knock on the bathroom door startled Susi and she turned to open it. Mandy Mosher stood in a shapeless lime floral nightgown with her hair sticking up over one ear and facial color that closely matched the nightgown.

"I need the toilet." Mandy's breath was shallow, her words clipped.

Susi stepped aside as Mandy dashed into the bathroom. Then she carefully closed the door on her roommate, went back into the main room of the cabin, and turned on a light. She found her watch on the bedside table. It was three-fifteen.

She sat in a somewhat lumpy armchair for a while until she felt a little less queasy. Mandy remained in the bathroom and Susi heard the toilet flush a couple of times.

Food poisoning, that had to be what was happening here. She might have known. Haul a bunch of perishables through that wretchedly hot San Joaquin Valley and then set them out for a couple of hours before you eat — you're just asking for trouble. She thought back over the dinner and focused on Lynne's potato salad. Mayonnaise was usually the culprit when this sort of thing happened, though given the disgraceful state of food safety in America today, it could easily be something else. Or several something elses. Salmonella in the chicken, perhaps, though she'd checked her piece carefully to be sure it was thoroughly cooked. Or maybe it was *E. coli,* though she didn't think you could get that from chicken.

Well, it was too late now, in any case. The damage was done. Susi's system was thoroughly scoured out by whatever nasty bacteria their dinner had harbored, and she could only hope this was the end of it.

Seven-Up. That's what she needed. But all of the food and drinks were in the communal cabin next door. She considered whether she felt well enough to make what seemed, in her current debilitated state, like a trek across the Rockies. Reminding herself that there was also a bathroom in the other cabin, she picked up the flashlight she'd left by the side of the bed — and completely forgotten when she was lunging toward the bathroom twenty minutes ago — and walked out onto the porch.

But it looked like she wouldn't need the flashlight after all. Somebody had thoughtfully left a light on in the communal cabin next door, probably as a bathroom beacon for the campers. She waited till she felt fairly confident she could get that far without collapsing, then made a break for it.

In the morning, Lynne was horrified to find that nearly everyone had been up in the night with intestinal distress. She herself had wakened around two with a sense that she had exactly three seconds to get to the toilet, and she'd gotten back to sleep fairly easily afterward. So far as she knew, Betsy hadn't been up at all.

Now, as they gathered in the communal cabin, the extent of the problem became clear and Lynne was dismayed. This was a terrible way to start a trip, with so many people sick, and the worst part of all was that she had prepared most of the dinner. What's more, she had thoroughly enjoyed the experience.

It was a kind of cooking she rarely did anymore — a full-scale leisurely session over a day and a half, starting with a cartful of groceries that filled her entire trunk. There had been years — quite a lot of them, actually — when she not only fixed dinner for five every single night, but also seemed to always be providing snack for Scouts or little league or Jenny's high school tennis team. Years of neighborhood barbecues and potlucks, of bake sales and covered dishes carried to end-of-season picnics, of PTA spaghetti dinners and teacher appreciation brunches.

For the Argonauts' Sunday night meal, she had slow-smoked the chicken in the bullet-shaped smoker, using last winter's prunings from the plum and apple trees for flavoring. This was a calculated emotional risk, because she so strongly associated this method of smoking food with Monty. The first couple of times she'd tried to use the smoker after Monty died, she'd been too upset to finish. This time she was fine, and it felt as if she'd passed another important milestone on the road she now traveled alone.

And, of greater relevance at the moment, the chicken *had* been thoroughly cooked, to the exact point where every morsel held the smoky fruitwood flavor, without being the least bit dried out. Any salmonella it might have harbored should definitely have been cooked away.

The potato salad was just her regular potato salad, the one she'd made hundreds of times over the years, a standard, middle-of-the-road mayonnaise-based, hard-boiled-egg-laced kartoffelsalat, with sweet pepper chunks in red and gold and orange. It had been refrigerated immediately and remained chilled all the way through the San Joaquin Valley in its cooler.

The eggs for deviling had been hard cooked at the same time as those for the potato salad, and though she'd bought them a week earlier for easier peeling, they hadn't passed the "enjoy by" dates that Trader Joe's stamped on all its eggs.

She'd made two batches of cookies, also standards: oatmeal raisin and chocolate chip, mixing the dough on Friday and baking it Saturday indoors while the meat smoked outside. She'd drifted through the cooking languidly, enjoying the experiences as if for the first time.

And now all the folks who'd eaten this special meal were sick.

Even Judith looked disheveled, and had

come out without putting on lipstick, or any makeup at all, for that matter. Judith was idiosyncratic about her appearance, with a trademark single braid hanging nearly to her waist. But she always appeared in public perfectly made up, looking as if she were about to be photographed for the cover of some glossy women's magazine.

Betsy had brewed a pot of coffee, but so far she was the only one drinking it. The thought of putting acid into her stomach was too much for Lynne just yet, and she sipped instead at a glass of water. The others, except for Nikki, seemed equally reluctant to eat or drink. Indeed, only Nikki, Marianne, and Betsy seemed unaffected.

"Well, it must have been the chicken," Nikki told them as she bit into a multigrain bagel. A food purist on the cusp of veganism, she'd skipped the chicken altogether. " 'Cause I ate everything else and I'm fine."

"Don't rub it in," Judith told her. She wore shorts and her Argonauts T-shirt and nibbled cautiously at a muffin. Lisa had yet to put in an appearance, but Judith had reported that her daughter was showering and had also been unwell in the night.

"Sorry," Nikki said, though she didn't seem the least bit repentant.

"I don't see how it could be the chicken," Lynne protested. "I fixed it on Saturday and ate it for dinner and I was just fine. What I didn't eat, I refrigerated immediately, and it was packed with tons of blue ice on the trip up here. Same as the potato salad, which I also ate Saturday night."

"Nobody's blaming you, Lynne," Judith said. "I got salads at the grocery store deli, and you never know where that stuff has been. Though I stuck with the potato salad and only had a little of the cole slaw myself."

"I skipped all the store salads," Marianne said, "just to be on the safe side. I'm allergic to peanuts and shellfish, so I have to be really careful with prepared foods."

"What, people slip shrimp into things?" Nikki asked. "Never happens to me."

"Well, yeah, shellfish isn't much of a problem most of the time. But you'd be surprised how many things have peanuts in them," Marianne said.

Lynne was shaking her head. "I knew about Marianne's allergies when I was planning and cooking, so I was even more conscious of what I was doing."

"In any case," Marianne said, "I ate the chicken and Lynne's potato salad and I wasn't bothered at all."

"I didn't eat any of the store salads," Susi put in. "So those can't be the problem. I can't help but think it *must* have been the chicken or Lynne's potato salad."

Lynne winced. "Look, I'm really, really sorry about this. I don't know what happened or why, but I was in charge of the food, so it definitely happened on my watch. How about if I run into town and get something for breakfast?"

Judith shook her head. "Don't be silly, Lynne. We've got muffins and bagels and cereal and I don't see how there can be anything wrong with any of them."

"I left the spinach dip out for about an hour on Saturday," Betsy admitted reluctantly, "and it has sour cream in it. Maybe that's what did it."

Judith shook her head again. "I don't think so. Lisa hates spinach so she wouldn't have eaten any of that, and she was sick, too."

"Well, that pretty much rules out everything but the s'mores," Betsy said, "and I've never heard of anybody getting food poisoning from marshmallows."

"Well, whatever it was, I guess it's over," Lynne said. "Maybe it'd be a good idea to wait a bit before we head into town, though."

"I need my medications," Susi reminded. Feeling too weak to walk down to the pay phone at the office, she had borrowed Nikki's super satellite phone to reach her doctor. "And even though I managed to find most of my regular vitamins and herbals from you, nobody has Coenzyme Q10 or zinc, and I need them both for proper healing."

"Guilty as charged," Marianne answered lightly. "I don't even know what Coenzyme

Whatever is. I do have the Vitamin E you're looking for, though I must admit I never heard of rubbing it into your skin."

"It minimizes scarring," Susi said curtly.

"I feel like the world's worst vitamin slacker," Nikki admitted, "but I think I can live with the shame. I'll run into town and pick up your stuff at the drugstore, Susi. Anybody want to come along?"

Perched on the front passenger seat of Nikki's Expedition headed into Nevada City, Betsy Danforth tried not to think about her friends back at Murmuring Pines and how awful they must feel. Getting away with Nikki and Marianne was quite wonderful, actually. Betsy had never been one to suffer from poor health and she wasn't all that keen on being around the ailing, either. Riding out her mother's last illness had cured her of any latent Florence Nightingale tendencies. Her own attitude toward illness was to retreat to her burrow until she felt fully recovered.

At least she could mail home the lamp she'd bought yesterday. She adored the lamp, and just looking at it transported her back through time to marvelous childhood visits with her Ohio grandparents. However, once they'd unpacked everything last night, it became clear that the lamp would be a continual annoyance if she tried to haul it around through the rest of the week. Not that it was fragile, of course, with that heavy bronze base, but it was bulky and — well, unattractive. Jim was going to think she'd completely lost her mind when he saw it, but that was next week's problem.

Then they could pick up Susi's fool medication. Betsy had been amused during Susi's pharmaceutical survey to discover that no less than four of them were taking gingko biloba to improve their memory. Though in Susi's case, it obviously wasn't working as well as it might, or she wouldn't have forgotten the pills.

"You know," Marianne said from the back seat, "when we were telling our scary stories last night, I can't believe that none of us mentioned scary things happening to our kids, or our students. I bet we all have a million of those."

Nikki glanced over her shoulder. "You're right! Kids getting knocked out on the playground, or hit by cars, or *almost* hit by cars. A little girl ran out in front of my car when I was a teenager and I had to swerve and hit a parked car to miss her. I didn't think my heart would ever beat normally again."

"I'll never forget when some moron holding a birthday party thought I was being overly dramatic about Briana's nut allergies," Marianne said. "She's even worse than me, and she ended up riding to the hospital in an ambulance when that woman gave her wontons fried in peanut oil. And Mark, of course, said it was *my* fault."

Betsy was starting to realize that while the Gordon divorce might be long final, the animosity level remained high. She decided not to follow up. "I lost count of the number of times I had my kids in the emergency room, and it was always a new and different emergency room because we moved all the time when Jim was in the Navy. If we'd lived in one town straight through, like Lynne did, my kids' files would've been so thick we'd probably have been turned over to Child Protective Services."

"I hate it when one of my kids gets hurt," Nikki said. "It turns me into a raging animal."

"I can see that," Betsy told her. "Something small and fast and snarly with a lot of very sharp teeth." Nikki laughed and flashed Betsy a quick grin.

"What do you think?" Marianne asked now, as Nikki drove into the heart of what looked like an altogether charming little town. "Are we going to be able to go up to Downieville this afternoon?"

"Not right away, I don't think," Betsy answered after a moment. "Lynne was planning to get up there in time to have lunch, but I don't think that too many people are going to be very enthusiastic about eating for a while."

Nikki headed up Broad Street, which featured sophisticated little shops and appealing restaurants and tourists in L.L.Bean walking shorts who probably belonged to the very expensive cars that lined the main drag. "I thought these Gold Rush towns were supposed to be rugged and basic and full of boarded-up buildings," Nikki said. "This looks more like Carmel."

"Most of them aren't this nice," Betsy told her. "I think that the reason Nevada City is so well maintained and prosperous is that folks from San Francisco have always come up here for their vacations." As they passed beyond the commercial district, they encountered quiet, tree-shaded streets lined with ornate Victorian mansions. "This place may have gotten its start during the Gold Rush, but San Franciscans kept on putting serious money into it afterward."

Nikki swung around toward the business district again, heading for the Post Office. "Hey, look! Mountain bike rentals!"

Betsy glanced at her watch. "Are you two thinking what I'm thinking?"

"I bet we could get them by the hour," Marianne said.

"And nobody else would want to do it anyway," Nikki pointed out.

Betsy smiled. Suddenly the morning seemed a whole lot brighter.

Chapter 6

Amos had been on the phone for what felt like hours, calling hotels, motels, and bed-and-breakfasts in the Nevada City area.

Tiffany hadn't taken down the driver's license information she was supposed to from the lady who bought the lamp, and in response to his frantic call to Visa, Amos had learned only that the James Danforth in whose name the card was issued got his bills at a post office box in Floritas. Tiffany remembered that the women had stopped in the shop because of car trouble, a fact Amos confirmed in an artfully nonchalant conversation with Al the mechanic. Amos used the pretext that one of the women had left behind some papers, though Al didn't seem particularly interested. He did recall that the women were on their way to Nevada City and that the driver, a Lynne Montgomery, had also paid by credit card. So now he had two credit card receipts to work from, and two names.

He'd called nearly a dozen places and thoroughly polished his patter by the time he reached Murmuring Pines. He'd grown so accustomed to being told no, or being given curt lectures on privacy, that when the woman who answered told him yes, his sister

Lynne Montgomery was staying there, for a moment Amos forgot what to say next. But he recovered quickly and enlisted her cooperation.

"Please don't tell her I called," Amos told the woman. "I want to surprise her."

And that, at least, was the truth.

Fifteen minutes later, as he prepared to close the shop and head north, the front door banged open and trouble walked in. Amos had never seen this man before, but he knew instantly who he was and what he wanted. The men who came and "bought" the items he brought to his shop from San Francisco usually looked very different from one another, but each had the same hard eyes and taciturn demeanor. And each looked as if he'd be comfortable taking on a drunken biker gang, all by himself.

This one was lean and wiry, vaguely Mediterranean with black hair in a buzz cut and brown eyes that took in the entire shop before his second step. He wore a cheap, shiny black shirt with Sansabelt trousers in a different shade of black, and he stank of musky aftershave. He offered the standard opening line and Amos responded correctly, wondering as he always did who had chosen such stupid dialogue.

Then the man asked for the lamp.

"There's been a misunderstanding," Amos spoke quickly, wishing he dared look away, but too terrified to move even his eye muscles. "An employee accidentally sold it yesterday. She didn't realize it was —"

Musk Man cut him off. "Get it back."

"I'm working on it," Amos assured him, with greater bravado than he felt.

Musk Man reached behind himself and turned the sign on the front door of Ledbetter Antiques and Fine Collectibles from OPEN to CLOSED. He never broke eye contact, and for one heart-stopping moment, Amos thought he was about to die.

"Work harder."

Actually, Amos had hoped to have the lamp back in his possession by the time somebody showed up for it. The pickup was supposed to have been — he glanced surreptitiously at a porcelain clock nearby — six hours from now. Twice before the pickup had been late, but nobody had ever showed up early. It was as if, with animal instinct, Musk Man and his compadres had sensed that something was wrong, then hurried to straighten matters out.

"Maybe I need to talk to that employee," Musk Man said.

Oh dear God. Tiffany really *would* pee in her pants if this creature showed up at her doorstep.

"She doesn't know anything." Now there was an understatement. "I can assure you that I got every scrap of information she had." Right now, Amos wanted only to get out of the shop while he was still ambulatory and breathing. "Actually, I just found out where the woman who bought the lamp is staying, and I was on my way. Would you care to join me?"

Once again, Musk Man reached behind him for the door. This time he turned the knob and motioned for Amos to come with him.

Years ago, a burly lumberjack on a clandestine visit to the Castro District had given Amos a crash course in how to walk with confidence, the better to avoid appearing vulnerable to muggers or thugs. As he followed Musk Man to a nondescript navy sedan parked outside Ledbetter Antiques, Amos squared his shoulders and lengthened his stride, wishing he'd paid much closer attention.

As Marianne Gordon sprawled with the rest of the group in the shade of a huge tree in Tin Cup Diggins beside the Yuba River, she decided that life wasn't nearly as bad as it had seemed lately.

Mark's newest lawyer — he'd run through several, probably because he was a little sloppy about paying his bills — was a real pit bull, and Mark's current set of custody demands was even less reasonable than usual. Marianne knew that he was mostly interested

101

in cutting his child support payments —
which he hoped to halve by having the kids
alternate weeks with their mom and dad —
than he was in spending more time with the
kids.

So far, Marianne had resisted the impulse
to trash this idea (and its proponent) to the
kids, who thought their father's gambling
rather charming and loved going along on his
impulsive jaunts to Las Vegas. Nor had she
spelled out the complexities of transportation — to swim lessons, soccer practice, the
beach, basketball games, math tutoring, and
the all-important mall — that would arise if
the kids spent half of each month in Mark's
Oceanside condo, twenty miles north of
Floritas. Just getting them to school on time
would be a challenge; Mark had never been a
morning person.

When Marianne began to notice that her
resolve was wearing down, that she was seriously considering yielding ground, she had
realized this trip was absolutely essential.
Time for a psychic recharge. And so far it
was working. She could feel her backbone
stiffening with every hour. Another week of
this and she'd be ready to take on both Mark
and his lawyer, with one hand tied behind
her back.

"So are you going to break out the pan
and the metal detector and start prospecting?
Or do we use it as a wok and fix dinner over

the campfire?" Nikki asked. She pointed upriver. "There's folks panning over there, if you want to take a look-see before you make up your mind."

Marianne checked it out. Sure enough, a man and woman stood knee-deep in the rocky water, wearing heavy rubber waders and dipping a pair of black pans repeatedly into the clear, swiftly moving river. There was a definite timelessness to the image. She squinted her eyes to blur away the edges of the town and remove the obvious trappings of twenty-first-century civilization, which were admittedly sparse to begin with. From this fuzzy perspective, she had no trouble imagining the river clogged with forty-niners swishing their pans determinedly from sunup to sundown.

Marianne had stuck a hand into the water, coursing downhill from the melting Sierra snowpack, when they first got to Tin Cup Diggins. She wasn't surprised that, even with fresh sunburns, the couple panning upriver looked cold.

Marianne loved the Gold Rush period and considered it a perfect microcosm of American history: adventure, expansion, grit, ingenuity, impulsiveness, determination, recklessness, failure, adaptation, and success, all seasoned with a generous dose of greed. Contemporary gold prospecting, however, was a fairly sore subject. Marianne's boyfriend Jeff, who specialized in get-rich-quick ideas that were longer on potential than actual reward, had urged her to make this trip profitable by bringing home some gen-yew-wine gold. *It's still there,* he assured her, having prowled the Internet and therefore knowing everything. *All you have to do is let the river run. Find enough and maybe we can take the kids to Hawaii.*

Yeah, right. She'd be lucky to find enough to take them to Burger King.

"I promised Jeff I'd check it out," Marianne told Nikki now, "and as you well know, I brought all the stupid equipment." Marianne's gear was extensive, and she'd been grateful for all the space in the back of Nikki's SUV. "But you know what? I think it's kind of a silly idea. Maybe I'll just break out the metal detector and walk around the grounds of Murmuring Pines tonight. Then I can honestly say I tried."

"We've got the pan with us," Nikki reminded, "so you could just stick it in the river here and then tell him that you gave it your all."

"Or better yet," Betsy suggested, "you could get a little gold dust and update the story of how the Downie party found gold here in the first place."

"Which was?" Mandy Mosher asked. Marianne hadn't known Mandy before this trip, though she remembered the girl in her high school years as a cheerful joiner, the kind of kid who eagerly does the scut work for homecoming float building, or the air bands competition, or after-game dances, even as elected student leaders take all the glory. At their planning meetings over the spring, the young woman had been bubbly and talkative. Today, however, she'd been uncharacteristically quiet. Like most of the others, she'd only nibbled at lunch.

"They'd packed over the mountains," Betsy said, "instead of following the river upstream the way most forty-niners did. Right after they got here, somebody caught a big salmon in the river and they boiled it for dinner. When they were cleaning the pot, they found gold dust in the bottom of it."

"Not bad," Nikki said. "And the story fits with camping, too. I think you could sell that line, Marianne. Does your boyfriend — what's his name?"

"Jeff."

"Does Jeff fish?"

Marianne shook her head. Not only did Jeff not fish, he wasn't even all that keen on camping. In fact, when you got him out of the bedroom, he was pretty much useless. Marianne had lately been thinking that for a generally competent woman, she made consistently pathetic and inappropriate choices in men.

"Perfect," said Nikki. "You can tell the

whole story, then, and make it really good. Tell him we made bouillabaisse over an open fire with fresh-caught salmon and herbs growing wild on the riverbank. And then, *voilà!* You volunteered for KP because you're such a good sport, and were rewarded by finding the gold dust."

"And what do I use for gold dust?" Marianne asked. "Flakes off Betsy's mother lode?" Betsy had brought along the full-scale reproduction of an enormous chunk of gold that she used in her classroom and in the annual spring "Gold Rush" when her fourth grade students searched for "gold" hidden in Pettigrew Park.

"Nah," Nikki told her, shaking her head. "Just tell him you cashed it in. We'll all be witnesses." She raised her right hand and grinned. " 'Jeff, Marianne was absolutely tireless in her quest for treasure. We had to rip her out of the water to get her to eat or sleep.' You think he'd buy it? I don't know him, after all."

"I'm not a very convincing liar," Marianne said, though she had to admit the scenario was tempting.

"Look at it this way," Nikki said. "If your ex is being such a jerk about custody, do you really *want* to have any more money? That'd just give him an excuse to cut his child support."

An excellent point. In the four years they'd

been divorced, Mark had repeatedly tried to poor-mouth his way into reduced support payments, even as his pool and spa business exploded. Lately there'd been a lull in the residential building boom that was turning the area around Floritas into a miniature version of Orange County. Mark was using this as an excuse to stint on some of his financial obligations, and child support was always the first one he dropped. The irony was that now that there actually *was* a sluggish economy, and he'd gambled away all the profits from the go-go years. Life would be a lot simpler if Mark could only stay away from the casinos.

"Plus, if modern-day gold prospecting were all that easy," Lynne Montgomery put in, "don't you think everybody would be doing it? At the very least, this whole town would be filthy rich. And charming though it may be, Downieville doesn't look very affluent to me."

Another excellent point. Marianne herself was quite taken with tiny, isolated Downieville, a wonderful town with a sense of stability that grew out of continuous occupation ever since Major Downie and his motley band had plopped themselves down to boil fish on this riverbank in 1849.

Downieville was also at an altitude that would guarantee a legitimate change of the seasons, something Marianne sorely missed

107

from her Wisconsin girlhood. The town was nestled in the flat area along the two streams that joined at its center, with steep mountains rising on either side, thick with evergreen forest. They'd passed a funky old fire engine parked on Main Street before walking across a quaint, one-lane bridge to reach this park. The place fairly reeked of rustic charm.

Marianne could easily see herself living here someday, when the kids were grown and gone, and her life was no longer governed — one might even say terrorized — by custody arguments and arrangements.

But that day was a long way off. Curt was only nine and Briana thirteen. And she could imagine the yowls of protest she'd get from both of them if she even suggested leaving Floritas. Up here there was no surfing, no Charlotte Russe, no cell phone reception.

"Hey!" Judith said, frowning down at the newspaper she had been flipping through as the others chatted. "How close are we to Truckee?"

Lynne cocked her head and seemed to consult a mental map. "About fifty miles as the crow flies," she said. "It's just inside the California-Nevada border, north of Lake Tahoe. Why?"

"There's a fire there," Judith said. "A pretty big one, sounds like. It's closed the interstate and stopped some Amtrak train from Chicago."

"That would be the California Zephyr," Lynne said. "It comes through the same mountain pass as I-80. The Donner Pass, actually."

Marianne shuddered. She had always regarded the Donner party as one of the saddest footnotes in Western expansion. Though she didn't think of herself as particularly squeamish, the notion of cannibalism went beyond her personal disgust factor. "Is the fire likely to get down here?"

Judith shook her head. "It says it's forty percent contained, whatever that means."

Lynne frowned. "It means not nearly out, that's what it means. But I'd say the likelihood of it getting this far is pretty remote."

"I hate California wildfires," Susi announced. As was her style, her tone suggested that the others might really find them swell.

"Fire was a huge problem in the early Gold Rush towns," Marianne told her. "A lot of them burned over and over again. They'd slap up some wooden buildings and tents, and then somebody'd knock over a lantern and the whole thing would go up in smoke in an hour or two. The gold didn't burn, of course, but everything else would." She smiled. "And then as soon as the embers were cool, they'd start building again."

"I've always been fascinated by the guts the forty-niners had," Betsy said. She was lying on her back with her hands locked behind her head, looking up at the sky. "I mean, think about it. They left behind everything and went off into totally unknown territory, looking for something as small and difficult to find as gold dust. When I was growing up, I sort of thought there was one little river and it had chunks of gold in it. I didn't realize until this trip just how huge this area was."

"And they were really running blind, heading into the wilderness," Lisa Limone added. "This was all unexplored territory — no roads, no rail lines, hardly even any maps. And the maps they did have just showed some random squiggles to represent rivers." Lisa had been in the first AP U.S. history class Marianne ever taught, and had been an utter joy as a student: enthusiastic, inquisitive, prepared. With any luck, Briana would be in Lisa's social studies class next year at the junior high.

"Like the map Betsy put up in the food cabin," Lynne said. "Which doesn't even show that the Yuba River has three branches. Probably nobody'd gotten up this far when it was drawn."

Marianne had spent some time looking at that map this morning as she waited for her tea water to boil. The map was artificially aged and resembled nothing so much as one of those genealogical charts that began with one name on the left and then doubled to the right with each earlier generation. Except that here the name on the left was the San Francisco Bay, moving east through a succession of smaller bays until it began splitting into rivers and their tributaries.

And Lynne was right. It showed only one Yuba River.

Betsy nodded. "Exactly. The forty-niners didn't have electronic communication, or any communication at all, really. Once they left home for California, whether they went overland or around the Horn, they were totally cut off. And after they got here, they weren't going to write home and say it was a colossal mistake. There was a good chance that their letters wouldn't get through, anyway."

"It wasn't always a mistake. Some of them *did* get rich," Susi noted.

"But not many," Betsy said. "I don't think anybody kept very accurate records, but even in the places where there was a claim every ten feet, most folks went bust pretty quickly. They'd run out of food, for one thing. The ones who made the big bucks were the entrepreneurs like Levi Strauss, who sold supplies to the miners."

"Hmmm," Judith said, looking up from her newspaper and frowning again. "If the fire doesn't get us, we're supposed to be on the lookout for escaped convicts."

"Oh, please," Susi said scornfully. "What

did they do, break out of some little frontier jail? Grab the keys from some sloppy old sheriff when he was bringing them gruel for dinner?"

"Not at all," Judith told her. "They escaped from a California Youth Authority work camp in Southern California two days ago. But apparently they were originally from this area, so residents are supposed to be on the lookout for them."

"If they were in a CYA camp, they can't be that old," Betsy said. "They'd be just kids."

Susi shot Betsy a disdainful look. "Obviously you haven't worked with high school students lately. They don't need to be old to be dangerous, Betsy. One of the scariest students I ever had was only fifteen when he took a ball peen hammer to his stepmother."

"So where were they from?" Lynne asked. "And where are they supposedly headed?"

"Grass Valley," Judith said. "Which is just south of here, if I remember correctly."

"You do," Lynne told her. "But I honestly don't think there's any reason for us to be concerned."

"And they could have gone a million other places," Judith added, flicking an insect away.

Marianne flinched as she watched a yellow jacket buzz around the remains of her sandwich, a smidgen of bread and onion in waxed paper sitting on the picnic table. She felt instinctively for the bee sting kit in her fanny pack, then stood and moved away from the table. "Anybody want to go check out the museum?"

"Hey, Lynne, look at this!"

Lynne pulled her attention away from a display of items discovered by local Privy Diggers. While excavating in areas that had housed nineteenth-century outhouses, they'd unearthed crockery, buckles, and miscellaneous bits of metal. Lynne had first encountered this universal archeological technique in Colonial Williamsburg, learning later that it was a common and useful technique in digs and excavations from all eras. Even before plumbing advances offered a swirling pathway of water, folks had apparently been unable to resist throwing things in the toilet. If anyone had excavated the latrines of Pompei, they'd probably found shards of Roman wine vessels and lots of broken toga pins.

She followed Judith Limone's finger to a display of liquor labels on the wall of the Downieville Museum, and noted with relief and pleasure that Judith seemed fully recovered from the food poisoning, or whatever it was that had crept up on them in the night. Lynne was gratified by how swiftly most of her group had bounced back, and relieved that her own stomach seemed to have settled pretty well, too. Coming up to Downieville could have been a disaster, given the fact that there was nothing on the forty-three-mile stretch between here and Nevada City but the remains of Camptonville and North San Juan. But blessedly, nobody'd needed an emergency stop by the roadside as they drove in.

Teachers, she decided, were a resilient lot.

"It looks like this local brewery brought in barrels of generic hooch and then prettied it up with fancy labels," Judith said. "Medford Rum, Holland Process Gin, Henry McGibbon Bourbon, Sparkling Champagne Cider. What do you want to bet that it all came out of the same barrel of rotgut?"

"No bet," Lynne told her.

"These settlers were a gullible lot anyway," Judith went on. It had been years since she taught fourth grade Gold Rush, but she sure seemed to remember a lot. Or maybe she'd put more time into background research than she was willing to admit. "The story goes that Major Downie and the other miners sent twenty-five thousand dollars' worth of gold down to be cashed out in San Francisco by some con man who promised them twenty-two dollars an ounce when the going rate was sixteen. And the next time anybody heard of the con man, he was in the Isthmus of Panama, heading back for New York."

"And after *that*," Marianne said, returning

from a visit to the Chinese joss house altar that had been reconstructed at the rear of the first floor, "he was reincarnated as one of my boyfriends."

Chapter 7

Winding back down Highway 49 to Nevada City, Lynne could feel herself relaxing, moving into the natural flow of both the gently curving road and the Highway 49 Revisited Tour itself.

The trip may have gotten off to a rocky start, but teachers were survivors, accustomed to encountering unexpected annoyances and swiftly resolving them. There was no reason to believe everything wouldn't go smoothly from here on out, and everyone but Susi seemed to be settling comfortably into personal rhythms for the trip.

Lynne herself had really been looking forward to this week. She did a lot of vicarious traveling through her clients, and while many of them went places she'd have found hopelessly boring — Disney World in Orlando, for instance, or Las Vegas — many others took some really cool trips.

In the past few months, Lynne had sent clients on a cruise to Lower Nubia and a two-week birding and music tour of the Czech Republic. She'd arranged for three couples to take a three-week China tour with a six-day add-on in Vietnam, where two of the men had served. And a few months back, she had sent her old friends Alice and Don

Harper on a fantastic — and fantastically expensive — three-week tour of History's Lost Cities: Lhasa, Tibet; Kathmandu, Nepal; Ulaanbaatar, Mongolia; Vietiane and Luang Prabang, Laos; Petra, Jordan; Muscat, Oman; Samarkand, Uzbekistan; and Angkor, Cambodia.

But for herself, this had seemed quite perfect, exactly what she wanted right now: a week in a historic natural location with a group of bright and entertaining women, some of whom had been her friends for decades. A grown-up summer camp, where you got to plan your own activities and hang out with your own friends and make your own rules.

The forest along this stretch of Highway 49 was dense and rich, with towering pines and sequoias hugging both sides of the roadway. The trees formed a distant V with the two-lane blacktop at its base, opening at the top to vivid blue sky. They were more than half a mile above sea level here, engulfed by the Tahoe National Forest, and all but alone on the highway.

Now and then they'd pass a road crew grinding dead trees into instant mulch at the edge of the roadway, taking advantage of the only time of the year when this sort of maintenance was feasible. Driving up to Downieville, the two-car caravan had passed several logging trucks laden with massive tree trunks, barreling down out of the Sierra as a reminder that man hadn't quite finished taking advantage of this region's natural resources.

But mostly today they'd had the highway to themselves in both directions, twisting along nearly close enough to reach out and touch the thick undergrowth that hugged the shoulders. On the CD player, James Taylor was going to Carolina in his mind, but Lynne felt quite content to be right where she was, on the back roads of Gold Rush country.

Their miniconvoy stopped briefly at the Canyon Creek trailhead, where they left Nikki, Betsy, Marianne, and Lisa, who planned a late afternoon hike and a possible dip in the icy South Yuba River. The afternoon was so deliciously warm and clear that Lynne was half tempted to join them, but as driver of the only vehicle returning directly to Murmuring Pines, that wasn't an option for her. She waited while another logging truck passed, then swung the van back onto Highway 49.

Her agenda for the rest of the afternoon was clear and simple: a nap, a glass or two of wine, and a shower. The order was negotiable.

Most of the others riding back with her had similar plans. Judith, who'd chosen to be a passenger rather than a driver today, was actually ahead of schedule, catching forty winks with her head resting on a rolled-up sweatshirt, just behind the driver's seat. Judith had always been noted for her efficiency. Mandy was lying down in the way-back. Susi squirmed uncomfortably beside Lynne, riding shotgun. Lynne mostly ignored her, singing along softly with "Sweet Baby James" on the CD player.

When Lynne pulled into Murmuring Pines, the place seemed deserted. The only vehicle on the grounds was Connie Caravaci's Toyota pickup, parked beside the office. She stopped and stuck her head into the office, but Connie wasn't in. Apparently the San Franciscans occupying the two cabins closest to the highway had checked out on schedule and nobody else seemed to have arrived.

Perfect.

It was, Lynne decided contentedly, rather like having their own private Gold Rush town, albeit one with far greater amenities than most of the forty-niners could even have dreamed of. She found a chilled bottle of Chardonnay in the food cabin, poured herself a generous glass, and wandered out onto the wraparound porch to enjoy the bucolic splendor of this tucked-away retreat.

The cabins were built along a ridge above a ravine thick with conifers and lush green underbrush. Somewhere off to the south a creek burbled below, while a scarlet cardinal swooped past the porch on his way to important bird business.

As Lynne sipped her wine, her gaze wandered down the steep hillside, then stopped abruptly at an out-of-place patch of cobalt blue. She leaned over the railing for a better look, then went back inside, frowning, to look for Betsy's binoculars.

The blue was an altogether wrong shade for this sylvan hillside, and the scene made Lynne uneasy. When she returned with the binoculars and focused on the patch of color, she realized with a rush of sudden horror that the cobalt blue was actually a plaid sleeve — with a pale hand extending outward into a fern. The hand wasn't moving.

Judith Limone came up behind Lynne. Her catnap on the way back from Downieville seemed to have revived her. "I had no idea this would be so peaceful," she sighed. "What're you watching, Lynne? Wildlife?"

"I don't think so," Lynne said grimly, handing over the binoculars.

Judith looked through the lenses and gasped. "Why, what on earth?"

"I don't know. But I'm going down to look. Could you run back to the office and find Connie? Unless — you don't think that *is* Connie down there, do you?"

"No idea," Judith told her, and before Lynne could add a request to call an ambulance, the principal had set down the binoculars and was racing through the cabin and down the road to the office.

Lynne looked down the steep hillside and

considered. She'd never been one for rock climbing, or any form of hiking that didn't involve clearly demarcated and well-graded trails. Still, this slope didn't look too difficult, and as she clambered over the balcony railing and dropped three feet to the angled ground, she decided not to think too much about what she was doing. This was a time to act, not to plan.

And naturally, right when she could really have used their help, all the truly fit members of their group were off cavorting in the South Yuba River. Nikki Mason and Lisa Limone would be down this hillside like mountain goats, most likely, leaping from branch to boulder with the grace of extras in a Tarzan movie.

Whereas Lynne Montgomery — fifty-something and accustomed to taking her exercise on the level pavement of the Floritas seawall above the Pacific shoreline — was reduced to backing slowly and deliberately downhill, moving on her hands and knees. Not until she was halfway into the ravine did it occur to her that she should have brought a first aid kit, not that she had a spare hand to carry one. In fact, she could have used two or three more hands just to keep from falling head over tin can down the side of the hill.

She was nearly at the bottom when she heard Judith yell down. "Lynne! I couldn't find Connie, but I called nine-one-one. They're on the way."

Lynne raised a hand to wave acknowledgment and felt her footing give way. She slid the last eight or ten feet down the hillside, grateful to be wearing jeans and not shorts that would have left her knees and legs exposed.

She turned sideways to break her fall, and as she crashed to a halt, she got her first clear look at the figure she'd been climbing down to reach.

Connie Caravaci sprawled on the ground like a forgotten doll, her limbs twisted and neck sharply angled, utterly still.

Lynne took a deep breath and turned to look up at Judith, silhouetted above her. "It's Connie down here," she yelled.

The owner of Murmuring Pines lay motionless with her eyes closed. But when Lynne touched her fingers to Connie's wrist, she was rewarded by a faint but steady pulse. And then she could also hear Connie's breathing, shallow and raspy.

Lynne moved cautiously around Connie's body. There was no obvious bleeding to be staunched, though a trickle of dried blood ran down the side of the woman's face, probably from an injury during her fall. Her short silver hair was matted with more dried blood, above and behind her left ear. Lynne took a deep breath and spoke Connie's name, softly at first and then more sharply.

No response at all.

Lynne backed away, wondering what, if anything, she could or should do. You weren't supposed to move people with head injuries, and the angle of her neck suggested a possible spinal injury as well. Connie lay on her side with her eyes closed, her skin tone almost white.

"Do you want the first aid kit?" Judith called.

"Nothing I could do with it," Lynne yelled back. "How long will it take them to get an ambulance here?"

"Not long. That's what they claimed, anyway." Judith's tone was hopeful but dubious. She'd spent a long career dealing with bureaucrats and civil servants.

Lynne took Connie Caravaci's hand in her own, settled herself as comfortably as she could, and waited for help, talking softly to the woman just in case she could hear, reassuring her that assistance was on the way.

Out-and-out kismet, Connie had said last night about finding this place. *Pure luck.*

"Hang in there, Connie," Lynne told her softly now. They said you couldn't ever know for sure if people who were unconscious could hear what was going on around them. So as she waited, Lynne told Connie about the day's travels: lunch in Downieville, Tin Cup Diggins, the displays of button strings made by women in the gold camps at the Downieville Museum, the breathtaking solitude of the towering pines, the huge logging trucks rumbling down Highway 49.

Surprisingly, the wait really wasn't very long. Barely five minutes later, Lynne heard the sound of a truck engine coming up the road into the Murmuring Pines property. Moments later four young paramedics looked down the side of the hill.

After that, things moved with gratifying speed.

Susi Braun lay on her uncomfortable bed in her wretched little cabin, pouting.

She didn't like much of anything about the way this trip was turning out. She wasn't happy about scrounging vitamins like some pathetic beggar, or sharing her cabin with Mandy Mosher, a virtual stranger, who once again was zonked out and snoring. She sounded like an overfilled balloon set loose to empty itself by *brrppping* around the room. Susi particularly did not appreciate spending half the night in the john because that Montgomery woman had been careless about food safety.

She was annoyed by the gung-ho camaraderie that the younger teachers exhibited, an enthusiasm that might work nicely with eight-year-olds but which left her cold. She found Nikki Mason particularly irritating, with her holier-than-thou attitudes about proper diet and physical exertion.

And she really didn't feel well.

While the others seemed fully recovered, Susi still had cramps and twinges and she was fairly certain she was running a fever, though her thermometer was in the meds bag that she'd inadvertently left behind.

But mostly Susi had to admit that she didn't like thinking about what her husband Rick was doing back in Floritas.

Rick was a gregarious charmer, currently working as marketing director for a sports card company up in Carlsbad. He'd been involved one way or another with sports memorabilia for the last twenty years, hobnobbing with deteriorating athletic legends and feisty up-and-comers, hanging out in hotel bars with perky little personal assistants. Fidelity had never been Rick's long suit, but Susi was willing to overlook his affairs because he was such a devoted father and family man. Mostly they seemed to be mindless flings: a Cowboys cheerleader in Dallas, a sportswriter in Philadelphia, a succession of pneumatic young receptionists.

Susi had always assumed that he'd stay the course in their marriage because he was so accustomed to the creature comforts that came with having a rich wife. Susi's father had been a petroleum engineer with a penchant for the stock market, and he'd amassed a sizable personal fortune before he and Susi's mother died, heavily insured, in a Venezuelan air crash. Susi had been a junior at USC at the time, majoring in education and shopping.

There was no doubt in Susi's mind that Rick was currently having an affair. Over the years she had learned to read the signs well. They were all in place right now: unexplained absences, late nights at the office, extra solicitousness of Susi when he did manage to get home, a certain indifference in the bedroom, flowers for no particular reason.

Now that both the boys were away at college, Rick and Susi were actually seeing less of each other than they had when the whole family lived together. There were no more water polo matches to attend, no more predawn swim practices or community service beach cleanup days. The boys didn't need carpooling or rides to Youth Group or laundry service, and the grocery bill was down by two-thirds.

The Braun nest, emptied over the course of the past two years, had become a lifeless husk. A well-decorated husk, to be sure. Susi had redone both boys' bedrooms, the family room, the downstairs powder room, and the patio landscaping. She was currently looking at fabric samples for a master bedroom makeover, and all that held her back was a sense that what her husband *really* wanted to make over in that room was the identity of his bedmate.

Mandy's snoring suddenly moved into a buzz saw crescendo. Time for some defensive music, Susi decided. And she needed to rub more Vitamin E into her toes. It seemed to be helping, actually, which was a good thing because the incisions were quite unattractive and Susi wasn't prepared to abandon her extensive collection of designer sandals.

Susi sat up on the bed, reached over into her suitcase for her personal CD player, and stopped abruptly.

Somebody had been messing with her things.

The CDs, which had been alphabetized and tucked snugly into the far side of the bag, were now both out of alignment and out of order. Her socks and underwear were jumbled, and two tightly rolled T-shirts had been unfurled and then folded sloppily atop her jeans.

She looked around the room. A nosy maid, perhaps? She never trusted the minimum-wage functionaries one encountered on vacation, though she'd expect less trouble here than down in Mexico, where you just never knew. Somebody had definitely been in the cabin to perform basic maid service. The beds were made, though the sheets hadn't been changed, and when she checked the bathroom now, she found a new set of threadbare towels hanging on the racks. The wastebaskets were empty.

Inside the bathroom she unzipped her makeup kit. The three twenty-dollar bills she had tucked behind the deodorant were gone.

Susi wasn't sure what to do next. What she *wanted* to do was march right up to Connie Caravaci and ask her what the devil was going on and who was stealing from the guest cabins. But that wasn't exactly feasible, given that just a few minutes ago, Connie's unconscious body had been loaded into an ambulance and rushed off to the hospital.

After Judith sounded the alarm, banging on the cabin door like some twenty-first-century Paula Revere warning of an imminent Red-coat invasion, Susi had stepped out onto her porch just long enough to watch Lynne crash down the side of the hill, landing almost on top of poor Connie. When the rescue squad arrived, Susi watched for a while, but quickly lost interest. The operation seemed compe-tent enough — young men in dark uniforms coordinating their efforts and working with quiet efficiency. But everything they did seemed to be in super slo-mo.

Super slow-mo. Like those sports replays Rick so loved to watch, the same event viewed over and over again, slowed to a crawl, then repeated from fifteen different an-gles. Funny that she kept coming back to

Rick, as if he — or his love of sports — had anything to do with this latest calamity. Whether she was ready to admit it or not, lately everything kept circling around and coming back to Rick Braun.

Something, Susi realized, felt different about Rick's latest dalliance. He seemed to be working harder at hiding his unaccounted-for hours, and to be offering larger and more extravagant bouquets. He was also exceptionally cheerful.

Good heavens, could this be the woman he'd actually leave her for?

Lynne listened to Susi Braun's complaint with growing anxiety. Lynne wasn't inclined to give much credence to claims that Susi's suitcase was mussed, but the missing sixty dollars worried her enormously. If Susi's cabin had been burglarized, Connie's accident took on an entirely new perspective.

Lynne swung into action. She knocked on Judith's door, asked her to look around and see if anything was missing, then returned to her own cabin.

It didn't take long for Lynne to realize that the contents of the cabin she shared with Betsy had also been disturbed. The place hadn't been trashed or searched too obviously, but there were subtle differences in the way things were arranged on tabletops. An Almond Joy bar was missing from beside her bed, its wrapper in the otherwise-empty trash can. And Betsy's jewelry pouch was gone.

Should she call the police right away or wait until the others returned? No reason to put things off, Lynne decided, and she was just stepping away from the pay phone down by the now-deserted office when Nikki's SUV roared up the drive. Lynne hastily filled in the four horrified returnees about what had happened, sending them off to check their tents and cabins. Then she trudged back up the hill to take another look at the communal food cabin.

When she reached it, Nikki was just opening the closet door.

"Oh, no!" Nikki cried. "Oh drat, drat, *drat!*"

"What?" Lynne asked, looking around the rest of the room. It would be much harder to check this place out than to investigate individual cabins, because everyone had been in and out of here repeatedly. Most of them had deposited things here and they'd all moved stuff around.

Nikki spat out a barrage of colorful epithets, then turned to Lynne. "My shotgun's been stolen," she announced.

"Your what?" Surely Lynne hadn't heard this correctly.

Nikki shook her head and paced. "My shotgun. I brought it along for my costume, for the Characters Dinner. You know, I'm coming as Black Bart, the gentleman bandit."

Lynne had read about Black Bart, a respectable San Francisco clerk who moonlighted robbing stagecoaches during the Gold Rush, always very politely. He had, in fact, been apprehended after a couple dozen robberies when police traced a laundry mark on a handkerchief he'd left behind. Nineteenth-century forensics.

"And for this you needed a shotgun? A *real* shotgun?"

"I didn't bring along any ammunition," Nikki explained, "and that's actually kind of the point. Bart's shotgun was never loaded. But I already *had* the gun, you see, so it seemed silly *not* to bring it. It's a period recreation of an 1897 Winchester, very cool."

"If you say so. But what was it doing in here?"

"Well, I couldn't very well leave it in my tent," Nikki answered irritably, "even though it's in a locked case. And I didn't want to keep it in the car while we were riding around places, since the SUV doesn't have a lockable trunk. I just slipped it in the closet here when nobody was paying attention, so it would always be locked up when we weren't here."

Lynne laughed. "Worked like a charm, I guess, at least till somebody stole it. None of *us* even knew it was here."

Lynne sat down at the kitchenette table

and idly picked up the "Mother Lode," the big lump of "gold" that Betsy had brought along. It was just a chunk of misshapen quartz, of course, painted with the kind of gold metallic spray used to make Christmas decorations. Betsy used it in the fourth grade Gold Rush that Pettigrew Elementary sponsored each spring. Along with other painted rocks, it was hidden in Pettigrew Park, to be discovered by the nine-year-old miners.

Beneath where the rock had been sitting on the table was a little puddle. Lynne frowned and leaned forward, turning the rock over in her hands. It was moist on the underside, as if somebody had washed it recently.

"Hey, Nikki," Lynne said. "Take a look at this. Betsy's Mother Lode is *wet*."

Nikki came over and took the rock. "You're right. But why would anybody wash a rock?" She looked around the room. "Looks to me like the maid service here is pretty rudimentary, actually. Has there even been a maid in?"

Lynne nodded. "The beds are made in the other cabins and the towels have been changed. The waste baskets are emptied. But you're right. The service is pretty basic. The kind of thing where they'd just slap a paper band around the toilet seat and call it disinfected."

Nikki grimaced. "So then why would anybody wash a rock?"

"To clean it off, I suppose," Lynne said.

"But we've been gone all day. And why would anyone need to clean a rock that was sitting, minding its own business, in an unoccupied cabin? Omigod!"

"What?" Nikki hadn't stopped pacing.

"You'd wash it if it had something on it that you didn't want anyone to notice. Like blood. I was the one who went down the hill and found Connie. There was matted hair and blood on her scalp, and a little dried trickle running across her cheek."

Surely, Lynne tried to tell herself, she was just being silly and melodramatic. But still, it couldn't hurt to look around a little more. She set down the rock and moved her gaze systematically around the cabin. The foodstuffs seemed more or less in order, the boxes of supplies still neatly arranged along the wall. The glasses they'd used last night were washed and drying in a drainer by the small kitchen sink.

"Nikki, do you remember when we were talking about these rugs in the cabins?" Lynne indicated the braided rag throw rug on the floor. Last night they'd discussed how all the rugs were different, that somebody seemed to have actually constructed them from real rags, perhaps even on the North American continent. Betsy, who'd made a few rag rugs in her younger days, had noticed similar fabrics in several of the different rugs in various cabins.

"Not really," Nikki admitted. "Rugs aren't very exciting to me."

"Me neither," Lynne said. "But I do remember that last night that little blue-and-yellow rug was sitting beside the bed. Now it's all the way over here." Lynne bent to take a closer look and picked up the rug, uncovering a dark irregular stain. She touched a tentative finger to it and realized it was moist, as if somebody had spilled something and then moved the rug to cover it up.

The door burst open.

"My CD player's missing," Betsy announced, "and my jewelry pouch, though you already noticed that, Lynne. And I just ran into Lisa, who said that it looked like somebody'd been going through her underwear, though none of it's missing. Judith doesn't seem to be missing anything. I guess even sneak thieves are afraid of her."

Lynne realized, with a sinking heart, that her trip wasn't on nearly as even a keel as she had believed when driving back down the mountain road from Downieville this afternoon.

Something very wrong was going on here.

Chapter 8

The sheriff's deputies who responded to Lynne's call were initially polite. They'd heard about Connie's accident and knew she'd been taken to the hospital. This was, after all, a small town with a presumably limited police blotter. Dramatic hillside rescues of unconscious innkeepers couldn't happen that often.

But their interest ratcheted up considerably when they heard about the stolen shotgun, and Lynne could tell that they were looking at the diminutive Nikki Mason from an entirely different perspective.

"You were carrying a loaded shotgun as a *prop?*" the older deputy asked. 'Older' was a relative term here. He couldn't have been more than thirty-five. His nameplate identified him as OFFICER M. WASHBURN and he was clearly appalled.

"First of all," said Nikki, trying without much success to hide her irritation, "it wasn't loaded. I didn't even bring along any ammunition. And it's perfectly legal for me to own it. I'm not a convicted felon or a drug user or a mental patient. I wasn't transporting it across state lines and it was in a locked case. And at the time it was stolen, it was on a shelf in a closed closet in a locked cabin that we had rented with an expectation of security."

Deputy Washburn nodded. "Are there other weapons missing?"

"Not mine," Nikki said, "and I think I'm the only one in this group who owns any. But others are missing things." She nodded at Lynne.

"Several items are missing from different cabins," Lynne told him, "and none of them appear to have been broken into. They were all locked when we got back. Most of us don't have real valuables along on this trip, other than Nikki's shotgun." *Nikki's shotgun* had such a bizarre ring to it. Lynne wondered if she'd ever get used to the notion. "Some of us brought cameras, but we had them with us today. This place is off the beaten path and the only other folks who were staying here left this morning. Suppose Connie interrupted somebody who was in the process of burglarizing the cabins? I only met her yesterday, but she spent some time with us at our campfire last night, and she seems pretty fearless and straightforward. I don't think she'd stop to call for help if she stumbled onto something going wrong at her place. She'd be much more likely to just march in and ask what the devil was going on."

The deputies exchanged looks.

"And then you're saying that this burglar

threw her down the hill?" the younger one asked. He was very fair, with a peaches-and-cream complexion and blue eyes. If Lynne had been thirty years younger, she'd be salivating. Because her son David was a police officer back home in Floritas, Lynne was quite familiar with the standard equipment carried by cops. This young man wore every possible accessory on his Sam Browne belt, including a few oddball items that she couldn't identify at all. Bear repellent, perhaps?

Lynne shrugged her shoulders. "Maybe. Or maybe the burglar picked up whatever was handy, like this gold-painted rock that was sitting right here on the table, and whacked her with it. And *then* threw her down the hill, so it would look like she had an accident and fell. There was a place on her head that had bled, and it could just as easily have happened in here as on the hillside. That would also explain the wet spot here on the floor. Somebody moved a throw rug to cover it up. They probably tried to wash the floor and couldn't get it all out."

Deputy Washburn, looking suddenly weary, turned to his partner. "Wait here, with these ladies. I'll be right back."

Lynne watched through the window as he went out to the patrol car, sat down, and used the radio. He was gone several minutes, and when he came back in, he didn't look happy. He walked around the porch outside the cabin and looked down the hillside for a few moments. Then he came to the doorway and motioned for Lynne to join him outside.

"Can you show me where Mrs. Caravaci was when you first saw her?"

"You mean go down there again?" Lynne tried to keep the anxiety out of her voice. Once was more than enough for this particular adventure.

"No, no," he reassured. "Just point it out."

Lynne aimed a finger down the hill. "She was behind that big bush there."

"Was her head on a rock?"

"Not at all. It was lying on a fern, actually. And the place where the blood had caked on her scalp was facing up."

"How would she have gotten down there?"

"When I found her, I just assumed she was on the hill for some reason," Lynne said, "and that she slipped and fell. It wouldn't be hard to do."

Deputy Washburn considered the incline. "Assuming you had reason to be on the hill in the first place. So. You went down after her?"

Lynne nodded.

"You do all that damage to the vegetation?"

Lynne turned to him. There was something vaguely accusatory in his tone that she didn't like at all. For the first time she noticed just how battered the shrubbery was between the cabin and the spot where Connie had come to rest.

"I imagine I did a fair amount of damage, yes. I was in a hurry to get down there and it's a pretty steep hillside. I wasn't worrying about protecting the wildflowers. In fact, I kind of fell the last part of the way. But don't forget that the guys from the Rescue Squad went down there too, and brought her back up. If anybody's to blame for messing up the hillside, I'd look at them."

Deputy Washburn shook his head. "I'm not blaming anyone, Mrs. Montgomery. Just trying to figure out what happened. Mrs. Caravaci's in a coma, so there's no way to ask her about any of this. I just talked to the doctor and he said she has a head injury that could come from hitting a rock or being hit by a rock, either one." He looked down the hillside again. "There's plenty of rocks on the way down, that's for sure. I think I'm going to see about having somebody climb down and take a look. What I don't want is you ladies going down there and messing things up."

Lynne squared her shoulders. "None of us has the slightest intention of going down there again. I would have preferred not to do it the first time." She hesitated. "With Connie in the hospital, is there a problem about us staying here?"

"Not with me," he told her, flashing a cockeyed smile. "She live alone here?"

"I think so."

"Well, then, I imagine somebody at the hospital is tracking down her relatives right now. It'd be up to them to decide if you can stay."

"She doesn't have any local relatives," Lynne said. "At least that's what she told me. She said her kids still live down in L.A. and she's been divorced for twenty years. We're supposed to stay here tonight and tomorrow night and then we're moving on south to Columbia."

"Sounds reasonable to me," he said. "Now, I'm going to have one of our detectives and some technicians come out here. Are you sleeping in that cabin, Mrs. Montgomery?"

Lynne shook her head. "Nobody is. We're using it to store our food and communal supplies. Oh, and the women who are camping in those two tents have been using the bathroom there."

"Excellent," he answered. "Nobody will need to move, then. And I'm sure the campers can use a bathroom in one of the other cabins. So there won't be any problem if we lock that cabin up for the time being."

Lynne smiled sweetly. "You say that as if we have a choice."

Half an hour later, Detective Jeff

McMasters arrived on the scene. He was about forty-five, a short wiry fellow with one of those odd complicated moustaches that paramilitary men are so inexplicably fond of. It swept across his face like a squirrel tail and curved up dramatically at both ends. It was a gold miner look, actually, one that would have been accompanied by shoulder-length locks a hundred and fifty years ago. Lynne wondered if that was why he affected it.

Lynne guided him on a fast walk-through of the food cabin, pointing out the rock, the stain, and the shelf where the shotgun had been.

"Side-by-side Winchester?" he said, a note of admiration and what might even have been envy in his voice.

"Yes. Mrs. Mason can tell you more about it. None of the rest of us even realized it was here. But all of our cabins seem to have been searched, and rather clumsily at that. They're mostly small things that are missing: a CD player, some cash, a leather pouch with some inexpensive jewelry in it."

He listened and nodded, then left the cabin with Lynne on his heels. He sat down at the picnic table outside and set his notebook on the table, then motioned for Lynne to join him. She sat across the table.

"Now. This is an organized tour group?" he asked, unable to keep a note of skepticism from his tone. He seemed to expect a bus with uniformed driver, cute little name tags all around, and an overextended itinerary. Also a classier clientele. Lynne herself sometimes led upscale special-interest tours, such as the Sonoma Sojourn that visited California's wine country, but she hadn't run across any fancy tours of gold country when she'd done her preliminary research. Of course, that didn't mean there weren't any.

"Very informally organized, Detective," she told him mildly. "I own a travel agency down in Floritas, in northern San Diego County. And I occasionally lead specialized tours. But I put this particular trip together as a favor for some old friends, a group of teachers." She explained that the trip had arisen out of a chance remark at Betsy's Christmas Open House the previous winter.

A pair of crime scene technicians drove up then, in a white van with NEVADA COUNTY SHERIFF'S DEPARTMENT on its side doors. Detective McMasters took them into the food cabin. While they were inside, Lynne noticed the other Argonauts peeking out of tents, sticking their heads out onto front porches, pulling aside curtains. It reminded her of the forest creatures cautiously surfacing in a Disney movie when the hunter is finally gone. Sure enough, the moment McMasters came outside again, they all disappeared once more.

It *was* like Disney.

The technicians gathered cases and equipment out of their van and went back indoors. As they began whatever they were doing inside the food cabin, Lynne took Detective McMasters around and introduced him to the others. They started with Nikki. His questions about the shotgun were precise and specific, and Nikki's answers were equally direct.

Next he talked to Marianne Gordon about what had been in her tent and what was missing. Then he visited the Limone cabin, the one shared by Susi Braun and Mandy Mosher, and finally the one where Lynne was staying with Betsy Danforth.

He was low-key and thorough, snapping pictures, asking questions, making careful lists of what had been stolen and from where. On his way to interview Susi and Mandy, he was stopped by one of the technicians, a tiny Asian woman with a sleek black pageboy. They stepped aside to confer for a few moments, and then he returned to Lynne.

"It appears you may have noticed something important here, Mrs. Montgomery. There's blood on both the rock and the floor."

"Connie's blood?"

"We won't know that until we run some lab work, or until she wakes up and tells us what happened. But it's a logical guess. And in the meantime, we'll need to get fingerprints from all of you for elimination purposes, so we can figure out which prints aren't supposed to be there."

"We were planning to go into Nevada City for dinner in about half an hour," Lynne told him. "Is there any reason we can't leave then? It would probably make things easier for you here, actually, if we were out of your way."

"It probably would," Detective McMasters agreed. "We can do the prints right now."

It was actually closer to forty-five minutes before the Argonauts left Murmuring Pines. When they returned two hours later after dinner, the police were gone and the cabins were locked. Lynne got back first, with Betsy, Susi, Marianne, and Nikki. The others had ridden with Judith.

Bands of yellow crime scene tape were crisscrossed in front of the door to the food cabin.

"Darn it," Susi said, "I really wanted to have one of those leftover brownies."

Lynne had a sudden memory of Susi beside her at the serving table the night before, stacking four of them on a plate. She'd been so busy worrying about her potato salad that she'd forgotten all about the brownies Susi had brought along. "Where did those brownies come from, Susi? Didn't you say somebody gave them to you? Maybe there was something wrong with them and *that's* why everybody got sick."

Betsy, standing nearby, perked up. "I'm allergic to chocolate, so I didn't eat any of them. You may just be right." She called across to Nikki, who was heading for her tent. "Hey, Nikki! Did you eat any brownies last night?"

Nikki shook her head and turned back to join them. "Nope." Hers was probably a refined sugar–bleached flour issue, and Lynne was relieved that she spared them the nutrition lecture.

Susi's eyes had widened so much they seemed to fill her face. "Oh my God, that could be *it!* I don't know where those brownies came from, actually. They were in the work room at school on the last day, with my name on them, and I just figured it was Moms in Touch or somebody like that."

"Moms in Touch didn't give *me* any brownies," Marianne said, "though I think I have a reputation as an atheistic heathen, so maybe they wouldn't." Moms in Touch was a Christian group who provided flowers and foodstuffs and inspirational notes for the faculty of the various Floritas schools.

"There wasn't a note saying who they were from?" asked Lynne, who had left plenty of things for teachers in various Floritas school work rooms over the years, generally without anybody noticing or challenging her.

Susi shook her head. "I didn't pay much attention, to be perfectly honest. I had a box of See's Candy, too, in my mailbox. And a nice note from a mom whose son just managed to squeak by with a C so he could stay on the football team. But the brownies didn't say who they were from."

Lynne looked at Betsy. "Bets, remember when we were on Guam and there was that big fuss because somebody sent the C.O. some brownies with laxative in them?"

Betsy's eyes widened. "Right, made with that chocolate-flavored laxative. And after all the hullaballo, it turned out to be his own son. Who was shipped off to military school shortly thereafter, as I recall, with a mighty sore fanny."

"I bet that's it." Lynne was feeling more vindicated by the second. "Marianne, did you have any brownies? I had part of one but I didn't like it so I didn't finish it."

"None," Marianne said. "I automatically avoid anything that might have nuts in it."

Susi's expression could have melted glass. "Well, I had a *lot* of them. Everybody knows I'm a chocoholic. I can't believe somebody would do this to me!"

"We don't *know* that's what happened," Lynne reminded her, though she personally felt pretty convinced.

"Well, if that *is* what happened, be grateful

you didn't get shot," Marianne told Susi. "Teaching's a risky business these days. And I bet that's exactly what happened. Whoever did it certainly wouldn't have any way of knowing you'd share the brownies."

"The little bastard!" Susi sat on the cabin steps, looking exasperated beyond her current strength.

"That sounds like you think you know who did it," Lynne said.

Susi slowly shook her head. "Not for sure. But there were a couple of real jerks in my tenth grade regular English class. Board boys."

Lynne knew that Susi referred to kids who skateboarded to the beach with surfboards tucked under their arms. If their families had money, they also went to the mountains in winter and snowboarded.

Lynne looked around the group. "Well, we'll have to check with the others when they get back, but it makes a lot of sense to me that this is what happened. You think there are some of them left, Susi?"

"There were this morning. I just didn't feel like eating them."

"Well, when we can get back into the food cabin, I'll wrap them up and take them home. Weren't they in some kind of disposable aluminum pan?"

"Yeah, but why take them back? To show how stupid I am?" Susi asked.

Lynne shook her head. "Not at all. I'll have my son the cop check it for fingerprints." Strictly speaking, this fell significantly outside of David's job description. He was a patrol officer for the Floritas Police Department. But she couldn't imagine him refusing. "And maybe it'll turn out to be somebody whose prints are on file, from some juvenile offense or something."

"That *would* be sweet," Susi said.

And sure enough, when Judith's Buick crawled up the drive five minutes later, each woman's gastric distress the previous evening turned out to be directly proportional to the number of brownies she had eaten.

Lynne felt relieved beyond all reason. It made perfect sense to think that the group indigestion rose out of one of Susi's students hating her. In fact, if she wasn't more pleasant in the classroom than she'd been so far on this trip, Lynne could imagine a scene like *Murder on the Orient Express*, with a whole group of Susi's students getting together to do a bit of special baking for the teacher.

Marianne built a campfire, as much out of habit as out of any real desire to sit around and commune with her fellow travelers. When you went camping and it got dark, you had a fire. It was as simple as that. As she gathered kindling and positioned firewood,

Marianne tried to concentrate on the wonders of this environment and avoid thinking about what she'd probably be doing right now if she were down at home.

There was a possibility she'd be in a steamy clinch with her boyfriend Jeff, who might well be the horniest man alive, but on a Monday night, the kids would probably be home and Marianne never violated her own rule about not having sex while the kids were under the same roof. The rule had actually gone into effect without her realizing it during the last couple years of her marriage to Mark, who'd grown so disinterested in her physical charms that she had suggested sex therapy. He'd countered by saying that what he really wanted was a divorce, which turned out to be a declaration of unconditional war.

No, on Monday night she'd be by herself, most likely online. It was awkward to admit it, out in this wondrous land of rushing rivers and towering pines and jagged mountains crafted by both God and Man, but Marianne was starting to feel the pangs of serious Internet withdrawal.

It had kind of crept up on her, the Internet, the way addictions so often do.

It all started when they got the new computer, the loaded Dell with up-to-the-minute everything. Up until then, she'd been vaguely aware of the possibilities of the World Wide Web without ever really investigating them.

It was a time issue, mostly. She had a full-time job and custody of two active — overly so in Curt's case — kids, both gifted athletes who participated enthusiastically in a year-round relay of sports. Little league moved into soccer, then segued into volleyball for Briana and basketball for Curt, both of whom seemed to have gotten all the height genes on both sides of the family. And then it was softball season again, with a new set of uniforms and team pictures and assistant coaches. Marianne was always schlepping somebody to practice or sitting in rickety bleachers or pulling together snacks and a cooler of Gatorade for the team.

So she always figured she didn't have time for anything else. But she'd been mistaken. There *were*, it turned out, things that could be cut from even the most heavily scheduled twenty-four-hour day. She couldn't stop reading the newspaper, because she taught history and loved the way current events evolved into contemporary history, but she discovered that she could do very nicely without television. She quit her book club and instead listened to books-on-tape while performing her chauffeur duties.

She hired a gardener and gave up any pretense of working in the yard. She increased both kids' allowances and tied the funds to additional chores, which they performed without too much hassle. That took care of a lot of the housework. She cut a separate deal with Briana, who was strangely fond of doing laundry.

She did her grocery shopping at Costco, and as much as possible, she did the rest of her shopping online. The delivery charges were more than offset by the time she saved, and often she could find terrific deals.

She had gotten in touch with some old high school friends from Wisconsin, and chatted back and forth with them online almost every day. She discovered some sites where you could click your mouse and somebody else would give money to worthy charities, and she faithfully bookmarked those and contributed daily. Then she joined an online list of environmentalists, and following up on a passing reference by one of them, hit the emotional jackpot, a list of mothers of kids with ADHD.

Here were women who understood exactly what it was like to live with a kid whose body chemistry was out of whack, who knew more about dosages and interactions of various drugs than any of the doctors Marianne had visited with Curt, and who offered an unbeatable combination of support, wisdom, education, and black humor. It was eighteen months since Marianne had discovered the group called "runningonempty," where even the name was gallows humor.

But even though she could no longer

imagine how she had ever survived without the Internet, she knew it could never take the place of these real, live, home town friends.

Amos Ledbetter was up before dawn on Tuesday morning, having once again tossed fitfully through the night. Yesterday had gone wrong beyond all imagination, but today — today he would make it all better.

Amos possessed a wardrobe that was the envy of every man who'd ever seen it. At least a third of its items could only be accurately described as costume materials. This afforded him great pleasure. Dressing up was one of Amos's favorite activities and most enduring entertainments.

There hadn't been much opportunity to develop this side of his personality as a child growing up in the San Joaquin Valley, where dressing up usually meant putting on a shirt. Now Amos again lived in the sturdy two-story Victorian house in Stockton where he had grown up. The present circumstances were considerably more enjoyable, however, with his social-climbing sister married to a Marin banker and both parents gone to what he fervently hoped was their eternal reward, a scenario he always envisioned featuring pitchforks and molten lava and huge vats of boiling tar.

So as a kid, he hadn't had the opportunity

to indulge his fascination with clothing and costumery. But a boy can dream, and an effeminate boy growing up in cowboy country dreams more than most. When Amos enrolled at UCLA, those dreams came true beyond anything he had ever imagined.

Appearances counted for everything in Los Angeles. The film industry relied on costume rental companies whose inventories could outfit anything from Henry VIII to a paramecium. Amos had worked part time at Hollywood Costume while an undergraduate, filching the occasional perfect accessory and buying overstock items outright. He'd tried on Bogie's suit from *The Big Sleep*, Anthony Quinn's Papal robes from *Shoes of the Fisherman*, and a slinky little number worn by Jack Lemmon in *Some Like It Hot*. One unforgettable evening in West Hollywood, he'd jammed his toes into a pair of the original ruby slippers from *The Wizard of Oz*.

When Amos had returned to the San Joaquin Valley for his father's eight-year death watch, half of the U-Haul truck that he drove north contained wardrobe. In a gesture as petty as it was symbolic, he had now outfitted his parents' bedroom to hold it all, with professional clothing racks and walls of shoe displays and a revolving hat cupboard designed for him by a clever San Francisco friend. He didn't dress up as much as he used to, these days, and a depressing percentage of the clothing no longer fit in any case.

Middle age was so cruel. And he wasn't really even middle-aged anymore, not unless he was going to live to be a hundred and eighteen.

But rusty or not, Amos could produce a particular look in a hurry when he needed to. He had assembled the various components of today's outfit last night, determining to his chagrin that the pants were a wee bit snug. While he thrashed around in his four-poster bed last night, he'd realized suddenly that the snugness actually served to make his costume all the more authentic.

Only then had he been able to doze off.

Humming a medley from *Cabaret*, Amos now donned sturdy hiking boots, knee socks, leather lederhosen, a blousy white shirt and a jaunty Tyrolean cap with a crisp white feather. Even under duress he still took pleasure from role-playing. He played his old Berlitz German conversational tapes while he breakfasted on bratwurst, washed down with a hearty Bavarian ale. He peeked out through the drawn blinds at regular intervals during this preparation period, terrified that Jed or Musk Man or one of the others would make an appearance. But nobody ever showed up. Amos could only hope that after yesterday's misadventures and unexpected booty, they had all gone to ground indefinitely.

Finally, feeling altogether in character, he slipped a Wagner CD into the unit in his pickup truck and headed north.

This had to work. If it didn't, his goose was cooked.

Chapter 9

Lisa Limone woke early on Tuesday morning.

She'd spent a restless night filled with disjointed dreams about Connie Caravaci lying at the bottom of the hill, intermingled with other terrifying experiences, both those relayed by the others on Sunday night and her own personal horror stories, tales she had no intention of sharing with her mother or anybody else. Not that Lisa couldn't have come up with a couple of amusing and relatively innocuous anecdotes, like the night she thought she was being followed on a deserted street in Berkeley, when in fact the jingling she believed came from a pursuer turned out to be the hardware on her own backpack.

It wasn't incidents like that that had caused her to toss restlessly through the night. It was the memory of her two truly terrifying narrow escapes from rape. The first, back in high school, had taken place at a party she wasn't supposed to be attending, on a night her parents thought she was sleeping over with a girlfriend. She'd held on to her virginity only by the fortuitous arrival of the cops, called by neighbors complaining of excessive noise. She had managed to slip out a back window when the police arrived, walking the mile and a half home shaking uncontrollably.

The second, on a date in San Francisco several years later, had begun as an innocuous excursion to a foreign film festival and ended in a drunken wrestling match in a grimy little third-story walkup apartment.

Right now, however, Lisa was more concerned about her morning tour guide chores than with the sordid details of her youth.

Lisa had inherited her mother's organizational talents, and knew there was no reason on earth to feel anxious about this morning's trip to Malakoff Diggins. She'd eagerly volunteered for the guide duty here because hydraulic mining was a subject Lisa knew inside out. She'd probably forgotten more about this sorry chapter in California history than any of the others on this trip — with the possible exception of her own high school history teacher, Marianne Gordon — would ever know.

But she wanted to do this right. She might be the most knowledgeable, but she was also the youngest, and she knew the older women thought of her first as Judith's daughter and second — a distant second — as a teaching colleague. Like Mandy, Lisa was a product of the Floritas public schools, and had been a student in classes taught by Susi and Marianne at the high school. It was, indeed, Marianne who had first cultivated Lisa's interest in history.

So Lisa reviewed her materials one last time, then wandered down the road listening to early morning bird calls and wondering if moving back to Floritas hadn't been a colossal mistake.

Mom and Dad were thrilled, of course, and her job at Floritas Junior High was a plum position. Floritas Unified was an excellent school system where any openings brought dozens of applications. Lisa was fairly certain she'd gotten her job the old-fashioned way, through blatant nepotism, but it didn't bother her at all. She knew she was plenty qualified.

Still, she was finding life in Floritas all too predictable. For better or worse, it was a small town, one where she'd spent most of her life. Lisa found herself frequently yearning for the spontaneity of her college days, when she and her roommates at UC Davis might wake up feeling restless and take off for a day or two to party in San Francisco, crash with friends at Berkeley or Santa Cruz, gamble in Reno, or guzzle wine at Napa vineyards.

With a start, she realized that she'd walked all the way through downtown Nevada City, which was just starting to wake up. Reluctantly she turned around and headed back, stopping to inhale the faint odor of garlic and ginger that lingered outside the Chinese restaurant where they'd eaten last night. The

National Hotel across the street looked wonderfully old and authentic, full of its own secrets and memories.

How many famous Californians, Lisa wondered, had stood here on Broad Street contemplating the National since it first opened in 1857? How many honeymooners had climbed the stairs to Victorian lodgings there? How many miners had celebrated lucky strikes buying a round for the house in its bar?

And how many others had trudged past its doors in defeat, starting the long journey back home, without ever striking it rich? "Seeing the elephant," they'd called it, a metaphor for experiencing California and all the wonders it seemed to offer. For most of the forty-niners, Lisa knew, seeing the elephant had been an experience longer on toil and frustration than on material reward.

It was, for the most part, the ordinary people comprising history who really interested Lisa. The human element. When her mother'd been in school, history meant facts about dead white men and the rote memorization of dates. For Lisa's generation, the discipline had metamorphosed into an intriguing and organic field of study. It had pleased Lisa to learn that her mother was actively studying the role of women in the Gold Rush on her own time, as part of her personal preparation for this trip.

Now Lisa picked up a blueberry muffin and a morning newspaper. She read the brief story on page 3 about Connie Caravaci's injury, which was being attributed to an accidental fall. The escaped convicts were still at large, the Truckee fire was under control, the governor was asking Californians to conserve energy, tax reform was in trouble in Congress, and a suicide bomber had blown himself up in a Tel Aviv café. Business as usual.

When she wandered back up the road to Murmuring Pines at eight-thirty, she found most of the group up and about, though moving at a very leisurely pace. She poured herself a cup of fresh coffee from a carafe on a picnic table and watched Nikki and Betsy finish up their morning yoga in a clearing beyond the tents. Marianne and Lynne were working independently on Susi's Gold Rush crossword puzzle, reading questions out loud and making a theatrical show of hiding their answers from each other.

But the detail Lisa found most fascinating about the group's morning activities was that her mother had wet hair and was just getting dressed when Lisa returned. For Judith Limone, this was the equivalent of lolling in bed till noon.

A bit later, everyone gathered around the picnic tables.

Lynne began with an announcement. "I just called the hospital, and they said that

Connie is still in a coma. They also told me that they haven't been able to find her kids, so until someone tells us otherwise, I'm going to assume we're all right to stay here through tonight. We'll pull out first thing in the morning as planned. Now, here's the lineup for today. This morning we'll head out to Malakoff Diggins, with me and Nikki driving, because the roads out there are a little iffy and we don't want to mess up Judith's car."

"But it's okay to mess up mine?" Nikki asked with a grin.

"Yours is meant to be messed up," Judith told her, returning the smile. "This is one of those rare instances where an SUV with off-the-road capability might actually get to *use* that feature."

Lynne nodded. She looked tired and a little distracted. "Lisa will tell us a little bit more about what to expect at Malakoff Diggins in a minute. We'll bring along lunch, and make sure you all remember to bring along your little neck coolers. It's likely to be really hot out there. This afternoon's schedule is wide open. You're welcome to go down to Grass Valley and Auburn, hang out in Nevada City, stick around here, whatever."

"You're also welcome to come white-water rafting with the Tough Chicks," Nikki Mason announced. "The river's running and it should be a blast. No previous rafting experience required, either."

Lisa was really looking forward to the rafting. Yesterday they'd merely waded in the river after their hike, but this was the kind of adventure she adored. She and a couple of college friends were planning a ten-day white-water tour on the Colorado River through Grand Canyon just before school started in the fall.

"Anybody who wants more info on the rafting talk to Nikki," Lynne said. "And then our dinner reservation is at seven. Steak and lobster night at the National Hotel in town. Anybody have any questions?"

"Have the police figured out what happened to Connie?" Judith asked, frowning. Lisa knew her mother hated loose ends and unfinished business. Judith made neat little boxes in front of the items on her to-do lists. Those items not checked off at the end of one day moved to the top of the next day's list until every one of them was X-d out.

"I wasn't able to get through to Detective McMasters," Lynne admitted, "though whoever answered his phone claimed he'd be in touch with us. Nobody would tell me anything, cops or hospital. I'll try again before we leave."

"Or maybe he could join us out at Malakoff Diggins," Betsy suggested.

"I'm willing to wait for him here," Susi

Braun said. "I'm half inclined to go back to bed."

Lisa thought Susi seemed crankier than usual this morning. She sat in an Adirondack chair examining her feet with irritation. Marianne's bottle of Vitamin E was uncapped beside Susi and she'd just popped open one of the golden gel capsules to rub more oil into her surgical scars.

"I'll leave you my car keys," Judith offered, "in case you want to run into town for anything. Or we could get you whatever you need before we go."

"I'll be fine," Susi assured her, in her best Camille tones. "It's probably a good idea for me to stay here anyway, so there'll be somebody available to assist the authorities when they arrive."

" 'Available to assist the authorities'?" Marianne snorted. "You've been watching too much *Masterpiece Theater*, girl."

Lynne paused for a moment. "Up to you, Susi. Let us know what you'd like us to do for you before we leave." She smiled and looked around the group. "And now, ladies, listen up. Miss Lisa Limone is going to tell us a little bit about what we're going to see this morning."

Lisa stood at the end of the table, aware that everyone was watching her expectantly. Suddenly she felt utterly calm. This was no different from teaching, really, with the distinct advantage that this group — unlike her students at the junior high — had success-fully concluded puberty.

"What we're seeing this morning," Lisa began, "is an abomination, pure and simple. And to explain what happened here, I'm going to run through a little background that most of you probably already know.

"When gold was first discovered in this area, some of it was actually lying around waiting to be picked up. There were nuggets in the rivers and gold dust was mixed into the topsoil. The easiest way to get at the gold — other than picking it up in chunks, which didn't last long — was placer mining, using water to rinse away the dirt and leave the heavier gold behind. What started out as simple panning developed pretty quickly into more complicated methods using specially constructed equipment. Some of those methods were rocking the cradle, the long tom, and increasingly longer sluices. Each of these was a lengthier and more sophisticated version of the same general principle. Dig up promising dirt, run water over it, collect the gold that remained."

Lisa looked around. Everyone seemed to be paying attention and they all looked interested. She went on, "But it only took a couple of years before all the easy gold was gone. Now they had to find a way to get at the veins run-ning through the mountains. Some miners, and mining companies, sank shafts to find them. And then in 1853, Yankee ingenuity changed everything. A Connecticut miner working near here rigged a big canvas hose with a metal nozzle to wash away the dirt, and hydraulic mining was born. Rather than go into the mountain to find gold, they'd use water under pressure to blast apart the mountain from the surface on down."

Susi Braun frowned. "I don't think I understand. Wouldn't that make an incredible mess?"

Lisa regarded Susi with curiosity. Prior to the trip, all the participants had been instructed to provide Susi very specific factual information so she could construct the crossword puzzle, and Lisa had found her own hydraulic engineering clues scattered throughout the puzzle. So either Susi was incredibly dense — which jibed nicely with Lisa's memories of being a student in her high school English class — or she'd focused solely on the mechanics of her project. Maybe both.

"It did make a mess," Lisa told her. "A *huge* mess, big enough that in 1884, a federal judge granted a permanent injunction against hydraulic mining. You might say that was the beginning of the environmental movement in California."

Amos Ledbetter arrived at the base of the road up into Murmuring Pines later than he'd intended. He'd been slowed down by heavy traffic and a SigAlert approaching Sacramento. It seemed incredible to him that these rinkydink roads headed for these nowhere destinations could actually suffer from traffic jams and rush hour. He had always regarded this area as the ultimate Hicksville, but now it was Suburban Hicksville. Overdevelopment had come to the Central Valley with a vengeance. Sacramento was surrounded by mushrooming subdivisions and vast expanses of new three-bedroom Executive Homes. Every one of those executives seemed to be driving an SUV on the freeways in the early hours of the morning.

Now Amos drank his coffee and worried. He knew there was only one way in or out of Murmuring Pines and he was fairly certain he'd tucked himself sufficiently out of sight so that they wouldn't notice him when they left. He couldn't decide what to do. If he let them leave, then he could really take apart their cabins and campsites, but if the lamp wasn't there, then they probably were carrying it with them. It would take only the most perfunctory of searches to determine that.

Or he could follow them. They must have just left it in that van, rather than bring it indoors. This made sense, since the lamp was so incredibly heavy, stuffed full of something that Amos really didn't want to know about.

Ignorance might not be bliss, but in this case it definitely beat knowledge.

If he simply followed the women, he was sure that sooner or later they'd get out to explore something. Then he'd have his chance to search the vehicles, if necessary by smashing a window. He was feeling more desperate by the minute.

When the SUV and the van came down the roadway, Amos made up his mind. He'd follow them.

Then if somebody hassled him in any way, shape, or form, he'd break into his German and be the most indignant tourist Stuttgart had ever exported across the Atlantic.

Lynne's first thought when she saw the ruined mountains at Malakoff Diggins was unexpected and disturbing.

The landscape was actually rather pretty.

A century's regrowth of vegetation had softened the hideous damage, as nature struggled to recapture its own. The mountains themselves had eroded down to beautifully layered shades of gold and red and white, frosted atop with dark green pines. More pines were also sprinkled along the sides and bottom of this unnatural valley. The whole thing, Lynne thought initially, bore a striking resemblance to the sandstone intricacies she loved in Bryce Canyon, in southwestern Utah.

On closer inspection, however, the comparison didn't hold up.

Odd bits and pieces of huge, discarded equipment lay along the roadside: twisted cross-sections of metal pipe, items rusted beyond recognition. Furthermore, these eroded peaks had their feet stuck in some very nasty liquids, in a palette of unnatural and unsettling shades. This locale bore no resemblance to the crystalline waters they'd previously seen, rushing from the melted snowpack down through the mountains. These weird shades of blue weren't as pure as the glacial lakes of the Canadian Rockies around Banff, and the greens were murky. None of the liquid looked like it would support any life, and a lot of it smelled. Posted signs warned not to drink the pastel waters in these sections of mining tailings, as if anyone would be tempted for even a moment.

Lisa had explained that she'd been out here several times when she researched hydraulic mining as a college student. Now she led them down a trail. "Along here you can get a sense of the enormity of the engineering involved. Keep in mind that this was just one tiny part of the tunnel and flume system that fed water down here from higher in the Sierra."

Lisa stopped to point down at the two sides of a narrow valley. A huge tunnel had been bored through the hills on either side of the valley, creating a faux streambed that connected the tunnel segments. She headed carefully down the steep, rocky trail. "Follow me, and watch your step. Notice how cool it's getting as we go down toward the tunnel."

Lynne was surprised at how quickly the temperature dropped during their descent. This entire area — the State Historic Park and the essentially deserted land around it — was hot and dry and dusty. The temperature had to be at least in the high nineties. All of them were wearing cooling neckerchiefs that Betsy had made, sewing into each a small amount of the sort of polymer crystals used to absorb and hold water when mixed with potting soil. When soaked in plain water, the crystals inside the neckerchief band swelled and the slow evaporative process provided longlasting coolness on their necks.

Lynne was grateful to have hers on this hot, dusty day; still, it was easily fifteen degrees cooler down here, where the tunnel had been drilled through the mountainside on either side of this natural gully.

"The tunnels to this area were seventy-eight hundred feet long," Lisa went on, when everyone had reached the bottom of the trail. "That's a mile and a half. Dams were built and streams were diverted so they could control the flow of the water. Most of the time it would be like this, just a little bit damp." A few inches of standing water had turned decidedly stagnant, emitting a most unpleasant odor.

"So it would usually be dry?" Judith asked.

"Yep," her daughter answered. "And then, when everything was ready, they'd signal by telephone and let 'er rip."

"Telephone?" Betsy asked. "How could they have had telephones out here in the eighteen hundreds? We can't even get cell phone reception now." The various members of the group had several different cellular providers, but none of them were in range out here. Everybody had experimented briefly with Nikki's satellite connection, but for the most part they'd communicated with the homefolk via land lines, generally from the booth outside the Murmuring Pines office.

"Pretty ironic, isn't it?" Lisa said. "But this was actually the first business use of long distance. Several companies got together and set up the Ridge Telephone Company. They dug tunnels and strung sixty miles' worth of wire and installed thirty phones to connect different parts of the operation. This was two years ahead of what AT&T claims was the first long-distance line, back in New England."

"Amazing," Nikki said, shaking her head. "Who'da thunk it?"

"But individuals didn't really talk to each other on those first long-distance lines," Lisa clarified. "They wrote down messages that were read by one operator to another operator at the other end, who transcribed them and handed them over. Twenty-five cents would get you twenty words to any phone on the line."

"It sounds more like a telegraph than a phone system," Judith noted. "Or actually, like a low-tech version of e-mail. The more things change, et cetera, et cetera."

Lisa nodded at her mother. "Anyway, they'd use the phone system to tell the folks up in the mountains when to turn on the water. They could regulate the flow that way, and keep things moving even in the summer when rivers in this area normally dried up."

"Was the Army Corps of Engineers involved in setting up this technology?" Lynne asked suspiciously. "It sure sounds like their kind of gig."

Lisa laughed. "I guess you're right at that. And the Corps of Engineers had a lot to do with expediting the westward expansion. But as far as I know, what went on here was all private engineering. When the water was actually released, it would come down under incredible pressure, pass through the monitors, and blast apart the side of the mountain. It was strong enough to kill a man two hundred feet away from the monitor, or nozzle. We've seen these monitors several places now, including in the town of North Bloomfield as we just came through there on our way here. They always look to me like cannons in some Civil War battlefield, but they were actually more like gargantuan metal garden hose nozzles. The miners would hook them up, aim them at the side of the mountain, and blast away. Instant disintegration."

"Why were they called monitors?" Mandy Mosher asked. "Did they keep track of something?"

"Not at all," Lisa answered. " 'Monitor' actually was a trade name to start with, for the company that made it. It just slipped into generic use."

"And they literally sprayed the mountain apart?" Mandy asked in a tone of wonder.

"Basically, yes." Lisa was perched on rocks above the muck in the opening to a tunnel maybe seven feet in diameter. There wasn't much water in the stream bed, and it didn't look any clearer than the stuff elsewhere in the valley. "Nobody paid any attention to the impact that this hydraulic mining was having downstream until things got really out of control. The rivers filled with silt and dirt and carried it clear out to San Francisco Bay. Towns like Marysville that were downstream flooded out, farmland was ruined, and everything was a mess. In a way, it's a shame they changed the town's name to North Bloomfield, because its original name was a lot more accurate."

"And that was?" Lynne asked.

"Humbug," Lisa answered with a grin.

Chapter 10

Amos had no difficulty following the two carloads of women north from Nevada City.
This didn't represent any particular skill at
surveillance, since there was only one road
and they were all on it. His biggest problem,
actually, was staying far enough back so they
wouldn't notice him, yet close enough to tell
if they did anything unexpected.

Like turn off.

He almost missed it at first, when they
turned right onto Tyler-Foote Crossing Road,
and he sailed right past. But he quickly doubled back and headed east on the cutoff to
North Bloomfield and Malakoff Diggins,
stopping for a moment to check his map
after turning off Highway 49. After that, he
wasn't worried. There was no way those ladies
were going anywhere without him knowing
about it. This was truly a road to nowhere.

He kept back, confident that while they
might be out of sight, they couldn't possibly
be out of reach. This country could be used
to illustrate a dictionary definition of "godforsaken."

Amos had never been to Malakoff Diggins
and had never wanted to go. But it was
clearly identified as a State Historical Park
and therefore offered tourist amenities: mu-

seums, gift shops, sightseeing lookout points, maybe some ranger-guided tours. He'd blend in, keep a discreet distance, and then break into the vehicles while the women were off goggling at some exhibit. With a little bit of luck, they'd strike off on one of those ranger hikes. In any case, it shouldn't take long to determine which vehicle held the lamp, smash a window, and flee with his booty.

Then it happened.

Ka-thunk, ka-thunk, ka-thunk.

The rhythmic jolting of a washboard road, except that the road here seemed no worse than it had been for the last few miles. Nope, this was more.

He pulled to the side of the road and stopped. When he stepped out of the cab, blast furnace heat assaulted him, but Amos barely noticed as he stood and stared in disbelief at the flat tire on his right front wheel. Swell and dandy.

No point calling AAA from out here, even if there'd been a pay phone on one of the scraggly manzanitas lining the roadway, or if there were cell phone reception, which didn't seem worth bothering to check. It would take forever for them to get here, and he didn't need help anyway. You couldn't grow up in the Central Valley without learning some basic auto mechanics, and he'd changed many a pickup tire over the years.

Cursing softly, Amos found the jack and

spare, sending a brief prayer of thanks for the streak of caution that had prompted him to equip the truck with a real spare tire instead of one of those cheapo little donut numbers the auto manufacturers provided. Once he managed to get the frozen lug nuts loose, it took only another twenty sweaty minutes to get the tire changed.

But now, of course, the women were far ahead of him. He could only hope that once they reached the park, they would stop to enjoy their visit. Amos thoughtfully surveyed the broken, chalky mountains and scrubby vegetation that surrounded him. "Enjoy" might be a bit much to expect, actually, unless the landscape got a lot more interesting very quickly.

He looked again at the map, then realized with alarm that this was not truly a dead end drive at all. The women had the option of driving all the way through the park, and if they did, it would be almost impossible to waylay them. A dirt road went directly back to Nevada City from North Bloomfield. Amos didn't maintain many illusions about such thoroughfares, which were usually more dirt than road, but the women were driving appropriate vehicles for one. The SUV could get certainly through and the van also looked pretty sturdy.

He might actually *lose* them, and then . . . and then he would have to report failure to

Jed, or Musk Man, or whoever showed up next time.

This prospect was too alarming to contemplate. Amos hustled back into the cab of the pickup and turned the key in the ignition.

When he finally pulled into the ragged remnants of North Bloomfield, he blinked in surprise. It seemed he had grossly overestimated the requirements for being a California state park. This was no San Simeon. It was, in fact, so bleached out and desolate looking that he almost cruised right through it, assuming it to be just another mining ghost town on the road to North Bloomfield. But no, there it was, the sign clearly identifying this as *being* North Bloomfield.

He returned to the cluster of abandoned-looking buildings and parked. He got out, scanned the horizon, checked out a handful of parked vehicles, and determined instantly that the ones he was looking for weren't there.

A Jeep sat outside a building near what looked like a pair of oversized cannons. Across the dusty square, half a dozen young boys were clambering into a once-white van now liberally coated with grit. They looked about nine or ten. A middle-aged man with the enthusiastic demeanor of a scoutmaster stood near the van, engaged in earnest conversation with a young woman in a ranger uniform.

What now? Best to inquire if anybody had noticed which way the ladies had gone. There couldn't be more than a couple of alternatives. He clamped the Tyrolean cap on his head and started across the square.

"Allo?"

Amos spun to the sound of a gruff masculine voice. The speaker was a stout, fiftyish fellow in a Caesar's Palace T-shirt and a Grand Canyon baseball cap. Behind him stood a plump lady with graying hair and a younger couple, probably in their early twenties. The young woman was a stunner, a slimmer, sexier version of what had to be her mother, with a blond ponytail and long tan legs. The young man — husband, brother, fiancé? — looked very bored. His baseball cap read NEW YORK YANKEES and his T-shirt was from the Hard Rock Café in L.A. All of them wore khaki shorts and sturdy hiking boots.

Amos shook his head regretfully. "No speak English," he told them, feeling particularly smug at having selected such a useful costume. The last thing he needed was to be engaged in conversation by some bowling alley yahoos, lost on their way to the nearest Indian casino. *"Sprechen Sie Deutsch?"*

The joyous expressions that flooded all four faces told him instantly that he had made a very serious blunder. The older man let loose a torrent of German, and the quartet rushed toward him.

Well, wouldn't you just know it? Here in the middle of nowhere, where even the lizards probably got lonesome, Amos had stumbled upon a party of authentic German tourists. And him in his lederhosen.

"Gruesse Gott," Amos told them, frantically sifting through the phrases he'd half listened to over his breakfast bratwurst.

He had actually studied German what seemed like a lifetime ago, and had traveled through Europe the summer after college graduation, using a smattering here and there. But all he'd needed then was the basics: a cheap pensione, a meal, a rest room, a hot nightclub playing pop music. He'd traveled with Americans, who all spoke English unless there was absolutely no alternative. In Berlin they'd been looking for the romance of Christopher Isherwood but had instead found a booming metropolis that got spooky only when you walked across the border into the rubble of East Berlin.

In any case, Amos's German had never remotely approached fluency. His pronunciation was excellent, but his vocabulary woefully limited.

The foursome regarded him expectantly, apparently anticipating more than a basic hello. *"Woher kommst du?"* This was, he was pretty sure, a query about their home town, and might buy him some time. Across the square, the van full of Boy Scouts revved its engine and headed back toward the highway.

Sure enough, the question elicited another torrent of guttural sounds, this time from the older woman. There were even a couple of syllables he recognized. Frankfurt. She concluded with another phrase he thought he remembered, *"Wie heissen Sie?"* *What's your name?*

Amos resisted the impulse to answer, *"Ich bin Liberace,"* and replied instead, "Jed." When their expressions suggested they considered this response inadequate, he added, "Guckenberger," which was the actual surname of a stunning young man who ran a bar in Palm Springs. He vaguely recalled that this translated as "looker."

The foursome's initial joy at meeting a fellow Deutschlander had clearly evaporated. They weren't buying his German act, lederhosen be damned, and it was definitely time to mosey along. How to do so discreetly, without calling undue attention to himself? There'd been something on the tape this morning asking where somebody went on their vacation. *"Wo bist du im letzten Regen, gewesen?"* It didn't sound quite right as it came out, but he was clueless about what or where the error might be.

"Regen?" the older woman asked, frowning.

Amos's brain was swimming with German words now, but none that wanted to combine in any coherent fashion. *Weiner schnitzel.*

*Reichsmarshall. Lowenbrau. Biedermeier. Lieb-
fraumilch. Kristallnacht. Verboten. Dachshund.
Kartoffelsalat. Volkswagen.*

"Der verbrecher," he began, and knew instantly from their expressions that this was another vocabulary error. He shook his head hurriedly, and offered what he hoped was a beguiling smile of apology. *"Nein, nein. Wo ist huren?"*

Uh-oh. Whatever he'd said here, it didn't seem to be *Where is your hotel?,* which was what he'd had in mind. The older man's face darkened until it resembled an enormous pickled beet. The older woman's entire body jiggled in rage, and the *fraulein* gasped in outrage, clasping her fingers dramatically across her mouth.

Then the young man popped out of his ennui and charged Amos, landing an excruciatingly painful blow to his nose and then launching a systematic beating. He settled in to his work as if he had all the time in the world.

Amos had always been terrible at self-defense, despite his father's efforts to provide his son with the necessary tools to survive playground taunts and teenage thugs. Now, Beetface joined in, too, and the German men pummeled him mercilessly in a depressingly coordinated show of teamwork. He formed himself into a ball like a giant pillbug and prayed for relief. As he cowered on the ground, arms cradled around his face, he heard a ripping sound, felt a sudden breeze, and realized that he'd split the seat of his lederhosen.

By the time two rangers intervened and pulled the outraged Germans off him, Amos was battered, bruised, filthy, and very grateful not to be wearing some of his more flamboyant boxer shorts. Blood dripped steadily down the once-white shirt from what Amos was fairly sure was a broken nose.

The rangers — there were three of them by now, the woman he'd seen originally and two men — were not happy. It took over an hour in a wretched little administrative office to convince them that this was all a terrible misunderstanding, that nobody needed to be detained, that certainly the police weren't required and that none of the parties was interested in pressing charges against anyone else. He learned that he had called the tourists criminals and then asked where they went whoring around. All four of the Germans, it turned out, spoke excellent English, and failed to see the humor in his costume. The office was small and stuffy, with uncomfortable wooden chairs and an asthmatic air conditioner wheezing ineffectively in one corner.

The Germans finally left, still in a huff. Amos continued apologizing to the rangers after their departure, acknowledging the folly of playing dress-up. The rangers took this entirely in stride, being employees of the State of California. Amos swore on his mother's grave that he'd never return to Malakoff Diggins, a pledge he knew he would keep through this lifetime and several more to come.

He slowly shuffled back to his truck, dirty and disheveled, aching everywhere, his ruined shirt tied around his waist to cover the exposed expanse of gray-striped boxers. As he leaned against the driver's door, bracing himself for the painful climb back into the cab, he heard the sound of female voices across the square.

He turned around slowly and watched the women he'd been following come out of the small museum, laughing merrily about some fool thing or another.

Before Amos could even get his door open, they piled into their vehicles and sped away.

For the second time in twenty-four hours, Lynne was heading south toward Nevada City on Highway 49, a repeat journey that allowed her to notice nuances of the landscape that she had missed the first time. As yesterday, they had the road pretty much to themselves, but today there were billowy cumulus clouds floating across an azure sky.

It was days like this that made her truly appreciate the glories of travel.

What Lynne loved most about the notion

of travel was its sense of infinite possibility. Within the space of a single day, you could go from the most technologically sophisticated locale on the planet to the most primitive, from the most congested urban to the most outrageously remote, from the most bustling to the most bucolic.

At any given moment, millions of people were actively traveling: sailing into Norwegian fjords, trekking behind Sherpas across the Himalayas, gambling in satin and sequins in Monte Carlo, exploring medieval dungeons, bouncing over African plains in search of herds of wildebeests. Tourists were scrambling up the sides of Aztec and Inca pyramids and crawling on their bellies inside crystal-filled caverns. They were floating up the Amazon and trudging across the polar ice caps, wandering the Alhambra gardens and rafting down the untamed Snake River.

Lynne didn't want to do all these things herself, of course. In fact, a lot of them sounded decidedly uninteresting, or unpleasant, or both. But she loved sending people on these trips, and hearing about their adventures when they returned, looking at photographic records that ranged from blurry snapshots of her clients in front of buildings and natural wonders to excruciatingly detailed video presentations complete with crawling credits and post-production soundtracks. Lately, some of her clients had taken to e-mailing digital photographs to her while they were still on the road.

One of the things Lynne had found appealing about the Argonauts' tour from the very beginning was the group's insistence on forgoing various modern amenities. They'd hashed out all the rules early on, deciding to severely limit their use of contemporary technology. Modern vehicles were permissible, of course, along with modern foodstuffs except for Hard Tack Day, which nobody seemed too excited about.

The group had agreed only after spirited debate that mothers of school-age children would be permitted to bring along cell phones, but the reality of that was that most of the providers they used didn't have coverage in the remote areas they were visiting. Only Nikki had brought along telephone technology that worked anywhere, the kind of astonishing space-age equipment that allowed folks on those aforementioned walks across the Himalayas or the polar ice cap to call home whenever they felt like it. They'd taken time at Malakoff Diggins for everyone who wished to make a brief call on Nikki's phone, just to say they'd done it.

Music was permissible now as during the original Gold Rush, though the nineteenth-century Argonauts had been dependent on their own talents rather than portable CD players and boomboxes. Television and radio, however, were strictly *verboten*. And nobody, under any circumstances, was allowed to have any sort of computer equipment — no organizers or address books or laptops or wireless wonders of any description.

It was turning out to be very satisfying, Lynne thought, being cut off this way. The group was never more than a short drive from civilization and all its wonders, but the self-imposed limitations offered a certain sense of authenticity and adventure that was actually enhanced by the restrictions.

And the restrictions were actually, when you came right down to it, a lot of fun.

Chapter 11

Mandy Mosher was so homesick she wanted to cry.

She'd been gone for only three days and already she had trouble remembering what her babies looked like. She had no business even being on this trip. She didn't teach the Gold Rush, was a primary grade instructor who moved between kindergarten and third grade. The history of Floritas was the most advanced social studies she ever taught, and all that required was a class trip on foot to the historic buildings downtown. Part of her wanted to stretch herself professionally, to be ready to move beyond the primary grades if Judith — who liked to rotate her teachers among grade levels to keep them fresh — asked her to move up.

But all she could think about now was home. She wanted to be playing trucks with the boys on the living room floor, while Tim worked on his current sculpture out in the garage. Tim's art didn't sell very well — actually, if you didn't count people who already knew them, it didn't sell at all — but surely it wouldn't be too much longer before the public began to appreciate his quirky vision. One of these days his art was certain to take off. In the meantime, he had agreed to find some kind of paid employment next fall so that she could take some time off teaching to be with her children. For now, Mandy knew she was incredibly lucky that he liked being home with the boys. Most of her friends with toddlers struggled to find acceptable day care, in a continual series of disruptions and traumas that never seemed to entirely resolve themselves until the kids started school full-time.

Mandy looked around the tables pushed together for the Argonauts in the crowded, bustling dining room of the Nevada City Hotel. In general, Mandy found Victorian decorating creepy, with its emphasis on formality and pretension and ugly, ornate carving.

Still, this room was wonderfully atmospheric, featuring pink flocked wallpaper, dark woodwork, red velvet draperies, and a central chandelier glowing from a dozen red globes. Lamps burned red oil on tables covered with crisp white cloths, and the room was packed with folks taking advantage of the special Tuesday night steak and lobster dinner. They didn't all seem to be tourists, either. This apparently was a bargain that the locals also turned out for in droves.

The group had been chatting about half a dozen different topics, everyone seeming to consciously avoid any mention of Connie Caravaci. Mandy knew that if she let herself think about Connie for more than a few seconds at a time, she was likely to burst into tears.

"Hey!" Lisa Limone said suddenly. "Am I too late to tell a scary story?"

Mandy looked at Lisa, who was sitting beside her. Lisa had been two years behind Mandy at Floritas High and they'd never known each other well. Lisa'd been valedictorian and Academic League captain, always spearheading lagoon cleanups or recycling on campus or some other worthy environment cause. Mandy, meanwhile, had worked on the yearbook and painted posters for ASB and fluffed countless tissue paper flowers for homecoming floats.

"Does this mean you finally thought of something you can say in front of your mother?" Mandy asked now.

Lisa laughed. "Well, yeah. But it *was* a very scary experience."

Judith looked over at Lisa and made a show of bracing herself. "I think I'm as ready as I'll ever be."

"It was when I was about thirteen," Lisa began, "and we were staying up at Grandma Limone's in L.A. You and Dad had gone out for dinner or something and I think Grandma was just out of the hospital."

"Her gall bladder surgery," Judith said, nodding. "I remember. She was being a real pain in the you-know-what. Your father and I

189

were probably out at some gin joint, fantasizing about orphanhood."

"Well, you weren't home, I know that," Lisa said. "I was in the kitchen and I looked outside and saw this red glow from somebody smoking a cigarette. I was totally freaked out. I went to check on Grandma, but she was asleep, and when I went back to the kitchen, he was still there. So I picked up the phone, getting ready to dial nine-one-one, when I realized I was right by the switch for the patio light. I took a deep breath and turned it on — and there wasn't anybody there. So I figured I'd scared him off and I went around making sure all the doors and windows were locked. When I got back to the kitchen, I turned off the patio light. And he was *back,* still smoking that cigarette."

Lisa acted out the next part. "I flipped the switch off and on a couple more times, and the guy vanished every time the light was on. Which was when I finally realized that what I'd been seeing was a reflection from the red ON light on Grandma's stove."

Judith looked at Lisa in amazement. "And you never said anything to us at all!"

"Because I felt like an idiot," Lisa told her. "And I believe if I remember correctly, you promised us all another scary story of your own."

Judith shrugged. "Not much to this one, really. When I was in Brazil as part of an

AFS exchange, three of us were on a bus trip heading somewhere and the bus took off without us after stopping in some desolate little town." She shook her head. "We ended up being stranded there for twenty-four hours till the next bus came through, with no way to even get in touch with anybody."

Their dinners arrived then, and Mandy looked at her plate in nauseated horror. Under other circumstances, she'd love this meal. But her stomach remained unsettled and the queasy tummy went with territory Mandy recognized all too clearly. She was fairly sure the others recognized it as well, and suddenly she was tired of hiding both her secret and her discomfort.

Impulsively, she picked up a fork and clinked lightly on her water glass. The others were mostly drinking wine, but even under normal circumstances, Mandy didn't drink. She'd become a teetotaler after a college trip to Mexico that involved vast quantities of tequila and a twelve-hour blackout — which was, as she thought about it, a scary story in its own right. Now her traveling companions broke off conversations and turned to her, looking puzzled.

"I have an announcement," Mandy said before she could lose her nerve. She avoided making eye contact with Judith, who was seated directly across from her. "I'm pregnant."

The response was wonderfully enthusiastic: squeals of glee and shrieks of excitement from the younger women and warmly maternal expressions of delight from the older ones. To her great relief, Mandy saw that Judith was beaming more broadly than anyone.

Judith raised her wineglass. "And I have a toast. To one of the finest mothers I've ever known, and one of the luckiest babies who'll ever be born."

Now Mandy looked her right in the eye. "You're not mad?"

Judith furrowed her eyebrows. "Mad? Why on earth would I be mad?"

Mandy hesitated. "Well, I'm due in December. On Christmas Day, actually. But my babies tend to come early. So I'll probably have to stop working right after Thanksgiving, and —" She hesitated again, then spit it out. "And I had an ultrasound right before we left. It's twins."

This brought shrieks and enthusiastic comments, but Mandy barely heard them. She was still looking at Judith. It felt as if they were the only people in the room. "I don't see how I can come back to work. At least not till they're all older." She could feel tears starting to fall. "I'm missing so much already, being gone all day. I feel like such a failure, not being there for my boys."

Judith reached across the table and took her hand. "Mandy, honey, there's nothing in the world more important than your kids. If you want to quit as of right this minute, there'll always be a spot for you in any school of mine. If you want to work this fall, you call the shots on how long you stay." She grinned. "And if those twins manage to wait till Christmas to be born, you can call them Holly and Rudolph."

By now Mandy was blubbering helplessly, but she didn't mind who saw. These were her friends and Judith understood and somehow she and Tim would figure out how to pay for all of this. Tim would find work, she knew it. Mandy remembered Judith telling her once that she wished she'd had a dozen kids of her own, that something had gone wrong at Lisa's birth so that she couldn't. Judith had fed her love for children by teaching and surrounding herself with them.

Whereas Mandy was feeding her own love for kids by what Tim only half jokingly called overly zealous breeding. Mandy raised her water glass. "I've got a toast of my own," she said between sobs. "To the greatest women in the world. I love you guys."

An hour later when the group pulled into the deserted grounds of Murmuring Pines, they were still feeling celebratory, stuffed with steak and lobster. The sun had vanished behind the tall pines, but plenty of daylight still remained.

Lynne steered the van up the drive first, realizing as soon as she rounded the bend to their cabins that they weren't entirely alone after all. Two Nevada County Sheriff's cars were parked outside the last cabin, where they'd stored their food and communal supplies. Where most likely somebody had attacked Connie Caravaci.

Detective Jeff McMasters was sitting at the picnic table with a uniformed deputy she hadn't seen before. The two men stood and crossed to meet the group.

"What's up?" Lynne asked, getting out of the van. She didn't like this nocturnal visit at all. The police wouldn't be dropping by in the evening unless something was really wrong.

"A couple of things," Detective McMasters said, looking past Lynne. He focused on Nikki, watching her park her SUV and jump down from the driver's seat. "Mrs. Mason? May I see you a moment?"

Nikki shrugged and hurried over. "Sure. What's up?"

"Mrs. Mason, I'm going to have to ask you to come with us."

Lynne looked first at the cop and then at the young schoolteacher. Nikki wore an expression of absolute incredulity.

"What on earth for?" Nikki demanded. Her tone turned suddenly anxious, her twang more pronounced. "Is something wrong with my kids?"

Detective McMasters regarded her thoughtfully. "Were you expecting a problem with them?"

Nikki shook her head, indignant again. "Of course not. They're with my sister-in-law and I just talked to them before we went to dinner. But what else would you possibly want with me?"

Lynne wasn't sure what to do. Nikki Mason was certainly able to take care of herself. She was one of the most self-assured and assertive young women Lynne had ever met. At the same time, this *was* nominally Lynne's tour and she was supposed to be in charge.

"Isn't this something you can take care of here?" Lynne asked.

"Mrs. Montgomery, this only concerns Mrs. Mason," the detective said. Politely, but with that dismissive tone cops use to tell buttinskis to mind their own damned business.

"If it concerns Mrs. Mason, it concerns all of us," Lynne answered quickly. "Now what's the problem?"

"Yeah," Nikki put in, a hundred and five pounds of energetic irritation. This afternoon she'd tackled and tamed raging rapids on a Gold Country River, and tonight she'd refueled by eating her own dinner and much of Mandy's, trading away the two steaks to Marianne for a third lobster tail. "I haven't

195

done anything wrong and I don't see what you'd need me to go anywhere for. So you'd better just tell me what's going on here. I know my rights." Her backbone stiffened with every word.

Detective McMasters gave her a contemplative look. "Hillandale, Texas," he said cryptically.

Nikki shrugged. "My hometown. What of it?"

"Mrs. Mason, there's a bench warrant for your arrest out of Hillandale, Texas."

"That's ridiculous!"

"Then we should be able to clear it up without any trouble," the detective said smoothly. "But you need to come with us."

Judith Limone stepped forward. "Not without a lawyer."

"Are you an attorney, ma'am?" Detective McMasters asked. "I thought you said you were a school principal."

"I am. But I'm aware of civil rights, and Mrs. Mason doesn't have to speak to you without an attorney." Judith was growing more indignant by the minute. "There's certain to be some logical explanation for this misunderstanding, whatever it is."

"I don't doubt it," the detective answered.

"And I don't understand how you'd happen to know this place in Texas was looking for her anyway," Judith went on. Attack one of her teachers and you were looking for trouble. It was probably safer to remove a grizzly cub from its mother.

By now the others had all gathered around and the mood was somewhat less than friendly. It was the cops against the citizens, and the cops were distinctly outnumbered. This might not be the same as being surrounded in an urban alley by gangbangers with automatic weapons, but Lynne could see and feel the detective growing uncomfortable. Behind him, the uniformed deputy had unbuckled his holster and rested his hand on his service weapon.

Detective McMasters considered for a moment, then spoke. "You may recall that we took all of your fingerprints yesterday for comparison purposes after you reported being burgled. Somebody in our office accidentally included those prints when we submitted the other prints we'd found to the national database. And that's how we learned that Mrs. Mason is wanted in Texas."

Wanted in Texas.

Lynne thought he made her sound like some nineteenth-century cattle rustler, a Bonnie to some lowlife's Clyde. She also recalled that contemporary Texas tended to execute criminals first and ask questions later, if at all.

"And what about those other prints you submitted?" Lynne asked. "Who do they belong to?"

"We're continuing to investigate," he answered. Which meant they didn't know.

Lynne turned back to the young teacher. "Nikki, it looks like you're going to have to go along with them, stupid as this all seems. Who do you want me to call?"

Nikki's voice was tight. "My husband, please." She glared at the cop. "He's an attorney." She turned back to Lynne. "Tell him he needs to get his tail up here right quick, and that I'm not saying anything to anybody till he's here."

"Your choice," Detective McMasters told her.

Nikki turned to Lynne, briskly efficient. "It'll take him most of the night to drive up here, and God knows how long this will drag on in the morning. If I'm not back by the time you all leave, Marianne can break my campsite and drive my car. Feel free to use the phone, either to get hold of Larry or to call home yourselves. I'll hook up with you all down in Columbia." She offered a wry grin. "Just don't forget about me, all right?"

"Of course not!" Marianne told her. "I can drive back to pick you up whenever you're finished here."

"I'll stay in Nevada City till this is taken care of," Judith offered.

Nikki shook her head. "Don't be silly." She turned to the cops and extended her hands. "Do you want to handcuff me? I'm a dangerous fifth grade teacher. Armed with a Swiss Army knife."

"I'm sure that won't be necessary, Mrs. Mason." Since learning Nikki was married to an attorney, Detective McMasters seemed a tad more deferential. "Though you might want to leave the knife with your friends."

"Omigod!" Mandy Mosher's panicked voice came from behind them.

As they all turned to see what was happening, Lynne saw the deputy draw his weapon. She hoped nobody would make any sudden moves. The guy seemed awfully jumpy.

Mandy stood on the porch of the cabin she shared with Susi. "Somebody's totally trashed the place!" she announced.

And indeed somebody had.

Detective McMasters took charge with commendable efficiency. First he locked Nikki in the back seat of the patrol car. Then he and the deputy moved from cabin to cabin, weapons drawn, checking to see if somebody might still be lurking on the premises. Finding nobody in the occupied cabins, McMasters went down to the Murmuring Pines office and returned with a master key. He didn't offer an explanation of how he got into the locked office and everyone was too shocked to ask. While he was gone, the young deputy waited with the Argonauts. Lynne was relieved to see his gun back in its holster.

The two police officers then systematically checked the empty cabins. These were, in fact, empty. Nobody was at Murmuring Pines who wasn't supposed to be there, unless you counted the cops.

Detective McMasters allowed each of them to look into their cabins briefly without entering. It didn't take long to determine that the two tents and all four occupied cabins had been systematically vandalized. Chairs were overturned and mattresses lay half off the beds. Suitcases had been dumped and their contents strewn everywhere.

In her own cabin, Lynne noticed with growing anger that the food that had been moved there from the former communal cabin had been — well, actually, it seemed to have been played with. The room reeked of peanuts. From the doorway she could see that the contents of a four-pound jar of chunky peanut butter had been smeared around the room. Two boxes of nutritionally correct, marshmallow-free breakfast cereal had then been flung around like snowflakes, sticking to the peanut butter in all sorts of unlikely places. A fair amount of it seemed to be on the lampshades. Through the open bathroom door, Lynne could see a couple of unopened wine bottles sitting in the toilet bowl. Or maybe they'd been broken into the toilet. She couldn't tell from the doorway, and at the moment she didn't want to know.

Then Detective McMasters went to his unmarked car to radio in for assistance. When he returned, his expression was even darker.

"You'll need to move into some of these unoccupied cabins tonight," he said. "We aren't going to be able to get this area processed before morning."

"But we're supposed to leave first thing in the morning," Lynne told him. "At least that was the plan before you arrested Nikki. We have a full day planned on the road and reservations down in Columbia tomorrow night."

"First of all, Mrs. Mason isn't under arrest," McMasters said. He was getting testy now. "She's merely being held until we can clear up whatever this situation is in Texas. As far as your travel plans go, I'll get the crime scene people out here at first light. That's the best I can offer, I'm afraid. But you won't be able to go into those cabins tonight."

"And how are we supposed to get our medications?" Susi Braun asked. "My cholesterol pill is supposed to be taken at bedtime." She'd been hovering at the rear of the group, after sticking her head into the cabin she shared with Mandy and viewing its wreckage. Susi had been exceptionally quiet at dinner, Lynne realized suddenly, and she didn't look healthy.

201

The detective closed his eyes for a moment. "If you direct me from the doorway, I can remove anything that you absolutely have to have tonight. I'll have an officer stationed out here tonight to protect the integrity of the crime scene."

"What about to protect *us?*" Susi asked. "We're out here in the middle of nowhere and terrible things keep happening here."

Detective McMasters nodded. "Of course my man will also be watching out for you all as well. Then when my people finish in the morning, you can pack up your things and move on if you still want to."

"Who's going to clean up?" Judith asked. Lynne knew that Judith detested clutter and disorder. "It'll take hours to get this place back in shape."

His expression suggested that cleanup had never once entered his mind. "That's not really your responsibility, Mrs. Limone," he told her. "We don't want to keep you folks from your trip any longer than necessary. I just need to know where to get in touch with you."

Lynne knew he already had taken everyone's home addresses yesterday, and she couldn't imagine what Nevada County law enforcement might require from them in the next few days. The Argonauts were victims, not criminals, though increasingly she believed that the distinction had escaped the local authorities. Lynne was trying very hard not to feel overly guilty about the fact that she — a seasoned travel professional — had apparently checked this group of friends into the Gold Country franchise of the Bates Motel.

"There's one more thing," Detective McMasters said now, with a tone of reluctance. "I'm afraid I've got some bad news."

A perfectly nice L.A. expatriate was in a coma, their cabins had been burgled yesterday and trashed tonight, and a fifth grade teacher was being arrested as a fugitive from Texas. What could possibly be worse?

Then, as the detective continued, Lynne realized exactly what could be worse.

"When I radioed in just now," he told them, "I learned that Connie Caravaci died about an hour ago. She never regained consciousness."

Chapter 12

"What's going on here?" Lynne asked the detective. "Who's responsible for all of this?"

She waved a hand around to take in the cabins, the woods, all of Gold Rush country. "I can't believe that all the things that have been happening are just random acts of violence. Somebody *killed* Connie Caravaci, and whoever it was seems to have it in for Murmuring Pines."

Night was settling into the woods now, and suddenly the prospect of another night at Murmuring Pines was extremely unappealing. The forest felt alive with menace, and every nature sound held an ominous edge. Forty-eight hours ago, they'd sat around a carefree campfire making s'mores and reveling in their communion with nature. Connie Caravaci had sat right over by that tree, telling them about her adventures in an L.A. earthquake. Now she was dead and the tourist court she'd been so proud of was under siege.

Lynne knew that she could, of course, pack everybody up and move somewhere safer, even if it was to some cheapo strip motel with cardboard walls and lumpy beds and questionable plumbing. But that wasn't much of a solution either. Even if she could find rooms for everyone on such short notice, they still would have to leave all their things right here. It was a classic lose-lose situation. And these women were on an extremely limited budget anyway. The big splurge was their historic hotel rooms for the next three nights in Columbia.

"Just a minute, all right?" Detective McMasters seemed to make a decision and he crossed to his car, returning in a moment with a file folder. "Have you people heard anything about some escaped convicts that we're looking for?"

Judith nodded, frowning. "I read about them in the paper. Why? Do you think they're responsible for all this?"

"We're looking at them as very serious suspects," Detective McMasters said. "They know the area well, and we believe they were headed in this direction."

"I thought they were juvenile offenders," Betsy said.

"Two of them are nineteen and the other one is twenty," the detective answered. "That's plenty old enough to be very dangerous."

"Were they in jail for violent offenses?" Judith asked.

Detective McMasters kept his expression noncommittal. "They'd all previously been in drug diversion programs, but at the time of their arrests they were using again. They were convicted of armed robbery in a series of home invasions. They were apparently using the proceeds to buy more drugs."

Home invasion, Lynne knew, was one of those new terms invented to cover a situation that didn't precisely fit the criminal code. "Isn't that armed robbery?"

"In a manner of speaking," the detective admitted.

And what manner might that be? Double-speak?

"The newspaper article I saw said they were incarcerated in Southern California," Judith said now. "Is there any reason to believe they were actually headed in this direction?"

"They're originally from Grass Valley," Detective McMasters told them, "and one of them has a girlfriend and kid still here. The others have family, but their relatives all say they haven't heard from them."

Which didn't mean anything, Lynne knew. "So you think these guys are behind all the trouble here?"

Detective McMasters nodded. "We're considering the possibility that Mrs. Caravaci confronted them burglarizing your cabins and that they may not have meant to hurt her. Nobody was injured in any of the home invasions, so the attack on Mrs. Caravaci may not have been intentional."

"That doesn't make her less dead," Lynne said sharply. "Why haven't you caught them?"

"Not for lack of effort, Mrs. Montgomery," Detective McMasters said. "But these are young men who grew up in this area and they know it well."

He opened the folder and brought out three sets of mug shots. They were surly young men, two with lanky, unclean hair and one shaven completely bald. Robert Hargrove. Samuel Watson. Kyle Burke.

The Argonauts gathered around the picnic table to look at the photographs, but if McMasters had expected a jolt of recognition from somebody, he was sadly disappointed. These guys didn't look like anyone Lynne had seen in the last week, if ever. Nobody remembered seeing anyone who looked like any of the pictures, though Marianne Gordon noted wryly that, as a high school teacher, she recognized the sullen expressions.

Finally Lynne turned to the detective. "Please let us get what we absolutely need tonight out of our cabins so we can move into those others." She turned back to the group. "In the morning we'll decide whether to leave right away or stick around until Nikki's released."

Detective McMasters gathered up the photographs and said goodbye, leaving with Nikki locked in his back seat. Nikki, bless her heart, managed a cheerful little wave as the cruiser pulled away. And Detective McMasters, as he took his leave, acted as if he wished he could lock the rest of them up with her.

Which might not be such a bad idea if the woods were full of bandits who knew the area well. Those were extremely unpleasant-looking young men, and they had some very bad habits. But Lynne forced those thoughts from her mind. Surely by now these young punks knew there was nothing of value belonging to the Argonauts, and if they listened to any news tomorrow — on Betsy's stolen CD player/radio, for instance — they'd realize they were now wanted for murder.

Certainly, Lynne told herself, they wouldn't be stupid enough to make yet another return visit to Murmuring Pines.

Would they?

Judith Limone's insomnia had returned.

Truth be told, she rarely slept soundly, and no longer required more than five or six hours a night. Since passing through meno-pause, she'd metamorphosed into one of those irritating early risers she had sworn as a child never to become. A day rarely passed when Judith didn't witness sunrise, and she often rose before the morning papers were flung onto her Floritas driveway.

This week of the summer solstice, off on vacation, she was a regular slugabed, sleeping much more than usual. She'd even turned over yesterday morning to sleep an extra hour and a half. Recharging, she suspected.

This had been a particularly long and difficult year at overcrowded Pettigrew Elementary, for Judith and for all her teachers. A greedy and shortsighted City Council had approved far too many housing developments, blanketing the town's rolling hills with huge red-tile-roofed homes on postage-stamp lots. Only after the houses sold to folks moving down from Orange County and L.A. — nobody in Floritas could afford them — did the local school board notice that most of these new families had kids.

A new elementary school was under construction, but in the meantime the physical plant at Pettigrew was strained to bursting, particularly when you factored in the one-to-twenty teacher-student ratio dictated for primary grades by the state. When Judith had first come to Pettigrew as a teacher, the student population was 437. It had passed the 800 mark back in April. Mobile classrooms covered nearly all of the asphalt where kids had once played Four Square and jump rope and dodgeball and a local form of hopscotch on a huge American map painted right on the pavement. You could see Florida and the tip of Texas peeking out from underneath Betsy Danforth's relocatable classroom. Relocatables, of course, almost never were.

This year had also featured an unusually high rate of parental divorces and juvenile delinquency. When you seasoned all this with continuing pressure to perform well on standardized tests and baked it in classrooms with no air-conditioning, you had the classic recipe for principalian anxiety.

Now, however, Judith seemed to finally be caught up on her sleep, and with the events of the past couple of days, she'd reverted to her customary anxious insomnia. She was, therefore, the first of the Argonauts to hear a car come creeping up the road toward the cabins, just after 3 a.m.

She didn't turn a light on, but slipped across the room and gently shifted aside the blue gingham curtain so she could peer out into the night. She was sleeping in her clothes, so there was no worry about being decent; her nightgown was in the locked cabin that the crime scene people would be going through yet again in the morning.

On her way to the window, Judith picked up Lisa's heavy Maglite flashlight. Even though a deputy was supposedly on guard outside, Judith had locked and bolted the cabin door, wedging a chair beneath the doorknob as added security. And right now, it couldn't possibly hurt to have a blunt instrument at the ready, one she could also use to momentarily blind an assailant. There was no telling who or what might be out there waiting to sneak up on them. She had been thoroughly repelled by the pictures the detective showed them. They looked like creepy, soulless young men.

The night was pitch black, two days away from a new moon. Glittering stars sparkled in the black velvet sky, but those stars didn't cast a lot of light.

Judith could see the police cruiser parked across the drive between the cabins and the highway. She watched an officer step out of that cruiser and move toward the nondescript white sedan moving slowly onto the grounds. The headlights of the sedan went out and she held her breath, then sighed with relief when the car door opened and the interior light went on. Larry Mason, Nikki's lawyer husband, stepped out of the car. He spoke to the cop, who shook his head firmly and pointed back down the road.

Judith decided it was time to intervene. She removed the chair from beneath the doorknob, undid the locks, and stepped out onto the porch. "Hey, Larry," she called softly.

Startled, he and the cop both turned. The officer was starting to draw his weapon, which thoroughly unnerved her. When he recognized Judith, he nonchalantly pushed it back into the holster.

"You know this man, ma'am?" the officer asked.

"Yes, of course," Judith answered. "He's the husband of one of our group members."

No point mentioning which one.

By all rights, no matter how he'd gotten here, Larry should have been exhausted. However, he clearly shared the same hyperactive metabolism as his wife and instead appeared peeved. Like Nikki, he was small and wiry and very good looking, a marathon runner who did rock climbing for pleasure.

"Hello, Judith," he said, extending a hand. No California hugs for this transplanted Texan, though when he got lickered up at Judith's annual faculty Christmas party, he tended to call all the women "darlin'." Even the most fervent feminists didn't object. Larry and Nikki had met and married in Houston. His twang was even sharper than hers. "What in the devil is going on up here?"

Good question, Larry. "Somebody seems to have it in for Murmuring Pines," Judith answered. "It looks like the woman who owned the place was murdered, at least if the police are right. Somebody apparently bashed her over the head with a gold-painted rock that we use for the Pettigrew Gold Rush, and then threw her down the hill behind the cabins."

"Yes, yes," Larry Mason said impatiently. "Nikki told me all about that when she called last night. And I've just been to the jail, where they told me I can't see my wife until tomorrow morning." He glared accusingly at the cop, whose expression remained impassive.

Judith pushed the button on her watch that lit up its face. In the warm blue glow, she discovered it was three-seventeen. Barely seven hours had passed since Judith called Larry from the pay phone outside the office down below, right after she watched the squad car carrying Nikki disappear into the pines.

"How on earth did you get here so quickly?" she asked. "I didn't expect to see you till tomorrow morning."

"It *is* tomorrow morning, Judith. I managed to catch the last Sacramento connection out of San Diego, with a change of planes in Las Vegas." He grinned. "Made sixty bucks on the slots getting from one flight to the other. Picked up a car in Sacramento and here I am."

"What about the kids?" Judith asked.

"My sister's staying with us this week, while Nikki's on this trip. I didn't have time to stop at home before I left, so I called from the plane and told her what's happening." He looked around. "Is there somewhere we can talk?" He nodded toward the deputy. "In private?"

Judith frowned and looked around, remembering how utterly charming and timeless this woodsy setting had felt the first night when they gathered around the campfire. Now, even with police protection, suspicious shadows seemed to be skulking everywhere.

"Of course," she told him. The seven Argonauts remaining at Murmuring Pines were sleeping two to a cabin, using the previously unoccupied units that the police had opened for them. If she took Larry into her own cabin, they'd surely wake up Lisa. "I think that this cabin over here is empty and open." She looked at the cop, who shrugged. "Come on and let's check."

Larry pulled a briefcase out of the front seat and they walked together down the drive, guiding their way with Lisa's Maglite. As they left, the officer got back in his squad car and Judith could see him using the radio, no doubt reporting back that a dangerous San Diego corporate attorney was now on the scene.

Judith was surprised at how relieved she was to have Larry show up. For all her bluster about sticking around to protect Nikki and her rights, Judith was painfully aware that the criminal justice system was far outside her areas of expertise. DARE officers she could relate to. She knew who to call in Floritas to get speeders ticketed in the school zone outside Pettigrew Elementary, and recognized most of the local patrol officers by sight. She was, of course, on excellent terms with Officer David Montgomery, Lynne's son, who had been a student in Judith's classroom for Gold Rush all those years ago.

But Judith had no idea whatsoever how to deal with strange police officers in a faraway jurisdiction, particularly since they were far more adept than she at asserting authority through virtue of their positions. She'd been bluffing last night when she offered to stay and help Nikki, and was grateful beyond all reason not to have that bluff called.

She also realized now that she hadn't been able to admit to herself just how worried she was about Nikki. Judith considered herself to be an excellent judge of character and Nikki had arrived in Southern California with glowing references from the Houston school where she had previously worked. Judith was not allowing herself to consider the possibility that this energetic young teacher might actually be a criminal on the lam. It was just too ridiculous.

Or was it?

Somebody in Texas considered Nikki Mason dangerous enough to have put out a warrant for her arrest. And there was the shotgun, too, though Judith was working overtime to be tolerant about it. Judith would look like an incredible fool if it turned out that she'd hired a criminal to teach the youngsters of Floritas. Times had changed since the era when teachers were expected to live monastic lives beyond reproach, but they weren't supposed to be hauled off to jail either, with or without shotguns. Even during summer vacation.

Inside the empty cabin, Judith turned on lights. The physical plan was identical to both of the cabins she'd stayed in here at Murmuring Pines, which was oddly comforting. She and Larry Mason sat in a pair of chairs and she stared at the young lawyer intently.

"Do you have any idea what this is all about?" Judith asked him, in her best no-nonsense tone, the one that could reduce full-of-themselves sixth grade boys to tears. "Nikki being arrested?"

Larry shook his head. "Not a clue. I tried to find out what's going on in Hillandale, but Texas is two hours ahead of California time and folks there don't answer their phones in the middle of the night. I left messages all over East Texas, and now I'm waiting for the callbacks. Nikki said she left the special phone with you all."

Judith nodded. "I believe Marianne Gordon has it. Can you wait till morning? She seems to be a pretty early riser."

Larry offered a little hmph. "Not a blasted thing I can do before morning anyway. Now, tell me everything."

It took a good half hour to fill in Larry about all that had happened here at Murmuring Pines. He listened intently, his brow furrowed, taking notes on a legal pad. He

216

asked a lot of questions. Judith had hoped, when this interrogation began, that matters would be clarified by bringing in a sharp outsider with legal training. It quickly became clear that Larry Mason could make no more sense of matters than she could.

Finally they both agreed it was time to get some sleep. Judith left Larry in the cabin, walked the short distance to her own cabin with the flashlight, and crawled back into bed, genuinely exhausted.

Moments later, she fell into dreamless slumber.

Nikki Mason was hating every minute of this experience. She had never been in jail, and even though they'd been exceedingly polite to her — being a lawyer's wife had its useful moments — it was just bloody awful. Once she'd made it clear that she wasn't saying anything to anyone without a lawyer, the Nevada County officials had backed off and left her alone.

Very alone.

She hadn't contributed any scary stories to the group collective, but she now realized she'd been tempting fate to bring up the concept in the first place. Because no two ways about it, Nikki was smack in the middle of her own most terrifying experience right now.

It could have been much worse, of course. She knew that. She might have been penniless, arrested alone in some third world country with no American Embassy and a hostile populace. Instead she was in California, with plenty of money and a devoted husband who just happened to be an attorney.

If you had to be arrested on unspecified charges, this wasn't an altogether dreadful way to do it.

Nor was it a good way, however. She fidgeted on a threadbare mattress in a bleak, impersonal cell, considering the irony that she had willingly spent the previous nights in a sleeping bag on the ground without ever feeling uncomfortable. She wondered how soon Larry would get here, and if he'd send over some attorney he knew in Sacramento, in the meantime. She wondered how her kids were, and what Larry and his sister had told Allison and Greg about their mother's current misadventure.

She wondered if she'd be fired from the Floritas Unified School District.

But mostly she wondered what on earth all this was about.

Hillandale, Texas. That was all they'd tell her.

Hillandale.

Nikki hadn't set foot in Hillandale for almost seven years now. After her father's suicide, her mother had decided she simply couldn't bear the xenophobic atmosphere of the small East Texas town, and she packed up and moved to Corpus Christi. By then Nikki was living in Houston anyway, so she helped her mother close down the house she'd grown up in and drove the U-Haul truck south, making an adventure of it. There were certain topics they did not discuss. They didn't talk about Daddy or the terrible mess he'd made of his finances, they didn't talk about the lawsuit, and they certainly didn't talk about the morning Daddy had gone down to the river with his forty-five.

Now Nikki tossed through the night, dozing fitfully, doing her best to go back to sleep again quickly whenever her eyes popped open and she realized where she was.

She was wide awake in the morning when Larry arrived. Nikki had never been so glad to see him, had never been so grateful that the coin he flipped his senior year at UT had come up heads for law school rather than tails for business school. Never mind that Larry was strictly a corporate attorney and that he hadn't been in a courtroom since moot court in law school. He was her knight in shining armor, come to her rescue.

"Do you know what this is about?" he asked, when they were settled in the small room open for attorney-client conferences.

She shook her head. "If it's Hillandale, I figure it must be something about Daddy. I always paid all my speeding tickets, and till last night, I sure never got arrested for anything. I've been trying to think who you could call to find out, but the only one I can come up with is Leander Trenton, and he's dead too, had a heart attack two weeks after that stupid judge dismissed our lawsuit."

Nikki's mother had brought civil action against Daddy's former business partner, who had commingled business funds with his own and generally screwed up the business beyond repair. Daddy had already discussed bankruptcy with Leander Trenton, Hillandale lawyer-of-all-trades, when he took his handgun down to the river.

"I talked to a Detective McMasters this morning," Larry told her. "He's trying to get through to somebody with the police there. But don't worry, honey. I figure it'll only take a couple hours before we get this all straightened out."

Nikki started to respond, then heard her voice begin to crack. For the first time in years, she started to cry.

Chapter 13

Amos Ledbetter was on the road Wednesday morning at dawn.

Today he had chosen to impersonate a city yuppie, which he was pleased to find wasn't all that much of a stretch, though he did need to put a little effort into youthening himself. He'd darkened his hair, applied a neat little moustache, and dressed in pure Eddie Bauer go-to-the-country wear. He'd also applied a bit of discreet makeup over a bruise on his cheek, and while his nose remained swollen, he didn't think it was broken. He'd been reluctant to visit the doctor yesterday after the debacle at Malakoff Diggins and had instead simply taken to his bed after picking up a rental car in Stockton.

He'd almost rented one of the new T-birds, tempted to be so flashy that nobody would notice him, other than that he was out of place. But cops *did* notice flashy cars, and that kind of attention he could do without. He'd settled instead on a white Hyundai, opting for anonymity.

He realized what a wise decision that had been when he arrived in Nevada City and cruised slowly past the road leading up to Murmuring Pines. A police car sat parked at the base of the drive, with a bored uniformed officer sprawled behind the wheel. Amos could only imagine what was going on up there on the hill, through the dense forest, beyond the cruiser.

Amos had learned a long time ago not to beat himself up for errors of judgment, since there always seemed to be plenty of people around to take care of that chore for you. Still, he sincerely regretted throwing the temper tantrum that he'd pitched last night at Murmuring Pines.

He was frankly desperate by now.

Amos had been quite certain that the lamp was not in any of the tents or cabins, and equally certain that this was the right group of women. He'd found some of the distinctive peach parchment tissue paper he used in the store in one of their wastebaskets, and had discovered a couple other items he recognized as his own stock, wrapped in the same parchment tissue. Amos was a firm advocate of subliminal marketing, and he absolutely believed that the expensive tissue enhanced the appearance of almost anything wrapped in it. This assured that when his customers got their purchases home, they'd remember his shop fondly and want to return, next time they drove that stretch of Highway 99. He had a surprising number of return customers with homes in L.A. or Palm Springs or San Francisco, people who came through three or four times a year and automatically stopped at Ledbetter Collectibles.

Amos headed for the coffee shop down the road from Murmuring Pines, settling in at a window table, a good location from which to watch the road. There was only one way to head south from Murmuring Pines, and the women would have to pass right by here to get on that highway. He was at a considerable advantage today, having filched a copy of the group itinerary last night, along with a list of the names and addresses of the participants. It was covering this theft which had led — admittedly by leaps and then uncontrollable bounds — to systematically vandalizing the cabins, so that the absence of the papers wouldn't be noticed.

The address list constituted a truly significant find, since it was beginning to look as if Amos would need to track these wretched women down to their hometowns. Hometown, singular. Most of them seemed to live in the town of Floritas. Amos hadn't paid much attention to Floritas, a sleepy little surfing and flower-growing town, but he had spent many a pleasurable weekend at La Costa, which was just north of the town. Going down there wouldn't exactly be a chore, though he had hoped it wouldn't come to that.

Maybe today he'd get lucky.

He still hadn't been able to look in the van and SUV, and maintained a forlorn hope that the bulky lamp had been left in one of them for the sake of convenience. If not, however, he'd have to assume they had somehow shipped it out.

The coffee shop where Amos settled in was a curious hybrid, a place that had obviously begun its existence as a coffee shop of the old school. Carryovers from that era included a long list of breakfast specials, most starting with two eggs and at least one side of meat. The waitresses wore tan nylon uniforms with little white aprons in a style they'd probably used for decades. One of the waitresses, indeed, looked as if she'd been serving coffee there since the doors first opened.

Still, the place had moved into the twenty-first century by adding an extensive line of designer coffees, and a fancy selection of takeaway mugs. A blackboard offered a bewildering selection of possibilities, things like Caramel Hazelnut and Mocha Raspberry.

Amos ordered a croissant and a decaf Kona, the last thing he needed being additional stimulation. He was already reverberating, so hyper that he'd brought along a paper bag to breathe into should he begin to hyperventilate. The croissant was stale but the coffee was first-rate, and he spent some time catching up on current events in the local newspaper. He went immediately to the story about the motel lady, who was still in a coma. He read that the police were "pursuing several leads" in what officials now described not as an accident, but as a deliberate criminal assault on Connie Caravaci.

Amos hoped that meant they had no idea what had happened.

A TV played above the counter where a number of apparent regulars sat chatting and wolfing down platters of cholesterol. On the television, a perky young woman was interviewing a man in a pinstriped suit and power tie, a combo that screamed *politician*. The interviewee leaned forward earnestly and used practiced hand gestures to make his points.

Then the program cut away to the local news and Amos listened numbly.

"Nevada City motel operator Connie Caravaci died last night without regaining consciousness." A rather unflattering photograph of the woman filled the top right corner of the screen.

Amos could feel his chest tightening. Suddenly he was unable to breathe.

"Police theorize that Caravaci may have confronted three escaped convicts believed to be in the area following a daring midday break earlier this week from a Southern California youth correctional facility."

Convicts? Amos had read of the wayward boys without giving them a second thought. A jolt of hope swept through him, and he began breathing again, shallowly.

"Our own Jessica Doolittle is with Nevada County Sheriff's Detective Jeff McMasters. Jessica?"

The picture cut to a brunette with big hair, wearing a short-sleeved tunic in an unfortunate shade of yellow. She stood beside a man in a beige summer-weight suit and blue tie. He appeared exceptionally fit for a man in his forties and also looked . . . well, he looked pretty competent, actually. Amos was truly sorry to see that. Good lord, what was he going to *do?*

"Detective, when can we expect new developments in the search for Connie Caravaci's killer?"

Killer.

Amos was horrified. He tried to pick up his coffee mug but his hands were shaking too hard. He couldn't believe that the woman was actually *dead.*

Surely they'd made a mistake. Or maybe — he thought with a fleeting sense of hope — they were claiming she was dead for some odd police reason, the way they faked and lied about stuff on TV cop shows. Cops on TV shows never told anybody the truth about anything.

Still, the term "Connie Caravaci's killer" had a dreadful ring to it. Amos wished he'd paid more attention to TV legal dramas when they described what constituted being an accessory. The whole business seemed wildly inconsistent and capricious. People were serving life sentences for stealing a pack of cigarettes or running over a dog. Meanwhile, O. J. Simpson still searched for the Real Killer on golf courses across the nation.

Amos was quite confident that if he ever got caught up in the legal system, he wouldn't come out of it playing golf.

He clenched his fingers tightly around his coffee cup and willed them to stop shaking. He felt sick to his stomach and didn't have a clue what to do now. Everything was changed, had grown suddenly far worse than he'd ever imagined possible. The only comfort he could find was that, starting off like this, the day surely couldn't get any worse.

Then Jed slid into the booth across from him, and he realized he'd been mistaken.

"You know," Betsy Danforth said as they headed south on Highway 49 midmorning on Wednesday, "I've lived in some godforsaken places, both as a kid and when Jim was in the Navy. We spent an entire year once on a barren island in the Aleutians where there wasn't anything to do but drink and wait for World War Three. But I'd be hard-pressed to think of a place I've been happier to leave than Murmuring Pines."

Beside her, at the wheel of the Booked for Travel van, Lynne shuddered. The two of them were cruising at seventy-five down a four-lane stretch of road near Auburn. Clearly Lynne was glad to have Nevada City in her rearview mirror, too.

"I really outdid myself this time, didn't I?" Lynne said.

"Oh, come on. This wasn't your fault."

"I found the place," Lynne noted grimly. "I made the reservations, I saw to it that we'd have Murmuring Pines almost to ourselves. Of course it's my fault."

Betsy could tell that Lynne was extremely upset. Lynne normally tended to keep her emotions pretty tightly controlled, but she'd been bustling about for hours now — gathering group possessions as the crime scene people finished with the various cabins, furiously packing the van and Nikki's SUV, even snapping at Susi a couple of times. Not that Betsy could blame her for being short with Susi, whose self-absorption was Olympian.

All of them were distressed, of course, and all felt guilty at leaving Nikki behind, even though they took secret comfort in the certainty that her lawyer husband was surely making Nevada County law enforcement thoroughly miserable. Betsy had spent enough time with the wily Larry Mason at bring-the-spouse faculty functions to know that he could be a first-class SOB if he so chose, and these were circumstances that would bring out the pit bull in even the gentlest soul.

"You didn't know that there were going to be escaped convicts on the loose," Betsy told Lynne mildly. Lynne had a tendency to over-personalize these things. "And face it, up until Connie's accident, Murmuring Pines was pretty close to perfect."

"Except that what happened to Connie wasn't any accident," Lynne shot back.

"But it didn't have anything to do with us," Betsy said firmly, and Lynne offered no argument.

Betsy had been hoping that once they got out of Nevada City, everybody would mellow out a bit. She and Lynne were traveling to-gether today to do some serious antiquing. They'd be covering more than a hundred miles before they reached Columbia, passing through dozens of past and present Gold Rush towns on the way — not to mention several tantalizing side roads leading off to even more isolated locations.

And who knows? Maybe they'd happen upon Betsy's dream shop, a quaint little cot-tage tucked into a birch grove, with a wishing well out front and cheerful scarlet geraniums spilling out of window boxes. In this fantasy location — which she always thought of as Ye Olde Antique Shoppe, run by Miss Millicent LeFleur, age eighty-three — Betsy would dis-cover so many unique and distinctive bargains that she'd need to rent a U-Haul trailer to get them all home.

In the meantime, back in the real world, her antiquing on this trip was off to a disturbingly slow start. Apart from the lamp, she'd gotten only a cut glass inkwell at that place where Lynne's van broke down, and she'd found a marvelous tortoiseshell hand mirror and some exquisite embroidered dresser scarves in Nevada City. Now, however, she was ready to get down to serious business.

"I'm giving notice right now that I don't plan on adhering to Hardtack Day," Betsy said. "If Nikki were along, I'd do it to humor her, but I'm too old to eat jerky just to make a point. I know those miners had a rough time of it, and I commend their fortitude. But I'm on vacation."

Lynne offered a feeble chuckle. "Are we going to tell Nikki that we did it?"

" 'We?' " Betsy asked sweetly. "Does that mean we can stop for junk food, Lynne? Contrary to the itinerary?"

"Screw the itinerary," Lynne answered. "I'm happy to fall off that particular wagon right this minute. In fact, what I'd really like right now is a perfect custard-filled éclair." She looked from one side of the road to the other. They were moving into more sparsely populated areas. "Where we're headed, I'll be lucky if I can find a Hostess Twinkie."

"*Tsk, tsk,*" Betsy said. "Have some sunflower seeds. Take the edge off your hunger before you do anything rash."

"It'll take more than sunflower seeds to take the edge off me." Lynne shook her head and looked over at Betsy. Highway 49 had narrowed again to two winding lanes and Betsy was relieved to see Lynne slowing to a more leisurely speed. "But I guess there's no point in dwelling on what can't be changed."

"I'm trying to figure out a way to demonstrate hydraulic mining when I do Gold Rush next spring," Betsy said after a while. "Do you think Judith would let me blast away with a high-powered garden hose on that hill above the playground at school?"

Lynne laughed. "The grounds staff would probably have a fit, but I don't think Judith would care. You just can't get too carried away or there'll be mud all over the playground."

"Which would perfectly illustrate what happened downstream from Malakoff Diggins," Betsy answered. "The kids really get into environmental stuff if you can make it relate to their lives."

"Their parents will get all pissy, though, when the kids come home with mud caked on their hundred-dollar sneakers. And then Judith *will* care. Now, not to detract from the educational value of this trip," Lynne said, slowing as they rounded a curve, "but I've been watching some cute little signs for about ten miles now. I do believe that we're approaching an antique shop just ahead on the left."

Betsy leaned back and sighed contentedly. For the past few months, she'd been quietly tucking away money whenever she could, skipping indulgences, scrimping wherever the budget would allow. She'd accumulated $300 in cash to spend on antiques on this trip, and so far she'd barely put a dent in her grubstake. The money she'd spent on the lamp was extra, and she didn't count it.

Lynne pulled off the road, parking the van behind a Winnebago with Minnesota plates. The back of the RV was covered with bumper stickers. The top ones supported athletic teams: the Minnesota Twins, the Minnesota Timberwolves, the Minnesota Vikings, and (at a guess, because the Twin Cities apparently had no hockey team) the Chicago Blackhawks and Toronto Maple Leafs.

Below those came a sprinkling related to education.

IF YOU CAN READ THIS, THANK A TEACHER. CHILDREN ARE OUT FINEST ACHIEVEMENT. TEACHERS DO IT WITH CLASS. TEACHERS RULE. IF YOU THINK EDUCATION IS EXPENSIVE, TRY IGNORANCE. And of course, the most famous education bumper sticker of all time: IT WILL BE A GREAT DAY WHEN OUR SCHOOLS GET ALL THE MONEY THEY NEED AND THE AIR FORCE HAS TO HOLD A BAKE SALE TO BUY A BOMBER.

The final, most extensive collection, seemed to chronicle a cross-country journey: Mount Rushmore, Deadwood, Chimney Rock, Fort Laramie, Craters of the Moon, Emigrant Pass, Virginia City.

"Hey, look," Betsy said, pointing. "Kindred spirits. Do you suppose there are groups of teachers roaming all up and down Highway 49, just like us?"

"Actually," Lynne answered, "I'd say one group like us is more than enough."

Betsy could tell without setting foot inside that this was not the shop of her dreams.

The flowers in tubs beside the front door were plastic and the place lost immediately points for unnecessary cuteness. The sign announcing KAREN'S KURIOSITIES went on to specify ANTIQUES, COLLECTIBLES, RARITIES, TREASURES AND JUNQUE. Betsy was so annoyed by the "junque" spelling that she almost didn't want to go in, but she knew she couldn't resist. She had never been able to pass up a room full of stuff. Any kind of stuff. When Jim spoke of finding her a Twelve-Step Program for antiquers, he no longer seemed to be entirely kidding.

Inside Karen's Kuriosities, a pair of women in their late sixties dickered with a young woman who was nursing a baby in a bentwood rocking chair behind the counter. Karen, presumably. She might have been considered to be at something of a disadvantage, what with the baby and all, but she seemed to be holding her own quite nicely. When the negotiation ended, Betsy introduced herself and Lynne to the two older women.

"I'm Harriet Wilson," a plump, cheerful woman with a sunburned nose and casually tousled short white hair told them. She leaned on a curved shillelagh in a way that suggested hip problems. "And this is my traveling companion, Stephanie Geller. It's a pleasure to meet you."

"We like your bumper stickers," Betsy told them. "I take it you're teachers?"

Stephanie Geller nodded. She was considerably taller and slimmer than her traveling companion, with long, straight, steel-gray hair tied at the nape of her neck in the fashion of Thomas Jefferson. She bore a passing resemblance to Jefferson, actually, in a not particularly flattering way.

"Retired," Harriet Wilson clarified. "As for the bumper stickers, there's plenty more that we didn't put on. I figure to cover the wall behind the bar in my rec room when we get back home. The only one I absolutely refuse to put anywhere is WALL DRUG IN SOUTH DAKOTA."

"Is this a historical tour?" Lynne asked. "You seem to be following the California Trail pretty closely."

Harriet nodded. "Two nights ago we stayed

up at Donner's Pass. Very creepy."

Lynne smiled. "I can imagine it would be. We saw a few artifacts from the Donner camp in the museum in Nevada City."

"Really?" Harriet's eyes glistened and a line furrowed between her eyebrows. "We missed that, darn it."

Betsy shrugged. "Not much to it, really. Very little survived. Just a few belt buckles and bits of metal. Apparently the folks who came to rescue them were so horrified by what they found that they burned the whole camp. Twice."

Stephanie seemed philosophic. "Oh well, you can't expect to catch everything. I imagine you could spend years traveling around the West without seeing it all."

"You certainly can," Lynne agreed. "Did you two work out your own itinerary?"

The women nodded.

"We talked about taking this trip for years," Stephanie explained, "but we both were taking care of relatives with health problems. Then my mother passed away and Harriet's husband died and there wasn't any reason to put it off any longer. So here we are. After we finish going through Gold Rush country, we plan to retrace the old El Camino Real and visit all the California missions."

Betsy burst out laughing.

The Minnesotans frowned.

"Is there something funny about that?" Stephanie asked.

"No, not at all," Betsy answered. "It's just that I teach fourth grade, which is when we do California history, and I've *never* been to more than a handful of the missions. We just take them for granted. The way folks who live in DC probably never visit the White House."

"I bet California history would be fun to teach," Harriet said, with a tinge of wistfulness in her tone. "Minnesota history has its high points, of course, but California history seems so . . . I don't know . . . glamorous. Father Serra and the missions, the Gold Rush. Even the modern stuff has more pizazz. We've got the Progressives and you folks have Hollywood."

Betsy was trying to scope out the store while she talked to these women. Nice as they were, Betsy was on the hunt and priorities were important. "It is fun," she said over her shoulder as she squatted to look underneath a little table just inside the front door. It had a Deco feel to it, with triangular legs and a geometric inlay of pale woods on the top. Too pricey for Betsy's current mission of making her $300 go as far as humanly possible, and she didn't like Deco all that much anyway. But she lingered for a moment, picturing the table in her front hall. Betsy was a sucker for inlaid anything.

Lynne explained the Argonauts tour to the Minnesotans, who seemed enthralled, and Betsy was grateful for the distraction. "The idea — very loosely, of course — is to enhance teaching the Gold Rush. Most of the folks in our group work at the same elementary school. I used to help out with the fourth grade Gold Rush reenactment when my kids went to that school."

"What fun!" Stephanie told them. "Do you do it in character?"

"Absolutely," Lynne answered. "The kids dress up like miners and the adults hide gold-painted rocks on the hillside in a park near the school."

Betsy thought briefly of her spray-painted rock, the weapon that had probably been used to kill Connie Caravaci. Where was it now, she wondered? Probably now locked away forever in a Nevada County evidence room. Not that Betsy would ever want it back anyway. It was just a prop, and a highly replaceable one at that. But she wasn't even sure she'd have the heart to paint another.

"And then the kids cash in their gold?" Harriet asked.

"Exactly," Lynne said. "There's an 'Assay Office' set up in a tent and they get play money that they can spend on food and games and prizes. When I helped out, I'd dress up in a lacy blouse and long flowing skirt and wear this really cool jewelry made of parsley dipped in gold. It looks like those crystalline gold nuggets you see in pictures. I called myself Miss Kitty from the Longbranch, though the kids didn't get the joke."

These women, however, were old enough to remember *Gunsmoke*, and they roared with laughter.

"Miss Kitty! That's priceless," Harriet said.

Lynne's smile was wry. "Actually, I always believed Miss Kitty had her price, though I sure didn't mention it to the students."

Realizing that she wasn't needed for this discussion, Betsy turned her attention to a group of old dolls, many of them in excellent condition and wearing what appeared to be original clothing, displayed in a corner arrangement. She checked price tags. Karen knew what her Kuriosities were worth, all right. There were no shocking bargains to be had in this store. But Karen's stock wasn't half bad. Some very interesting metal canisters stood on shelves in the back of the store, right next to — could it be? — a sugar bowl in the shape of an orange that perfectly matched a set of salt and pepper shakers Betsy had found last fall up in Julian.

Caught up in the hunt, she barely even noticed when the Minnesotans left.

Chapter 14

Amos couldn't believe his good fortune.

Well, "good fortune" probably wasn't the best way to put it, and a better description might be something like "not altogether calamitous," but things had been going so spectacularly wrong for him since Sunday that he was willing to take joy in even the slightest hint of progress. And this was more than a hint.

After taking his leave from Jed at the coffee shop, Amos had waited outside in his car, slouched behind the wheel, trying not to look at the newspaper beside him with its now-out-of-date information about the well-being of Connie Caravaci. He waited and waited and waited some more. He saw families of tourists come and go, obvious locals drop in for lengthy midmorning coffee breaks, even a couple of cops who went inside and came out with steaming go-cups. He'd chosen his spot carefully and nobody paid him any attention at all, not even the cops.

Finally, when it seemed that he would have to either risk going inside or pee in his empty coffee cup, he saw movement on the road coming down from Murmuring Pines. The SUV and Buick came out first and turned onto the road leading to Highway 49 south, but he'd decided to go for the van first, since that was the vehicle that the women who stopped at his store and the gas station Sunday had been driving.

After about five more minutes, his patience was rewarded when the van came down the road and passed him. This was his first real look at either of them, and they looked disconcertingly alike — short-haired blondes in their fifties wearing sunglasses and sleeveless tops. He assumed the driver was Lynne Montgomery, since she was the one who'd signed for the auto repairs. That meant the passenger was the Danforth woman, who'd bought the lamp.

He followed them south on Highway 49 at a bit of a distance, wishing he'd used the bathroom at the coffee shop one last time. Then finally, he rounded a curve and saw them pulling into — could it be? — an antique shop. He all but swooned with joy. He drove on past and turned around at the first opportunity, pulling cautiously off the road near the shop.

He couldn't have asked for better. The van was tucked away beside a huge RV, making it almost invisible from the highway, and there were no other cars at the shop, except a battered Subaru behind the building that probably belonged to the owner. Amos had the advantage here, since they had no idea who he was. Even if they saw him, he wouldn't need to panic immediately. And if all else failed, he could go in and check out the shop.

He stepped behind a bush and emptied his aching bladder, then picked up a brick from a border around a kitschy little garden. Moving with the sort of purpose that absolute terror can instill, he walked around to the passenger side, took a deep breath, and smashed the window. The noise seemed incredibly loud to him, but nobody came out of the shop, so he reached a gloved hand inside and opened the door.

Once inside the van, it took no time at all to determine that the lamp wasn't there. He left everything as tidy as he'd found it, backed out of the van, and hurried up the road. A line from an old cartoon show kept running through his brain.

Curses! Foiled again!

Given that Marianne Gordon hadn't met Nikki Mason before the first Argonauts meeting last spring, she had grown remarkably fond of the young woman, and felt as if they'd known each other a long, long time.

Nikki's high-energy dash through life might be exhausting in the long run, but in small doses, it was great fun. Yesterday's white-water rafting trip had been an absolute blast, and Marianne had really been looking forward to today's drive south to Columbia. She and Nikki had talked generally about stopping to do some hiking en route, and it was clear that Nikki would be up for just about any kind of physical exploration they might encounter.

So much for plans.

Now Nikki was in the hoosegow and Marianne at the wheel of her friend's very large, very expensive vehicle, chauffeuring a load of invalids. This must be what it was like, Marianne thought, to drive folks from the assisted-living facility to community theater productions or the ophthalmologist or Bingo night at the parish hall.

Actually, there were only two passengers, Susi Braun and Mandy Mosher, but it felt like an army. Susi was never one to suffer in silence, and since Mandy had come clean about her pregnancy, she'd stopped making any pretense about feeling well. It seemed a safe bet that neither passenger would be interested in any spontaneous hiking. At this rate, Marianne might have to carry them both to the picnic tables for lunch. Which they probably wouldn't eat anyway.

Marianne knew she shouldn't feel surprised. Susi was always bellyaching about some physical ailment or another, foot afflictions and headaches being perennial problems. Their side-by-side home rooms at Floritas High were surrounded on all sides by male coaches who viewed academics as a burden to be endured solely for the reward of getting out there with the team every afternoon. Much like prisoners of war, Marianne and Susi had banded together — cohorts, if not precisely friends.

This morning Susi had relinquished the back seat to Mandy. She now sprawled in the passenger seat with her bare feet braced on the dashboard. She was rubbing another Vitamin E capsule into the scars on her toes.

"I don't know why I bother," Susi complained.

Marianne didn't either. "Susi, they're your *toes*. What if they *do* have a little scar or two? Does it really matter?" Even as she spoke, Marianne knew the answer.

"I've always thought my feet were one of my best features." Susi stuck her lower lip out in a pout that might be amusing on someone forty years younger.

"Look, vanity is all well and good, but unless you have something kinky going on with those feet — and if there is, I don't want to know about it — I just don't see what difference it makes."

Susi sighed deeply.

Marianne decided to let it go. "How's your stomach doing?"

Maybe moving to a different organ system would help. Because now that Marianne thought about it, Susi's bellyaching had been quite literal ever since Sunday night. She'd been bitching about stomach cramps on and off through the entire trip, and her face was pale this morning, the same shade of washed-out beige as her hair.

For the first time, Marianne considered the possibility that something might legitimately be wrong with Susi. One of the problems in dealing with hypochondriacs was that you tended to forget that they actually do get sick now and then.

"Not too good," Susi answered. She continued rubbing the Vitamin E into her toes. "I don't see how this can still be from those damned brownies, and I've been really careful what I've eaten since then. This feels more like — actually, it feels more like labor pains, if you want to know the truth."

A moan came from the back seat. "I don't," Mandy wailed. "I hate labor."

Marianne laughed and looked over her shoulder. Mandy lay on her back with her knees bent, sticking up in the air. A position not unrelated to childbirth, actually.

"I smell peanuts," Mandy said, "and it makes me nauseous."

"Probably something that was in Lynne's room," Marianne said. "Somebody did some impromptu decorating in there with our food supplies. Listen, you guys just hang on. We'll go straight to the park and just wait for the others. I'll find someplace cool where we can park in the shade and you can both sleep all day if you want."

The Argonauts were rendezvousing for lunch at Marshall Gold Discovery State Historic Park. Marianne had assumed Nikki's responsibility for supervising Hardtack Day, which in practical terms only meant that she was carrying the hardtack and jerky for lunch. Everybody had been issued special Hardtack Day water bottles this morning, with instructions to drink nothing else.

Marianne would normally be drinking water anyway, and maybe nibbling some trail mix. But there was something about being told she couldn't make her own menu choices that made her yearn for Cokes and Big Macs, for tacos and fried chicken. She slipped her hand into her left shorts pocket and surreptitiously transferred half a dozen M&Ms to her mouth.

"It's not precisely cheating to drink wine," Judith told Lisa as they cruised sedately south on Highway 49. "And we're not really drinking it anyway. We're just tasting."

Lisa laughed. "Mom, I'm not going to rat you out. And if you want to get blitzed, I'll be your designated driver. No problem. Just stop justifying it and get going."

Judith Limone *was* having trouble rationalizing the side trip, actually. The vineyards she'd researched in Amador and El Dorado counties were all located beyond their lunch stop at Marshall State Park, and Judith wasn't the sort to backtrack. The imp of the perverse had shown up this morning, however, whispering in her ear that it might be fun to bring a bottle or two of wine to the Hardtack lunch. She could claim, with a reasonably straight face, that it was an indigenous beverage.

Judith grinned now and looked over at her daughter. "Have I ever mentioned how much fun you are to hang out with?" It was true now, and always had been. From birth, she and Lisa had shared a special bond. Nate Limone appreciated the closeness between his wife and daughter, and respected it, though he did occasionally mention feeling a bit left out. When that happened, Judith and Lisa both instinctively moved to include him. The Limones formed a nuclear family in the truest and purest sense.

"You have, and I thank you. How do you suppose Dad is doing on his own?"

Judith considered. "Well, let's see. He's probably been taking all his meals at Denny's and Garcia's. He'll have misplaced his keys and the universal remote at least twice. The load of towels that was in the dryer when I left is probably still in the dryer. And I'm sure he's started two or three projects that involve getting out a lot of tools and materials."

Lisa laughed. "None of which will be finished when we get back."

"Of course not. And I'd bet money he didn't remember to call about that odd charge on the Visa bill. And if I don't specifically remind him about watering my tomato plants each time we call, they'll be dead as doornails when I get back."

"Mom? What's a doornail, and when is it alive?"

"I have no idea," Judith told her. Then she chuckled and glanced at her daughter, repeating a statement she'd made hundreds of times over the years. "But keep asking those questions, honey. It's the only way you'll learn."

As they laughed together Judith offered a silent prayer of thanks for Lisa. If she could only have one child of her own, this was the one she'd have special-ordered, from the tousled mop of curls on her head down to her endearing crooked little toes.

Lynne was furious about the smashed window in her van, even though nothing appeared to be missing. The Argonauts seemed to be riding the crest of a gold country crime wave, and she was sick of it.

"Random violence happens," Betsy told her. "That's why it's called random."

"But it's spoiling the trip!"

"Only if you let it." Betsy finished brushing the broken glass off her seat and carried the shards behind the store to a trash can. Karen Kuriosity had given them some cardboard and duct tape to close the gap, and had also offered to call the police, but Lynne was sick of the police and it didn't seem worth waiting around. They'd only tell her there was nothing they could do, and she already knew that.

She managed to regain most of her good spirits by the time they arrived at Marshall Gold Discovery State Park. From a tour guide's point of view, this was the perfect meeting point for the Argonauts tour, being the origin of it all. And while it wasn't precisely halfway between Nevada City and Columbia, it was plenty close enough.

Here was where James Marshall, constructing a sawmill in the river for Captain John Sutter, had noticed a shiny nugget in the river, setting off the entire California Gold Rush. To determine that the rock really *was* gold, Mrs. Jenny Wimmer, the mill crew's cook, had boiled it in baking soda and lye.

Lynne had seen the actual piece of gold in an exhibit case at the Bancroft Library at Berkeley. It wasn't very big, really, barely as large as Lynne's thumbnail, but it had an appealing, almost crafted shape. The nugget looked like something that might have been created as a ring or pendant by an artisan jeweler.

The group had left their rendezvous site vague, figuring that they would connect in the general vicinity of Sutter's Mill. Then they could either set up lunch right there or move as a group to a more congenial location. Lynne decided to cruise the parking lots and see if any of the others had arrived yet. She and Betsy had stopped at a couple more antique shops, taking turns waiting outside with the no-longer-lockable van. It was a fairly safe bet they'd be the last arrivals.

Sure enough, Nikki's SUV was parked in shade not far from the Visitors' Center. When she stepped out of the van, Lynne realized the van was almost as hot as the outdoors. She'd continued to run the van's air-conditioning out of sheer spitefulness, but even with the cardboard taped over the broken window, a lot of the chilled air vanished immediately. She turned her neckerchief over, putting the cool side next to her skin, thinking that she really ought to be used to the heat by now. High noon on the American River in June was a pretty unpleasant experience.

Somehow when she'd previously thought about the Gold Rush — generally only during her long-ago stints as a fourth grade room mother — she hadn't considered weather. But this weather was truly beastly, and July and August could only be worse. Lynne's respect for the endurance of the forty-niners increased with each passing day.

"The windows are open," Betsy noted, looking at Nikki's SUV. "I'll go see if somebody's taking a nap in there and then watch the van while you check inside."

Inside, the Visitors' Center was cool and dark and full of the kind of museum exhibits that don't get changed nearly often enough. Marianne stood over by an exhibit about the indigenous tribes, Native Americans who for centuries had blithely ignored the impractical soft yellow metal littering their landscape. She wore belted khaki shorts and a peach tank top and had gotten a fair amount of sun. Her cheeks and shoulders were rosy through the pale healthy tan she seemed to carry year round. Marianne was a handsome, vital woman, though never obnoxious about it.

Now Marianne beamed a greeting. "Man, am I glad to see somebody who's ambulatory," she told Lynne. "Between Mandy's morning sickness and Susi — well, Susi just being Susi, I guess — it's been one long and winding road. I feel like I'm driver for a M*A*S*H unit or something."

"That bad?" Lynne asked. She could feel herself switching into Tour Guide mode. It wasn't fair to have Marianne burdened with sick travelers. They'd need to switch off passengers so Lynne could haul the ailing. Though diminished air-conditioning wouldn't please Miss Susi one little bit.

"That bad," Marianne said. "I mean, I'm not complaining, but . . . oh, hell."

"We'll work something out after lunch," Lynne promised. "Betsy can ride with you and I'll take Susi and Mandy."

"I wasn't fishing to trade," Marianne protested. Mildly. The expression of relief on her face was all Lynne needed to see.

"Of course not. But I know that you and Nikki had plans for some hiking today and I can't imagine that your passengers are interested in hitting the open trail. Although there's one little problem."

"Only one?" Marianne's tone was wry.

Lynne explained about the smashed window on the van.

"Do you suppose you can get it fixed before we go back?" Marianne asked.

The prospect of 400 miles through the San Joaquin Valley with cardboard taped over her window was unthinkable. If it came to it, Lynne would stay over to get the glass replaced, which she ought to be able to do in one of the larger towns. Just when she'd finally gotten that lyric about being stuck again in Lodi out of her mind, *this* had to happen.

Betsy was standing in shade near the van when Lynne and Marianne emerged from the Visitors' Center. "No takers for lunch," Betsy said, "even when I promised they wouldn't have to eat jerky."

"Well, I'm getting hungry," Marianne said, "so why don't we at least get set up for lunch somewhere? Then we can start whenever Judith and Lisa get here."

Lynne shrugged. "No real reason to wait for them if you're hungry now, I don't think. It's not as if we have to be sure the steaks come off the grill precisely medium rare for their arrival."

Marianne chuckled. "No, it isn't. I staked out a place down by the river, within view of the recreation of Sutter's Mill. We can cool off with our legs in the river while we eat."

"Sounds cool," Lynne said, "quite literally. I could use that, so long as I can park the van close enough to keep an eye on it."

They retrieved the alleged food for the hardtack luncheon and confirmed that neither Mandy nor Susi was interested in joining them. The two had the windows of the SUV open and were catching a pretty nice breeze. Both wore their cooling neckbands and Mandy had a spare draped across her forehead. Susi was running a battery-operated fan attached to a spray bottle of water. She squirted this at regular intervals to shower her face and exposed limbs with chilled water from the ice melting in the cooler, and she appeared damp all over.

As for Mandy — well, Mandy woke up just long enough to assure everyone that she wasn't hungry, just exhausted, then turned on her side, rearranged the cooler bands, and promptly began snoring.

Leaving their comrades, Lynne and Betsy and Marianne got in the van and drove toward the potential picnic spot Marianne had located. They were halfway across the parking lot when Lynne spotted the Winnebago belonging to the St. Paul schoolteachers, parked in a remote corner. Though the area was far from deserted, most of the huge parking lot remained empty.

"Hey," Lynne said, turning toward the big boxy vehicle, "I want to see if they noticed anything when they left that antique shop." The Minnesotans had departed about ten minutes before Betsy and Lynne left the shop. She explained quickly to Marianne about meeting the women at their first antique stop of the day. "And maybe they'd like to join us for lunch."

"Good idea," Betsy said. "They're welcome to all of my hardtack, that's how generous I feel today."

Lynne parked the van near the RV and the three women got out. Almost immediately, Lynne heard what sounded like an angry male voice coming from inside the vehicle. She stopped abruptly, but couldn't make out what it was saying.

"Did you hear that?" Lynne asked the others softly.

"What?" Betsy stopped beside her and cocked her head.

Silence.

"It sounded like a guy yelling in there," Lynne said. Surely she hadn't imagined this.

Betsy nodded, looking worried. "It did indeed. They said they were traveling alone, didn't they?"

"Yeah," Lynne answered. They huddled together, some eight feet away from the RV, listening.

The voice came again, angrier and louder, and definitely male. "I said fuckin' forget it!"

The three looked at each other in alarm. Lynne knew now that something was definitely very wrong. They hadn't spent much time with the two Minnesotans back in Karen's Kuriosities, but neither had seemed the type to develop fast relationships and the women had definitely been alone two hours ago.

Marianne nodded toward the RV. "I'll make a fast circuit and see if I can peek in a window." She slipped off to the side and disappeared behind the RV from the left, moving lightly on her feet. A few moments later, she reappeared on the right, shaking her head.

"All the windows are buttoned up tight. The only way I could look in the front would be to jump up on the front bumper," Marianne reported. "That seemed a bit . . . well, obvious."

"Let's just pretend we didn't hear any-thing," Lynne suggested, "and knock on the door." Something about being with the others emboldened her. Because, face it, whatever was happening in this home on wheels was really none of their business.

Lynne took a deep breath and walked up to the back door of the RV. She raised her hand and knocked three times. Silence. She banged again. "Hey," she called, "Harriet? Stephanie? It's Lynne, from the antique shop."

Still no response. In fact, the silence from inside seemed rather ominous.

Lynne thought a moment, then called out again. "Did you know that you have a flat tire? Maybe we can help you all fix it."

A few moments later, the back door opened slightly, about eight inches. A young man, holding his head to one side, spoke. "Thanks," he said. "I'll tell my auntie."

Auntie?

Not bloody likely.

Last night in Nevada City, Lynne had in-stinctively recoiled when studying the unap-pealing mug shots of the three escaped convicts from Southern California. These were guys trying hard to look tough, and it wasn't much of a reach. Despite their tender years — none were old enough to vote, even if there hadn't been that pesky felony issue — the photographs had not seemed youthful. All three young men had a scary, hardened appearance.

And the gentleman on the other side of this door was one of them.

Robert "Robby" Hargrove, far too cuddly a nickname for this creepy dude, wore baggy jeans and a T-shirt. Hargrove's fingernails, wrapped around the edge of the door, were deeply stained and there seemed to be a snake crudely tattooed on his inside wrist. He'd shaved off the unkempt, shoulder-length locks he wore in the mug shot, and the scraggly growth on his chin suggested that he was trying, without much success, to grow a goatee.

The door wasn't open very wide, but as Lynne's eyes adjusted to the darkness inside, she could make out the figure of Harriet, cowering against the opposite wall. She couldn't see Stephanie, but there appeared to be another young man inside, behind Harriet. This would be either Sam Watson or Kyle Burke.

Marianne had slipped up beside Lynne and stood out of sight of the door, against the trailer wall. Betsy seemed to have disappeared altogether, and Lynne hoped she'd gone for help. Knocking on this door hadn't been the brightest move Lynne had made lately. For one brief giddy moment, Lynne had a flash of *Charlie's Angels*, the old TV show. She, of course, was Kate Jackson.

Marianne seemed oddly empowered. She drew herself to her full height and moved forward with sudden grace and speed, pushing the back door all the way open and yanking the stunned young man right out onto the parking lot.

Robby Hargrove was so startled that he literally flew through the air, his slight arms and legs flailing like a rag doll. Marianne flipped him effortlessly and he landed on his right side with a screech of pain. In moments, Marianne had a foot planted on his butt and his arm twisted high behind his back.

"Harriet! Stephanie! Are you all right?" Lynne yelled into the trailer.

"We will be," a voice called back. It sounded like Harriet. "Now listen here, young man —" Harriet's voice as she addressed her unwelcome guest wasn't quite as loud, but it was remarkably firm. "This has gone just exactly far enough."

An engine roared toward them. Now what?

Lynne turned her head to see Judith Limone's Buick squealing to a halt a few feet away. Lisa was behind the wheel.

Judith jumped out of the passenger door and marched toward Robby Hargrove, who remained firmly pinned to the ground. Marianne's captive was now cussing a blue streak. His grammar wasn't very functional, but he compensated with a colorful and inventive vocabulary.

A crash came from inside the RV. Lynne moved cautiously toward the door, alarmed. This entire business was careening out of control. There were still two escapees unaccounted for, men, who had been described as "armed and dangerous." She was not the least bit inclined to go inside the RV looking for them.

Another heavy crash came from inside, one that actually rocked the RV from side to side. Judith appeared ready to intervene, squaring her shoulders as if literally preparing to march into battle.

Then Lisa pushed her aside. "Out of the way, Mom," she ordered, peering inside the RV. Lisa was the calmest of them all, possessed of the invincibility of youth.

But before Lisa could move any farther, Harriet pulled the door open all the way and stumbled outside, followed closely by Stephanie. Both looked disheveled and frightened, and Harriet had a nasty bruise rising on her cheek. They blinked rapidly in the bright noonday sun.

"Are the others still inside?" Lynne asked. The dude on the ground might be out of commission, but he represented only a third of the danger. If this were a movie, the two thugs inside would be preparing a sneak attack to rescue their buddy, and they'd come flying around the front of the RV any moment now in a surprise ambush, brandishing tire irons.

"There's only one more," Harriet announced, "and he's out cold. Stephanie smashed him on the noggin with my shillelagh. Though he probably won't be very happy when he wakes up." She looked inside with a slight shudder.

Stephanie frowned. "Why did you ask about 'others'? Do you know who these wretched boys are?" She sounded almost hysterical.

"They're escapees from a correctional facility in Southern California," Lynne told her. "And if what you say is true, one of them is still at large. Three of them broke out together last Saturday."

"Oh, dear God," Harriet murmured. She looked a little woozy.

Lynne grabbed her elbow in support. "Are you two all right?"

Both women nodded slowly.

"Mostly my pride is hurt," Harriet admitted.

Judith shook her head and looked around. "Could somebody explain just what on earth is going on here?" she demanded, in her most principalian tones.

The young man on the ground let out another torrent of profanity.

"That's enough out of you," Judith snapped at him. "It's absolutely disgraceful what you boys did to that poor woman in Nevada City."

"Dunno what you're talkin' about," the guy on the ground responded. He tried to spit the words out, but ran into difficulties because Marianne had his face twisted so he was talking into the asphalt.

"The woman you threw down the side of the hill at the Murmuring Pines Cabins," Judith continued. "The woman who died last night."

On the ground, Robby Hargrove froze, instantly still and quiet.

"Oh, man, I don't know *what* you bitches are talkin' about," he said after a moment, speaking very slowly. "We ain't been to Nevada City. You bitches are crazy."

"We may be crazy," Judith announced crisply, "but we aren't the ones who've escaped from custody, and we haven't killed anybody. You boys are in an enormous amount of trouble, you know."

Standing next to Judith, Lynne could detect the faint odor of red wine on her breath. Good God, had Judith become a morning drinker? Well, it hardly mattered. Lynne had forgotten what an awesome force Judith Limone could be when cloaked in her Authority Figure persona. And when you put a little wine in her, she turned into the Queen of England.

Stephanie pointed. "Look, here come the park rangers!"

They all turned to watch the official vehicle bearing down on them. It squealed to a halt beside Judith's sedan. Two rangers rushed forward as Betsy climbed out of the back seat. One of the rangers moved to handcuff Robby Hargrove, who seemed almost relieved to be in the custody of actual law enforcement officers.

The other ranger, after conferring briefly with the Argonauts, moved cautiously into the RV, weapon drawn. "This one looks like he might need an ambulance," he called out a moment later.

"I hope the shillelagh isn't broken," Harriet murmured.

Chapter 15

Lynne was starting to feel more than a little cranky. The day was broiling hot, far worse than she'd expected. She no longer had a passenger window in her van, and the interlude with the two young felons had put a significant damper on everyone's spirits. By the time local authorities carted away the escaped convicts, Lynne was ready for a high tea on a Victorian porch.

Instead, she was facing dried meat scraps in the blistering sun.

The lunch spot Marianne had tentatively chosen on the gravel banks of the American River was proximate to the recreation of Sutter's Mill, but it didn't offer any comfortable picnic area, and it was notably lacking in shade.

"If Marianne doesn't object, I vote that we move to that nice picnic area upriver," Betsy suggested, reading Lynne's mind. "This isn't where the mill was originally anyway. I think we've all earned a bit of creature comfort. Or at least something to sit on that isn't covered with gravel."

"I've got no vested interest in being uncomfortable," Marianne answered immediately.

"Then that's settled," Judith announced

crisply. "Perhaps we should leave a note for Harriet and Stephanie so they can join us when they're finished with the police."

Lynne shook her head. "A nice gesture, but I have a feeling they'll be tied up for hours. And Stephanie was quite adamant about going into Sacramento and spending the night at the nicest hotel in town."

"Can't say that I blame her," Judith agreed. "Now, let's get on with lunch."

They set up in a shaded picnic area nearby, Marianne neatly arranging the various types of jerky on paper plates. It was quite an impressive array, actually, mostly turkey and beef, in a range of flavors from mesquite to teriyaki. Nikki'd sent away for some of it, ordering chunks of surprisingly tender beef from a smokehouse in Fredericksburg, Texas, and slabs of very salty salmon from a fish-monger at the Pike Street Market in Seattle.

Lynne picked up a piece of hardtack and sucked on it. "Are you sure this is supposed to be edible?" she asked after a moment.

Betsy checked the wrapper. "So they claim. But you know, I saw a piece of hardtack in a museum once that was left over from the Civil War. And it looked just like this."

"Perhaps we can help a little," Judith said sweetly. "Lisa?"

Lisa nodded and walked over to the Buick. She unlocked the trunk and carried over two canvas bags. From one she pulled a stack of small clear plastic tumblers and placed them on the table. Next she dug her Swiss Army knife out of a pocket and set it beside the tumblers. Finally, with a flourish, she brought out two bottles of wine.

"The Chardonnay was chilled when we left the winery," Lisa explained, "though it may have warmed up a bit since then. But the Zinfandel should be just the right temperature to accompany a fine peppercorn jerky."

Betsy laughed in delight. "I can't remember a time I've been happier to know you, Judith. Or was this Lisa's idea?"

"It was Mom's," Lisa said quickly. "But I added a little wrinkle of my own." She looked at her mother. "Before we get into that, do you want to give them your little speech about Father Serra and the mission grapes and how this is really terribly authentic?"

Judith looked around the table. "I haven't noticed anybody protesting, have you?"

"Well, you might have brought it out a little sooner," Betsy muttered, "but other than that, I think you've come up with a crowd pleaser here."

Judith took the Swiss Army knife and located the corkscrew. After she fumbled for a moment, she handed it over to Betsy. "You can do a much better job of this than I."

Betsy cheerfully used the tip of the corkscrew to peel away the foil on the Chardonnay. "I'll give it my best shot. Or would you rather that I get the real corkscrew out of the van?"

Judith offered an exaggerated shudder. "And sacrifice authenticity? I don't think so."

When both bottles were open and glasses poured for everyone, Judith raised her own tumbler. "To the finest teachers I know, a stupendous tour guide, and the best sports imaginable. And because I think so highly of you all, we have one more little surprise."

Now Lisa opened the second canvas bag and carefully removed a cherry pie. As she set it on the table, everyone stared dumbfounded for a moment. It was a beautiful pie, a world-class pie, a knockout with a lightly glazed lattice crust in a tantalizing honey brown. This was a pie that would be at home on the cover of *Martha Stewart Living* or gracing the most sophisticated gourmet restaurant dessert cart. On a state park redwood picnic table surrounded by leathery chunks of jerky, it was a true showstopper.

Betsy spoke first. "Lucy Whipple!"

Lisa nodded with a grin. "Exactly. I'm so glad I didn't have to explain."

As the others nodded, chuckled, and announced "Of course!" Lynne took another welcome sip of her Zinfandel, then set down the cup carefully. She wouldn't ordinarily have indulged, but there wasn't anything ordinary about this day or, for that matter, this trip. "I hate to sound so ignorant, but I have absolutely no idea what you're talking about. Who's Lucy Whipple?"

Betsy turned to her. "A new wrinkle in teaching Gold Rush, Lynne. Back when your kids were in fourth grade and doing Gold Rush, they probably read *By the Great Horned Spoon.* Which is a fine book and all that, but it's kind of a — well, kind of a *guy* story. A few years ago, a new kids book was published that gives a girl's view of the Gold Rush. *The Ballad of Lucy Whipple.* Lucy was trying to earn enough money to leave California and go back home, because she hated being here."

"Imagine wanting to leave this paradise," Lynne said laconically, wiping a sheet of sweat off her brow.

Betsy ignored her. "And so Lucy started a business baking pies. But Lisa, where *ever* did you find this?"

Lisa was already hacking at the pie with her Swiss Army knife. "We followed signs off Highway 49," she explained, "and we stumbled onto an amazing orchard. They had mountains of Bing and Rainier cherries, more than I've ever seen in one place." She gave an orgasmic little shudder. "Cherries are my absolute favorite fruit, so we got about forty pounds of them. But the orchard also had a little bakery."

Judith smiled serenely. "And I absolutely

could not resist. Besides, while you could probably make an argument that the wine isn't terribly authentic, thanks to Lucy Whipple, nobody can claim that this pie isn't pure Gold Rush. Which means we're in keeping with both the letter and the spirit of Hardtack Day." She lifted her wineglass. "The spirit, of course, being quite literal."

"I've made it a practice never to argue with you," Betsy told Judith cheerfully. "You're smarter than I am, and better educated. Plus you write my performance reviews."

Nikki wasn't sure what to expect when she and Larry strolled into the picnic area. They'd tracked the group down by waking up Susi and Mandy in the SUV at the Visitors' Center, and neither had been terribly coherent. Nor had they sent the Masons in the right direction, dispatching them to the riverbank. Nikki and Larry had looked all up and down the waterfront before finally locating the Argonauts.

It had already occurred to Nikki that, in her absence, Hardtack Day might have been observed with less than total enthusiasm. Even so, she was startled to find the group lounging around a picnic table that held two half-empty bottles of wine and what looked suspiciously like a cherry pie.

"I see y'all are really roughing it," Nikki

told the group, grinning. "Is this what happens when I get arrested? The standards all fall to hell and gone?"

The cries and shrieks of greeting were so wildly enthusiastic that they actually brought a tear to Nikki's eye. Sheesh, this was the second time today. Was she going soft already, and only halfway through her thirties? At this rate, by the time she reached menopause, she'd be a blubbering wreck.

Only now, as she hugged everyone and tried to decide which questions to answer first, did she realize how traumatic the past eighteen hours had been.

"Tell us everything," Judith demanded.

Nikki took a moment to collect herself as she inspected the jerky selection on the table. "You know, maybe this wasn't such a great idea after all. I'm starting to be really glad Larry and I stopped for brunch before we left Nevada City."

"You ate real food?!" Marianne had a note of indignation in her voice, but she also had a tumbler of wine in her hand and a plate of pie crumbs in front of her. "On Hardtack Day?"

Nikki nodded. "Guilty as charged. But only of having an omelet," she added hastily.

There was probably, Nikki decided, no need to share any of the particulars of her late morning with the others, and certainly not while Larry was still around. After her release, she and her husband had eaten an enormous breakfast, then taken a motel room and shared a long shower and some spirited lovemaking in air-conditioned quiet and blessed freedom. By then, the jail interlude was already starting to feel like an odd dream. And afterward, when Larry suggested trying to catch up with the others, Nikki had been more than ready to resume her vacation.

Larry planned to leave her with the Argonauts and drive his rental car back to Sacramento this afternoon, catching a San Diego flight that should get him home before sunset.

"Don't be a tease," Marianne told her. "We're all dying to know what happened."

"It was a big old mistake," Larry said, "pure and simple."

"Easy enough for him to say," Nikki said, shaking her head. "He wasn't the one who spent the night in a cell. But it *was* a mistake. A Texas-sized one, to be sure, and a giant pain in the ass."

"Fortunately, we were able to get it all cleared up," Larry put in.

Nikki grinned. "It can be very useful, having a lawyer in the family."

"Nikki!!!" Judith's tone was firm. "What *happened?*"

Nikki smiled at her principal. "Are you worrying about whether you're going to have to fire me for moral turpitude?" Nikki watched Judith's eyes, which didn't quite meet her own.

"It's crossed my mind," Judith admitted.

"Not to worry." Nikki scouted the table. "Where's that salmon jerky? Any of it left?"

"Most of it," Betsy admitted. "It's kind of salty. Nikki, don't make us beg."

Larry had poured them both tumblers of Zinfandel. Nikki picked hers up, swirled it slightly, and sniffed. "Nice bouquet. Okay. Here's what happened. Some of you know that I grew up in a little town in East Texas, Hillandale. A pretty little place in the Piney Woods. My daddy and another man had a couple of gas stations there. Daddy was a mechanic, the kind of guy who can fix anything that's ever been made, but he didn't have much of a head for business. His partner, Joe Bob Stewart, was in charge of all that. And Joe Bob made some really bad business decisions."

"He was an embezzling crook," Larry put in, showing remarkable restraint. The things he'd said earlier about Joe Bob had been considerably more flamboyant and a lot less pithy.

"That he was," Nikki agreed cheerfully. "Anyway, I was living in Houston and teaching when it all fell apart. They lost the business and there were huge debts, and Daddy . . . well, Daddy killed himself."

Nikki deliberately avoided looking at anyone when she made this statement. Her friends and coworkers in California knew that her father was dead, but this was the first time she'd ever told anyone out here how he'd died. Oddly, it wasn't as difficult as she'd imagined it might be to make the confession.

"How awful," Judith murmured. "That must have been just dreadful for you and your mother."

"It was." Nikki could feel herself tearing up again. She wasn't, it seemed, as comfortable with all of this as she'd deluded herself into believing. It still hurt, really hurt. And a night in jail was absolutely the least of it. "Anyway," she went on, "it gets kind of complicated here. It turned out that Joe Bob had actually moved the money into some land deals. There were major problems with the land deals, but about a year after Daddy died, some big company out of Texarkana bought Joe Bob out, for a bundle. And Mama sued."

No need explaining that it was Nikki who'd pressed for the lawsuit, who had urged her mother on, swearing that Daddy would have wanted it that way. "The suit was ugly, but it would have been all right except that it was heard in front of this old nutcase judge who was married to Joe Bob's sister." Nikki realized as she explained this that the whole business had the kind of incestuous back-woods flavor that gave country folk their bumpkin reputation.

Well, no matter. It was what had happened. Stereotypes tended to grow out of realities.

"And he didn't recuse himself?" Lynne asked. She looked and sounded horrified. Outraged, too. Nikki was liking Lynne more and more.

"Nope. I suppose Mama should have just dropped it all once it was clear we were in front of that judge, but Leander Trenton, her lawyer, said it would all work out." Nikki sighed. "Well, Leander was wrong. And I guess I made a bit of a scene in the court-room when that judge dismissed Mama's case. We stalked out after that and left town immediately. Mama was living down in Corpus Christi by then, so she and I just headed for Corpus that morning and never went back. Then our lawyer had a heart at-tack and died a couple weeks later."

"It seems that the judge decided after the fact that Nikki had been in contempt of court," Larry explained. "He issued a bench warrant for her arrest, but because she'd left town, she didn't know about it."

"Until last night," Nikki put in. "Actually until this morning, when we finally figured out what happened. Larry and Detective McMasters were able to get through to the authorities back in Hillandale. They were just

272

as surprised as we were to find out about the warrant."

"But what did the judge have to say?"

Larry Mason grinned. "That's where it gets *really* good. The judge isn't available for comment, because he's in jail himself, the slimy crook."

"I'm confused," Lynne said. "Why is the judge in jail? And if you left not knowing you were" — she hesitated briefly — "wanted, then how'd they have your fingerprints?"

Nikki rolled her eyes. "I had a summer job at the courthouse during college. They took my prints then. Until this morning, I'd forgotten all about it."

"And the judge was convicted of bribery charges," Larry added.

"So you're free and clear?" Marianne asked Nikki.

"Free as a bird and clear as moonshine," Nikki answered. "So. Have you guys been staying out of trouble while I was gone?"

The entire group erupted and Nikki stared in stupefaction as they all spit out details. Lynne's van had been broken into and it sounded very much like they'd participated in a free-for-all right here in the parking lot. Most remarkably, these events had transpired within the hour, involving two Minnesota schoolteachers nobody had met before this morning.

"Wait a minute," Nikki said finally, holding

up both hands to silence them. "When we stopped and saw Susi and Mandy over by the Visitors' Center just now, they didn't say anything about this."

Judith looked suddenly very guilty. "Oh my heavens, we never told them!"

Considering how grumpy and out-of-sorts both women had seemed Nikki could understand why nobody'd be racing back to share news. But still . . .

Nikki listened as Lynne outlined what had happened barely an hour earlier. When the story was finished, Nikki felt more confused than ever.

"So wait a minute. I thought there were three of those guys."

Lynne nodded. "There are. But the two who were here claim that the third guy split up with them immediately and went to Mexico. Which maybe he did and maybe he didn't. I don't think that these guys are normally too careful with the truth, so I'm not sure their information's entirely correct."

Judith shook her head. "I don't know, Lynne. Once they realized that they were wanted for murder, they started singing like the Mormon Tabernacle Choir. I've listened to an awful lot of young people telling me they didn't do something they were accused of. Unpalatable as these young men were, I had the sense they were telling the truth."

Lynne continued, "They swear — and I

mean that very literally — that they never were in Nevada City at all. They say they've been sleeping in the woods and fields, trying to get back north, but that this is as far as they've gotten."

Nikki shook her head. This was all far too confusing. "Then who trashed our cabins? Who broke into your van? And who threw Connie Caravaci down the hill?"

Chapter 16

Amos was not having a very good day.

He'd risked breaking into the van, only to find that the lamp wasn't even there. He had no idea how he would explain this to Jed, who had let Amos know in no uncertain terms that his failure to produce that miserable lamp was causing serious concern to Jed's people.

Jed's people, he implied, were even more ferocious than Jed himself. Amos pictured a rustic cabin filled with wiry hirsute men field-stripping automatic weapons and the occasional shaven-headed commando picking his teeth with an eight-inch Bowie knife. They'd be milling about at this very moment, oozing testosterone and gunpowder, waiting for . . . whatever. Whatever was in that wretched heavy lamp that Amos had brought back from San Francisco on Friday night in a load of otherwise innocuous merchandise to be displayed and hopefully sold at Ledbetter Antiques.

Like so many dreadful deeds, Amos had come to this miserable arrangement through intentions that were, if not precisely pure, at least well intentioned. Not that it mattered any more, of course. He was well past the point where he could extricate himself gracefully, or at all. In his heart of hearts, he kept hoping that the Bureau of Alcohol, Tobacco and Firearms — the folks who most often seemed in direct conflict with those of Jed's ilk — would arrest the sorry lot of them and release Amos from his Mephistophelian bonds. Alas, the ATF, like other government agencies, never seemed to be around when you needed them, and Amos had seriously considered ratting them out himself on occasion, stopped only by his realization that he knew next to nothing about their operation other than his own sorry involvement in it.

Amos had deliberately avoided learning what it was that he channeled from the man in San Francisco to Jed and his cohorts. Nothing good, he was sure. He'd long suspected drugs, except that the folks who "purchased" these items in his shop seemed so naturally psychotic that surely they'd require no chemical enhancement. Maybe they sold the drugs to further their programs, which he was pretty sure had to do with violent actions against the government, or against somebody.

His short-term goal was to keep that somebody from becoming himself.

More likely this had nothing at all to do with drugs. Once a skinny little guy with a shaven head and tattooed snakes curling up both arms had picked up a chest of drawers so heavy that they'd needed both of them and a dolly to load it into his truck. But usually the pieces that Amos channeled through Ledbetter Antiques were small and heavy. Very heavy. Gold bullion seemed unlikely, so he had to accept that it was probably some kind of armaments — and *that* he really wanted to know nothing about.

He'd never meant to get into this in the first place, had only agreed when he was so desperately short of cash and anxious to buy the stock from Bruce Warburton's antique shop. Bruce and his partner Ed had both been terminally ill and frantic to cash out so that they might spend their final months in Hawaii. Amos had been as eager to facilitate that dream as he had been to acquire Bruce's truly exquisite collection of antiques.

He remembered everything about that first time with terrible clarity. He had no idea how they came to learn of his need. A deceptively mild-mannered fellow who told Amos to call him John Smith had met him in the back of a dingy San Francisco bar and outlined the proposal. From time to time, someone would send Amos a coded e-mail inquiring about the availability of nineteenth-century porcelain. Embedded in the text of the e-mail would be a date and a time. Amos would drive his truck to San Francisco and pick up a small load of collectibles — nothing terribly remarkable, but acceptable pieces, the kind of job lot a dealer might purchase from time to time. Within that load would be a specially marked item that someone identifying himself by a coded password would come by to claim within the next couple of business days.

The little man had given Amos cash on the spot, a down payment. If everything went smoothly with the first transfer, he said, a second would follow a week later. Upon delivery, Amos would receive the remainder of his initial payment. It was, with the other funds that Amos had already scraped together, enough to buy Bruce Warburton's stock, all but two or three very high-end pieces of furniture, which Bruce left with another dealer on consignment.

It all went so smoothly that Amos was truly frightened. But once he'd taken that cash in the back of the bar, he knew he was committed. Within two weeks he had taken two deliveries and endured his first two encounters with Jed, who was nothing like the man in the back of the bar and who scared the bloody blue hell out of Amos.

And after that first time, there was no turning back.

A few months down the line, Amos had told a gaunt, blond-haired man that he wasn't interested in participating anymore, thank you very much, and Ichabod Crane had grunted that Amos didn't have the option of quitting. Actually, what he'd said was,

"You'll do it," and he'd said it in a way that brooked no disagreement whatsoever. When Amos ignored the next e-mail about nineteenth-century porcelain, he went out to pick up his morning paper the day after he'd failed to make the assignation and found Fluffy, strangled on his doorstep.

Now here he was, accessory to things he couldn't bear to think about, chasing a group of schoolteachers through gold country. The ridiculous part was that he hadn't been able to catch them, and in his more reasoned moments, he realized that the smugglers were well within their rights to consider Amos uncooperative.

He was in a terrible pickle. The lamp had not been in any of the cabins at Murmuring Pines or in the Montgomery woman's van. He had been positioned today to watch the opened trunk of the Buick while one of the young women brought out what turned out to be a pie. He could see clearly into the trunk and there wasn't any lamp in it, not unless it had been broken apart and packed in suitcases. He knew that those suitcases — he'd been through them twice — were jammed full of books and clothing, including some very interesting vintage clothing and wigs. At least one of the schoolteachers, it seemed, occasionally dressed in drag.

His last hope was the Expedition, but when he found the SUV parked outside the Visitors' Center, there'd been two women sleeping in the back seats, both of them a little too plump to be comfortable in this heat. They'd rearranged everything to provide themselves with the maximum possible comfort. Opened sleeping bags were spread over a jumbled base layer of suitcases and boxes and — well, *stuff.* There was no telling *what* might be in the back of that vehicle, apart from the reclining women. A troupe of juggling dwarves, for all Amos could tell.

As if that weren't bad enough, when the van showed up, cardboard covering its broken window, there was that entire baroque scenario with the old ladies and the RV and what turned out to be escaped convicts, for God's sake, those young men who'd been mentioned in the newspaper.

And *that* had turned into a bloody nightmare, bringing a veritable flood of police officers to the area. Before things ended, there'd even been a Nevada County Sheriff's car on the scene, and Amos had taken that as his cue to leave. High on the list of things that Amos was trying very hard not to think about was the Nevada County Sheriff's Department and the crimes they were currently investigating.

So Amos had decided to cut his losses for the moment. His best approach would almost certainly be to waylay them in Columbia, where they would be spending the night. Columbia was a quiet little town and he would lurk on its fringes until after dark, when he ought to be able to easily smash and grab while the SUV was parked unattended overnight.

Except.

Except for a bozo from Boise.

The bozo from Boise was turning left onto Highway 49 from a side road that really should have been much better marked. The bozo was fiddling with his CD player as he shot across the highway and he didn't notice Amos until he had broadsided him.

The crunch was spectacular.

The pain was excruciating.

Amos's left arm was smashed and he remembered thinking, just before he passed out, that his father had been wrong when he ridiculed the nine-year-old Amos who wailed and screamed after breaking his wrist. His father had told him he was being melodramatic and that it really wouldn't hurt at all if Amos weren't such a little baby.

Well, Amos was as grown up now as he was ever going to be. And it hurt like fury.

Chapter 17

Frogs were a take-it-or-leave-it proposition as far as Nikki was concerned, but she found herself oddly charmed by Angels Camp, home of the annual Jumping Frog Jubilee.

Angels Camp — which had nothing to do with heaven or religion, but had been named for either George Angell or Henry Angel, depending on whose history you accepted — nestled in a steep-sided canyon with Highway 49, its main drag, running along the canyon floor.

And Nikki felt quite certain she was going to like it.

Of course she was ready to enjoy just about anything, with a vengeance. Being on the road again felt absolutely wonderful. Larry was on his way back home and all Nikki wanted to do was move forward. No point nursing a grudge against the judge who had caused the problem, and no reason to ever mention any of this to her mother, who had remarried and seemed blissfully content selling time shares on South Padre Island with her husband.

Nikki was genuinely sorry to have missed the episode with the escaped convicts, and she figured that their ignominious capture by a group of teachers had probably confirmed every prejudice they'd ever held against education. She wished more than anything that she could have been there when Marianne flipped that young punk out onto the asphalt.

They'd reconfigured the passengers for the afternoon's drive, moving Mandy and Susi and their respective pillows into the two back seats of Lynne's van. Betsy continued riding shotgun to keep Lynne company and watch for promising antique shops, since Mandy and Susi had both — between moans — assured them that they wouldn't mind waiting in the car for brief intervals. This would also solve the problem of leaving the van unlocked till the broken window could be fixed.

Judith and Lisa Limone had continued toward Columbia by themselves, doing a bit more mother-daughter bonding and talking about driving out to Indian Grinding Rock Historic Park, some ten or twelve miles east of Highway 49. Since this was Lisa's idea, the park being devoted to Miwok culture and featuring some 1,200 mortar holes once used for grinding acorn meal, Nikki figured it was a safe bet that Judith would willingly go along.

Now Nikki parked high above Angels Camp, at the top of a multilevel lot. "You want to call home?" she asked Marianne, pulling out the fancy satellite phone. "Tell the kids you're in jumping frog territory?"

"Curt loves frogs," Marianne said. "But I

can't use your phone. Didn't you say that thing costs about a million dollars a minute?"

Nikki grinned. "After a night in jail, I'm inclined to be extravagant. It's Larry's treat anyway, and I'm sure he's figured out some way to write it all off, so go right ahead. Tell you what, I'll meet you down at the Visitors' Center." She pointed. "It's that way, at the corner of Main and Hardscrabble."

"You're making that up," Marianne told her.

"Oddly enough, I'm not. Take all the time you want. I'll be down there doing sprints, savoring my freedom." Nikki took a moment to show Marianne how to operate the phone, then vaulted down two flights of wooden stairs to street level. The metal handrails were blazing hot in the early afternoon sun.

Marianne had used Nikki's phone once before, when they all tried it out at Malakoff Diggins a couple of days ago. No, she corrected herself, not a couple of days ago. *Yesterday.* These days were turning out to be mighty long and action-packed.

She tried Briana's cell phone and her daughter picked up immediately. In the background she could hear sounds of the midway: screams and clanging bells and the roar of a roller coaster.

"Oh. Mom." Briana managed to pack a stunning amount of disappointment into those two basic syllables.

"How's it going?" Marianne asked. She felt too good to let her thirteen-year-old daughter pick a fight with her.

"Okay. This is, like, totally boring and Daddy keeps saying we *have* to come with him each day." Briana's voice was remarkably clear, considering the route it was traveling: cell phone in Southern California to various transmitters to outer space to a parking lot above Angels Camp, five hundred miles north of Del Mar.

"Did Curt get to his softball game all right yesterday?"

"Sure. The Engtroms took him." Until this year, Briana had also played softball, and been quite good at it. But she'd kicked up a fuss about registering this spring, and after arguing halfheartedly at first, Marianne had agreed to let her skip the season, knowing this meant her daughter would probably never go back to the sport. The time Briana might have devoted to practice and games all seemed dedicated now to mall pilgrimages. Her baby was growing up.

"And what've you been doing?" Marianne asked.

"You mean besides being bored out of my mind here at the fair?"

This was new.

"Honey, I'm sorry you have to be out there this week, but you know it means a lot to your father to have you at the fair."

"Oh, right, like he's even noticed we're here. He keeps running off so I can't even find him, and half the time he wants me to stay at the booth and watch it for him."

It would be just like Mark to find some backroom poker game, and leave the kids to their own devices. Between exhibiting at the fair and all but bunking down at the stables during horse-racing season, Mark knew every square inch of the place, as well as most of the fair regulars.

Best to leave this one alone. "What's Curt been up to? Has he been taking his pills?"

Nine-year-old Curt was such a textbook case of ADHD that Marianne, who'd once believed Ritalin to be a pharmaceutical plot against the children of America, had totally reordered her thinking.

"Yeah," Briana said, "I think he's taking them. Daddy told him it was up to him to remember, but I told Curt you'd kill him if he didn't."

Murder. Now *there* was a cure for hyperactivity. "How'd his game go yesterday?"

"They won, but he'll want to tell you himself. Mostly he's just eating cotton candy and going on rides." Briana lowered her voice confidentially. "I think he almost barfed when he got off the Loop-the-Loop this morning. He'd just had two corn dogs and a blue snowcone."

"Yuck! Have you been going to the contests?" Marianne and the kids had hit them all during the fair years: twin contests, freckle contests, mother-daughter lookalike contests, baby crawling races, table decorations, livestock judging, piglet races.

"Oh, Mom, those are so boring."

Marianne sighed. This might not be a bad time to actually let Mark *have* custody of Briana. Her moodiness and volatility would cure him pretty damn quick of his delusion that there was anything easy about being custodial parent. And it would free up whole huge chunks of Marianne's own time.

"Sweetie, I'll be back Saturday night and I'll pick you guys up Sunday morning before Daddy heads off for the fair."

"Do you have any idea how *long* it is till Sunday morning?" Briana asked.

Actually, it was hardly any time at all. So far the relaxation in the out-of-doors that Marianne had anticipated on this trip hadn't been nearly plentiful enough. And in less than seventy-two hours, she'd be headed home again. "It'll pass, sweetie. Is your brother anywhere around?"

Briana said she thought he'd gone on the Killer Mouse, and used up about five minutes walking over there and looking for him.

"You know, he could be anywhere," Briana said finally.

This was true enough, though hardly reassuring. Mark's idea of fair supervision was to give each kid a wad of bills and a farewell wave. It was getting harder and harder to avoid criticizing him to the kids. While Marianne had stopped trying to cure Mark of his gambling addiction years ago, she still wanted him to stop.

In their years together, Mark had gambled away everything but the house, and in the divorce settlement, they'd left the house in joint tenancy, with an agreement that they'd draw on the equity to pay for college for the kids. Marianne lived there and made the mortgage payment, but that hadn't stopped Mark from trying to borrow against it, several times.

"We're, like, having an incredible heat wave here," Briana went on, "and I'll probably pass out from heat prostration if I rush around trying to find Curt."

It occurred to Marianne that, in hot weather, Briana was likely to be clad in teeny little shorts and a scanty, skin-tight top, the kind of clothes her mother wouldn't let her wear out of the house. Mark saw nothing inappropriate about having his daughter dress like a streetwalker, yet another reason he was a poor bet for joint custody.

She realized she was listening again to dead air again and took the offensive. "So, Mom," Marianne chirped, in a tone of perky curiosity, "are you having a good time in

Gold Rush country? Did anybody guess what your costume is? Have you been to the caves yet? How's the rafting?"

She'd been hoping to shame her daughter and it worked. Briana sounded moderately contrite, and these days moderately counted for a lot. "I'm sorry, Mom. How's your trip?"

Of the thousand possible answers to this question, only one seemed reasonable at the moment.

"Remember that Chinese curse I told you about," Marianne told her, " 'May you live in interesting times'? Well, this week we're living in *extremely* interesting times. A couple of hours ago, I captured an escaped convict, single-handed."

At street level, Nikki was tickled to find what could only be called a Walk of Frogs, in the tradition of the Walk of the Stars on Hollywood Boulevard. Big, specially poured squares in the sidewalks on both sides of Highway 49 celebrated the winners of each year's jumping contest, dating back to the first competition in 1928, held to commemorate the paving of Main Street.

"How could you get a frog to jump seventeen feet?" Nikki asked Marianne when she rejoined her on Main Street. She looked down at a square in wonder. "Are these superenormous gargantua-frogs? Like in a science fiction movie?"

"Well, I do think they're pretty big," Marianne told her. "I looked it up this morning in one of Lynne's guidebooks while we were waiting to leave Murmuring Pines. They actually have to be longer than four inches to compete, and they measure three consecutive leaps for the contest. As I understand it, a big part of the fun is watching the trainers urging their amphibians on to glory. I believe you can even rent a frog if you happen to have left yours in your other purse."

"Rent a frog?"

"All the convenience of ownership with none of the responsibilities," Marianne said. "You don't have to worry about little Kermit going on a bender and getting out of shape just before the event, or getting squished by a car in the driveway, or being stolen by some French restaurant with grenouilles on the menu." She looked down at the sidewalk before her. In 1948, a frog named Heliotrope, out of Berkeley, had taken the championship by jumping eleven feet and five inches.

"The whole *idea* of having a frog-jumping contest is what really fascinates me," Nikki said. "I mean, 'The Celebrated Jumping Frog of Calaveras County' has a great title, but beyond that, I think the story's kind of dumb. I realize that's sacrilege in some circles, but I just busted out of jail so I'll say whatever I feel like."

Marianne laughed. "You're not stepping on my toes if you don't like Mark Twain."

"I don't have anything against Mark Twain," Nikki said. "It's his story that I don't like. Somehow or another I never got around to reading it until right before this trip. What a disappointment!"

"Well, Twain didn't get to these parts till most of the Gold Rush was over," Marianne pointed out, "so his information was third- or fourth-hand at best. I always thought the word 'Calaveras' seemed terribly romantic, until I found out it meant 'skulls' in Spanish."

Lynne gazed upward at the three-story building in Mokelumne Hill, then turned to Betsy. "I give up. What's I.O.O.F.?" She pronounced it. "Eeeyuuffff? It's on at least one building in every one of these old mining towns, and it's usually the tallest building."

Betsy waved her arm excitedly. "Teacher! Teacher! I know that one! Call on me, teacher, oh *please!*"

Lynne pretended to consult a seating chart and peer out into a classroom, squinting. "Elizabeth Akers?"

She liked using Betsy's maiden name, the name she'd first known her by, the name she always used when she thought of her oldest friend. Betsy today looked very much like Betsy back then. Her skin was more weathered and her laugh lines now permanently etched. But she wasn't an ounce heavier than she'd been at thirteen, with the same lithe fitness, the same sparkling green eyes, the same shining hair, cut shorter now and silvered through the blond. Betsy and Lynne had been blondes in bikinis on the beaches of Guam three-quarters of a lifetime ago, basting themselves with iodine-laced baby oil in the tropical sun.

"Those are Odd Fellows halls," Betsy said, nodding toward the building and returning to the present. "I.O.O.F. stands for the Independent Order of Odd Fellows. I know about them because my grandfather was one, in Ohio."

"The grandparents who had the lamp?" Lynne asked.

"The grandparents who had the lamp. Exactly. The petty bourgeoisie of Fostoria, Ohio. My grandpa was a manager at the glass factory and he belonged to the Odd Fellows lodge there. It was like Elks, or Moose, I think, the club for middle-class burghers. Out here during the Gold Rush, there wasn't anything for the guys to do when they weren't standing out in the middle of the river, and most of them had left all their family and friends behind. They were lonely. The Odd Fellows provided companionship and filled a kind of a void."

"Makes sense to me," Lynne said.

"I've been noticing the Odd Fellows halls in all the towns where we've been," Betsy went on. "They're usually something else today, like a bank or a museum or a saloon, but they've survived. And they survived because they're beautifully constructed."

"And tall," Lynne added, with a nod toward the building behind them.

"And tall," Betsy agreed. "You're right. They're usually the tallest building in any town. When guys struck it rich, they'd kick in toward first-class materials. And I think it was also a point of pride for the members who were craftsmen to do the work really well. They'd use brick or stone, usually, so the buildings could also survive fires."

This seemed entirely reasonable to Lynne. If you were out here in the middle of nowhere, standing all day in icy water with the sun blazing down on you, and maybe not finding any gold at all after that, you'd want someplace nice to hang out. Since you probably were living in a tent. Life hadn't been too pleasant for the forty-niners.

They continued walking back toward where Lynne had parked the van in shade.

"Hey, Bets," Lynne said, "I'm starting to get a little worried about Susi."

Betsy grimaced. "Me too. At first I thought she was just a complainer —"

"Because she *is* a complainer."

"Exactly. And a hypochondriac, too, no

question about it. But she really seems pretty sick to me today. She's bitched so much about being hot that she has to be running a fever. And her stomach shouldn't still be upset from taking that laxative Sunday night, even though she had more than the rest of you and I'm sure it wasn't easy on her system."

"It wasn't easy on anybody's system," Lynne pointed out. "Mine included."

"Yeah, but the rest of you got over it. And it's been three days now. Nobody else is still complaining of stomachaches. Not even Mandy. She's just nauseated. And she's got an excuse."

"So what do you think's the matter with Susi? Food poisoning?"

"I guess that's possible, and it could even date back to something she ate before the trip. Sometimes it can take days for food poisoning to affect you. But you know, Lynne, this sounds like my sister's symptoms when she had appendicitis. I don't suppose you know if Susi's had her appendix out?"

Lynne laughed. "I somehow missed that detail of her medical history. But we can certainly ask. I had appendicitis and her symptoms would fit. Except I seem to remember throwing up, too."

"Oh goodie!" Betsy said. "Something to look forward to." She shook her head. "You know, I'll feel like a real idiot if she *does* have appendicitis and we've been telling her to shut up and lie down."

"We haven't been telling her that," Lynne protested.

Betsy grinned. "But we've been thinking it."

Chapter 18

"Actually," the woman in the modest nine-teenth-century frontier dress at the hotel desk in Columbia said, "your group has the Fallon Hotel entirely to yourselves."

Lisa Limone stood with her mother in the tiny lobby of the City Hotel on Main Street of the restored Gold Rush town, as they registered for the final three nights of the Highway 49 Revisited tour. Lisa had been to Columbia before, when she was in college, and she liked the town's quiet authenticity.

"Really?" Judith asked, surprised. "You mean we've taken over the whole hotel?"

"Oh, there are other rooms," the woman explained, "but midweek this time of year, they're not occupied. In fact, the Fallon's only open on weekends till mid-June." She issued them keys and a passkey to the hotel lobby, explaining that while there was no on-site evening staff at the Fallon the building was kept locked and a night watchman slept on the premises.

The Fallon Hotel was only a short walk from the City Hotel and Lisa and Judith were happy to stretch their legs after their long drive. The quiet dusty Main Street was deserted except for a few stragglers, clearly also tourists. A sleek gray cat crossed in front of them, well aware that vehicular traffic wasn't permitted on this road, and a calico comrade lay curled asleep in a drinking fountain bubbler. The road curved gently to the right onto Washington, past the panning operation, taking them to the Fallon, which like its sister hostelry, the City Hotel, dated back to 1857. Catalpa and sumac trees lined the street, and Judith remarked in delight on an English walnut across from the hotel.

As they unlocked the outer door and entered the lobby of the Fallon Hotel, it was all Lisa could do not to laugh out loud.

The lobby was furnished in a style that Lisa always thought of as Victorian Nightmare, all very dark and gloomy, with heavy draperies and dark flocked wallpaper and an oddly shaped green velvet double chair sitting smack in the middle of the room. A courting chair, most likely, S-shaped with one side facing in one direction and the other in the opposite, to keep young couples at a discreet distance by means of the center divider. Not that anyone could get very comfortable in this monstrosity anyway. It might have done for a San Francisco socialite, but it was tough to imagine any of the rugged men who'd built this mining town perching daintily on its velvet cushions.

"Hey, guys!" Lynne Montgomery came down the hall toward them, with a spring in her step. She'd showered and changed into

298

white denim shorts and a turquoise tank top that matched her eyes. "We were just about to start worrying about you."

"We went over to Indian Grinding Rock Park," Judith told her, "and it was farther than I expected." She cocked her head, and Lisa noticed that her mother looked tired. Well, wine before lunch would do that to you. "Actually, everything's been farther apart than I expected. Somehow I thought that Gold Rush country was smaller. A lot smaller."

"Me too," Lynne admitted. "It's actually not much more than a hundred miles from north to south as the crow flies, but Highway 49 is no crow. How was the Indian park? Can I help you bring anything in?"

Lisa shook her head. "I'll go back out for it all in a minute. Right now I think Mom just wants to collapse for a while. The park was terrific and the actual grinding rock was fascinating. All the mortars are hollowed out of the limestone, hundreds of them. It makes the rock look sort of pockmarked, like it was bombarded by cosmic hail or something. The Miwok tribe were hunter-gatherers, and they used to assemble there in the fall and grind acorns for meal for the winter."

"Yum," Lynne said, making a face. "Acorn meal bread, acorn meal pancakes, acorn meal biscuits . . ."

"Do I have time for a nap before dinner?" Judith asked.

Lynne glanced at her watch. "I don't see why not. We're going to walk down to a natural foods restaurant just outside the historic area in about an hour. Mandy and Susi are both sleeping right now. Betsy's reading and the others went out exploring."

Judith chuckled. "If Nikki's gone exploring, with or without companions, there's no telling when she'll get back. How's Susi feeling? Any better?"

Lisa had been watching her eleventh grade English teacher's descent into medical affliction with great interest. Mrs. Braun — Lisa had trouble thinking of her as Susi and found it absolutely impossible to regard her as a colleague — had often complained of headaches when Lisa had been in her class. But the class met at the end of the day, and the complaints were so much a part of the teacher's personality that Lisa had never really regarded them as ill health.

Lynne shook her head. "Betsy and I are trying to talk her into going to the emergency room, and I'd've thought she'd jump at the opportunity, frankly. But all of a sudden she's saying she's fine and that all she needs is a good night's sleep. She has her own room upstairs, right next to the one you two are sharing, in front with a balcony. But I honestly didn't think she was going to make it up the stairs."

"Hmm," Judith said, frowning. "I guess she

could be really sick. I was thinking on the drive that she didn't look good at lunchtime. Is she running a fever?"

"None of us have a thermometer," Lynne said. "It's not the kind of thing you pack when you don't have little kids along." She considered a moment. "Although now that I think about it, even when I did travel with little kids, I never brought a thermometer. Anyway, she's flushed and sweaty. Betsy and I are guessing she might have appendicitis."

"Appendicitis?! Then why on earth won't she go to a hospital?" Judith asked irritably. "This isn't the frontier anymore."

"My sentiments exactly," Betsy told them, coming down the stairs. She grinned. "I think I'll go check on her. I've got an excuse, in any case. I believe I'm the first one finished with the Gold Rush crossword puzzle, and I need to turn it in. What do you suppose my prize will be?"

"Taking her to the ER?" Lynne asked sweetly.

The hospital turned out to be small and folksy and almost — could it be? — charming. When Lynne and Betsy arrived with Susi, who was now too sick to argue, they snagged a wheelchair to bring their patient inside, where they turned out to be the only people in the emergency room. An efficient but friendly Filipina nurse listened to Susi's symptom recital, whisked her into a back cubicle, and called for lab work. The local doctor on call showed up within ten minutes. He was sharp and focused and just a little too young to be believable, but he wasted no time in tentatively diagnosing appendicitis and calling a surgeon.

He also told Lynne and Betsy there was no reason they couldn't wait with Susi, which hadn't been precisely what Lynne wanted to hear. Right now, she'd have preferred some Big Nurse announcing that hospital policy forbade company in the ER. Betsy offered to stay and Lynne took her up gladly on the offer.

Susi had already collapsed in tears twice. She made it three when Lynne asked how to get in touch with her husband.

"Call him at his girlfriend's," Susi wailed. "Of course I don't know who that is right now, but that's where he'll be. With the woman who's about to destroy my marriage." Then she dissolved into hysterical sobs.

Lynne had assembled emergency contact information for everyone when she set up the tour. Hoping that Susi was being needlessly melodramatic, Lynne tried Rick Braun's cell phone first, getting no answer, then punched in Rick's home and office numbers, reaching recordings in both cases. She phrased her messages carefully, stressing urgency without panic.

The surgeon arrived, comfortably middle-aged and laconic. He introduced himself and went back to the examining room. A moment later, Betsy returned to the waiting room, just as Marianne arrived, driving Nikki's SUV.

"I thought you'd be back at the hotel," Lynne told her, "resting up for the next time we need you to apprehend a wanted criminal. I still can't quite believe the way you flipped that guy this afternoon."

"It was pretty basic," Marianne said, with a shrug. "I learned it in that self-defense class I took last fall." She looked around the small room, with its linoleum floor and scrubbable Naugahyde chairs. "How's Susi?"

"Getting ready for surgery, it sounds like," Betsy said. "I just wish we could get in touch with her husband."

"Rick's unavailable?" Marianne asked. She didn't sound surprised.

"Not answering any of his phones," Lynne said. "And Susi keeps bursting into tears and saying he's off with his girlfriend."

Marianne nodded. "Probably true. Rick's a notorious tomcat, but Susi normally goes to a lot of trouble to pretend he's faithful and devoted. She must really be scared. What about her boys? Have you tried to reach them? Bobby's all the way down at Caltech, but Rick Junior goes to UC Santa Cruz and I think Susi said he's staying up there this summer, working as a lifeguard at one of the hotels down by the boardwalk. And Santa Cruz isn't all that far away."

Lynne had found Susi's address book in her purse when they took her back to the examining room. Now she flipped to the B page and found listings for both sons. Bobby, down in Pasadena, wasn't answering his phone either, and he had some kind of goofy message, delivered in a tinny, robotic tone. Maybe even delivered *by* a robot, quite possibly of his own creation. He was, after all, at Caltech.

Rick Junior, however, was more old-fashioned. He was home, picked up on the second ring, and didn't sound drunk. For a college student in summer, quite remarkable. Rick Junior listened to Lynne's account of his mother's medical condition, then sighed. "I think I know how to get in touch with my dad, but I don't know how soon he can get up here. Tell me where she is, and I'll drive over tonight. It shouldn't take me more than about three hours."

While the others went back to the Fallon Hotel, Lynne and Betsy settled in at the hospital. Susi signed her own release, sobbing, burst into a new eruption of tears at the news that Rick Junior was coming, and was finally wheeled away, not a moment too soon for Lynne.

"I still don't like hospitals," Lynne told Betsy now, looking around the waiting room.

It wasn't bad, as hospital ER waiting rooms went: no noxious odors, no screaming babies, nobody limping in from the parking lot, dripping blood.

"I know," Betsy said. "I'm not too nuts about them either. But you've been back since Monty . . ." She let her voice trail away.

Since Monty died.

Since that terrible January morning when Monty suffered a fatal heart attack while surfing and Lynne had driven, blinded by tears, to Floritas General, where the man she'd thought would live forever had just been pronounced dead.

"Yeah," Lynne said. "A couple of times recently, actually. When I had to get those stitches on my palm from the broken glass somebody threw into my front garden, and then a couple months ago with my neighbor Ellen."

When she'd cut her palm back in March, out of a sort of poetic justice, Lynne had called David, who was off duty at the time from his job as a Floritas PD patrol officer, and asked him to bring her to the hospital. She'd taken David to the ER more times than she could count when he was a kid. Something about being with her strapping son, who so resembled his father and was quite wonderfully alive, had taken her over the hump. And after that it had been a piece of cake to go with Ellen and her father.

As they waited now, flipping through old copies of *People* and *Sports Illustrated*, Lynne wished somebody else were in charge of the tour. Finally the surgeon came out into the waiting room, still wearing his surgical scrubs, cap, and fabric booties. He offered a wide mellow smile.

"Got that old appendix out just in time," the surgeon told them. "It was right on the verge of rupturing, so that little lady's lucky she came in when she did."

"She'll be relieved to hear that," Marianne told him, with a hint of a smile. And after the surgeon had left, she turned to Lynne and Betsy. "I'll wait here for Rick Junior. You guys go on back to the hotel and get some rest, okay?" She hesitated. "I've been feeling kind of bad that I invited her in the first place, to tell the truth. It's one of those things that I've wished a hundred times I could undo."

"Don't be silly," Lynne told her, "and for heaven's sake don't worry about it. You sure you're okay here by yourself?"

"Absolutely," Marianne assured them. "It's nearly ten, Lynne, and you must be exhausted. This has been a really long day. Now go!"

And Lynne did, without protest.

The cast on Amos Ledbetter's arm was a discreet dove gray, and he wore it strapped tight to his chest with a charcoal gray sling. Slings had come a long way since the last time he'd worn one, when his mother took an old white bed sheet, ripped it to size, and tied it behind his neck with little wings sticking out on either side, just below Amos's nine-year-old ears. The entire affair had been bulky and voluminous, rather like a wayward parachute.

This one was almost fashionable, as close to sleek as an orthopedic appurtenance was ever likely to be. And thanks to the Vicodin, Amos himself was feeling rather sleek and mellow. He wasn't supposed to drive while taking the Vicodin, of course. But he'd thought this all through and formulated the plan before the bozo from Boise plowed into him on Highway 49. Tonight was the best — and for all he knew, the only — opportunity to get into the SUV.

Besides, Jed had issued a deadline, adding a certain menacing emphasis to the first syllable of the word.

The rental car company had towed off the remains of his vehicle, and had been surprisingly churlish about providing another. He'd been forced to call and beg a ride from Tiffany, who had prattled all the way back to Stockton. Tonight he was driving his own pickup, the one he used for transporting merchandise. He was still a little woozy, no doubt about it, but he stopped at Starbucks on his way out of Stockton and got a double espresso, so he was at least wide awake and woozy.

Highway 4 heading east out of Stockton was pretty much deserted by the time he set out, and he cruised east toward Columbia in a daze that would have been almost pleasurable had the images of Jed and Musk Man and Ichabod Crane and their cohorts not been hovering at the edge of the dashboard. He encountered very few cars along the way, which was just fine, since he noticed now and again that he was drifting a bit across the double yellow line in the center of the road.

Finally, what felt like hours later, he reached Columbia and drove around town slowly, looking for the cars. He hadn't anticipated any difficulty finding them, since the place was all but deserted. The large parking lot down behind the Fallon Hotel was entirely empty, and as he cruised up Parrott's Ferry Road, he saw the sedan, parked beneath a tree near the Masonic Hall.

But the others weren't there. Neither the van nor the SUV. Where in God's name could they be?

He cruised the town so many times that he knew he was becoming conspicuous, then finally parked near the Fallon Hotel, two cars down from the Buick, and got out of the truck. He was definitely in the right place, he realized with a heart-stopping jolt, when he recognized the older woman with the braid, the one who drove the Buick, sitting out on the second-story balcony running across the front of the Fallon. She appeared to be reading, and he didn't think she noticed him as he sauntered nonchalantly north, just taking the sights in an old historic town on a warm summer evening.

He went clear to the north end of town, then decided it was probably a good idea to sit down for a while. He entered the St. Charles Saloon and ordered a Coke, certain that it would be the worst kind of folly to mix alcohol with the Vicodin. He nursed the drink and waited, then realized suddenly he had reached the limits of his own endurance. If he didn't start back to Stockton right now, he was likely to fall asleep right here on the bar. Or pass out back in his car — a car, he suddenly realized, that was parked across from a state park office.

Then he'd have to explain himself to yet another set of park rangers.

So far he'd tangled with the authorities at Malakoff Diggins and narrowly escaped the ones at John Marshall. He'd rounded off his adventures with gold country law enforcement by riding to the hospital in the back seat of a sheriff's deputy's cruiser, a trip that would have nourished his sense of irony if he hadn't been in such pain.

He got into the truck, cruised two more times around town in a futile search for the van and the SUV, then headed back to Stockton. He passed by the hospital without even glancing at its parking lot.

Chapter 19

"Breakfast in an ice cream parlor," Betsy said contentedly. "Now *that's* my idea of how to get a day off to a good start."

Of course they weren't consuming sodas and sundaes, but Lynne had to concede that the Thursday morning breakfast buffet set up for the Argonauts in the ice cream parlor off the Fallon Hotel lobby was quite a sumptuous spread. The room itself had the feel of a former saloon, which it probably was — with huge beams on its vaulted ceiling, wainscoting, and more of the spectacularly ugly wallpaper that appeared wherever historical buildings had been restored throughout gold country.

"You think they'd give me some hot fudge sauce for my coffeecake?" Lisa Limone asked.

Betsy shuddered. "I guess it couldn't hurt to ask. But why stop at that? Maybe you could get whipped cream and nuts on the quiche, too."

They were down to four at breakfast. Nikki and Marianne had set off an hour earlier for Calaveras Big Trees State Park, where they planned to hike among the giant sequoias. Mandy had announced her intention the previous night of sleeping till she woke up, and

Susi was no longer a part of the Argonaut equation.

Judith asked, "How's Susi doing this morning, Lynne?"

Lynne had just used the phone in the Fallon lobby — there weren't any phones in the rooms — to call the hospital. "Well, she was asleep when I called, but I did talk to her husband."

"The philanderer?" Judith asked, eyes narrowed. Judith held strong and inflexible views on the subject of marital fidelity.

Lynne nodded. "He got in around sunrise, apparently. Said he drove straight through from Floritas, as if I ought to be impressed." Lynne didn't much care for Susi, but it angered her that the woman had to endure the embarrassment of an unfaithful husband at the same time she faced emergency surgery.

"Yeah," Betsy said. "Very impressive. He probably didn't even have to stop at home to pick up a toothbrush, if he was at the girlfriend's house. Just grabbed his dopp kit, pulled on his pants, and hit the road."

"We don't *know* that's where he was," Lisa said mildly.

"I don't *know* that the government's going to take a big chunk out of my paycheck," Judith answered, "but it's a pretty safe bet."

"Are he and the son going to stay here in Susi's room?" Betsy asked.

Lynne shrugged. "I kind of doubt it. Marianne said she offered the room to Rick Junior last night after he got in and he recoiled in horror. Told her he'd be fine sleeping in the back of his pickup."

Lisa laughed. "Can't understand *that*. Most college guys would just love to spend a couple of nights alone in a historic hotel with a bunch of schoolteachers."

"Well, I'm sure his father won't want to sleep in the truck," Lynne said, "though he might not find the prospect of sharing a hotel with us any more appealing. Marianne knows the Braun family better than any of us do, and she sounds as if she'd like to slice up Rick Senior's liver and serve it with some fava beans and a nice Chianti. But I'll offer them the room again when I go over there this morning. And if he doesn't want it, I'll try to get her a refund."

A young woman in a frontier calico dress came into the room and approached the table. "Is one of you Mrs. Montgomery?"

"That's me," Lynne said. "What can I do for you?"

"I have a couple of messages for you," the woman said, handing over two slips of paper. "You can call out from the phone in the lobby here if you'd like."

"Thanks," Lynne told her, looking over the messages. "My, my. One of these is our buddy Detective McMasters up in Nevada City, and the other is Stephanie Geller."

Judith's eyes widened. "Stephanie, the teacher from Minnesota?"

Lynne nodded. "I think this is a Sacramento number. I'll try them both before I head out."

"Speaking of heading out," Judith said, "what's on the schedule today?"

"Entirely up to you," Lynne told her. "I was planning to run over and check on Susi after breakfast and then I thought we could meander through Jamestown and Sonora. They're both really nice little restored towns with some good antiquing. And some of you might be interested in the Railtown Museum in Jamestown."

"Sign me on," Betsy said immediately, "though I could take or leave the trains. And Susi too, for that matter. Will we be gone all day?"

Lynne shrugged. "Doesn't matter to me. I was thinking we'd have lunch out somewhere and then come back and prowl around Columbia this afternoon. That'll give everybody time to get duded up for the Characters Dinner."

"I'm really looking forward to that," Judith said. "Is there a prize for best costume?"

"You bet, Mom," Lisa told her. "The winner doesn't have to visit Susi."

Detective McMasters didn't seem particularly pleased to be hearing from Lynne, even though the conversation had been his own idea.

"I wanted to see if any of you had any further thoughts about what happened to Mrs. Caravaci," he said. "Particularly in light of the episode at Marshall State Park yesterday. Sometimes something like that can jog a memory."

"It hasn't jogged mine," Lynne told him regretfully.

"Then let me ask you something. Do you recall encountering a man with a long beard at Murmuring Pines? Or anywhere else in your travels?"

"Long beard? You mean like ZZ Top?" Or that guy, whatever his name was, from the band Alabama? Something about ill-kempt facial hair seemed to appeal to Southern musicians.

He laughed. "Yeah, like that, I guess. Why? Did you see somebody?"

"Afraid not," Lynne told him, "but I can ask the others if you'd like. I take it those two fellows we captured yesterday at the Gold Discover Park haven't confessed to killing Connie Caravaci? They were certainly carrying on enthusiastically about not having been to Nevada City."

Detective McMasters sighed. "Well, it's a funny thing, Mrs. Montgomery. When you start dangling a capital murder charge in front of somebody who's already in the

315

system and also facing a slew of fresh new charges, one of two things happens. Either he clams up and you can't get him to tell you anything at all, or he starts singing his heart out. Hargrove and Burke have turned out to be a matched set of canaries, and they've admitted sneaking into the park and overpowering Mrs. Geller and Mrs. Wilson yesterday morning. But before that, they swear they were down around Bakersfield for two solid days, and they even confessed to a residential burglary down there."

"A residential burglary?" Lynne repeated. This didn't sound too plausible to her, but McMasters was the cop.

"Actually, they swiped some clothes off a backyard clothesline," the detective explained, "and grabbed some lunchmeat out of a kitchen refrigerator because the back door was unlocked. The incident hadn't been reported, but the boys told us exactly where it was and officers down there located the place and confirmed that the clothes were missing. The house was on a small farm on the edge of town, apparently, and the homeowner noticed the clothes gone and figured it was migrant workers. It all checks out, down to the missing package of bologna."

"The fingerprints of those two didn't match up with the ones you found at Murmuring Pines?" The young men might be criminals, and unsavory ones at that, but

Lynne had heard nothing to suggest that they were clever. And whoever'd trashed the cabins was really on a tear. It was hard to believe that the young escapees wouldn't have left fingerprints somewhere.

Detective McMasters sighed again. "Nope. And if we can't match them up to that location, it puts us back at square one."

"Indeed." It seemed to Lynne that it put them farther back than that. Not only did they not have viable suspects, but they'd also lost three days' time trying to figure out who actually was responsible. "I wish I could help, Detective. And I'll ask the others again. But I don't think there's much we can do for you. Sorry."

Harriet Wilson picked up the phone on the second ring. "Lynne! Thanks so much for calling back, and so promptly, too."

"I just got the message," Lynne told her, "so I can't take credit for anything but getting to a phone. How are you two doing today?"

"Much, much better," Harriet told her, sounding remarkably rejuvenated. The Midwesterners Lynne had known over the years shared the same enviable resiliency. "We'd been intending to splurge a bit somewhere down the line, and this was probably as good a time as any. We had a perfectly lovely room service dinner last night, and we're about to go down for massages."

"Sounds great," Lynne said, wondering why Harriet had called. Surely it wasn't to gloat about ordering from room service.

"The police called again this morning," Harriet said, after a moment's pause. "Not the ones from the park, but that nice detective who came down just as you all were leaving yesterday, the one from Nevada City. They don't seem to be making a lot of headway in getting those young men to confess to murdering that poor woman up there, and they're hoping that one of the boys had said or done something that would help them."

"I got the same call," Lynne told her, "and you're right. They sound stymied. But I don't know how we can do anything more to help them."

"Actually, I *did* think of something," Harriet said, "but they didn't seem terribly interested in it."

"What's that?" Lynne asked. And why on earth wouldn't Detective McMasters jump at the information?

"Well, we'd spent the night at a campground near Nevada City ourselves, night before last," Harriet explained, "and we stopped for a good breakfast on the way out of town. There were a couple of men seated near us and one of them seemed . . . well, he seemed rather rugged and frightening, actually. He had one of those long mountain man beards like you see on cartoons about survivalists. You know what I mean?"

Aha! This explained Detective McMasters's query about the mountain man.

Before Lynne could respond, Harriet continued. "Anyway, I would have sworn that he was threatening the fellow who was with him, and he seemed like a very nice gentleman, the one without the beard, that is."

"Uh-huh." Lynne realized that Harriet was going to tell this story in her own sweet time, and she could appreciate why Detective McMasters had been less than excited by her information.

"The mountain man said something to the other man that I couldn't help but overhear, about how if he thought what happened to that lady — that was how he described her, just 'that lady' — was bad, then he had no idea what bad was all about. And then he got up, deliberately knocked over his coffee cup, and stalked out of the place."

"And you think he was talking about . . . what?"

"Why, that woman who owned the motel in Nevada City, of course. Because I realized once we unpacked everything and I started organizing and refiling maps and brochures and what not, that the coffee shop where we ate was right near the motel. Murmuring Pines, that is. Am I making any sense?" she finished, sounding surprisingly helpless.

"I'm afraid you might be," Lynne told her. "Thanks for letting us know."

Mandy Mosher awoke with a sense that something was wrong, and it took her a moment to realize that it wasn't that something was *wrong* so much as that it was different.

She didn't feel like throwing up.

She had carefully set out her crackers and lemon drops last night, on the glass top of a bedside table draped in brick-red velveteen festooned with gold dangly fringe. Through trial and error (and two previous pregnancies) she'd learned that she needed to be able to reach these first thing in the morning without attempting to raise her head.

But today the waves of nausea which had greeted her daily for months didn't come. Could she possibly be moving out of morning sickness? Could having two babies at once somehow accelerate the process? Were they — dare she hoped — girls? The ultrasound had clearly shown two babies, but they'd both been positioned to hide any revealing appendages. Mandy knew she'd love any baby, but it sure would be nice to have at least one daughter.

She decided that she wasn't ready to tempt fate by actually getting out of bed, reached cautiously for her watch, and discovered it was nearly 10 a.m. The others were probably all bustling about Columbia already, hiking and visiting museums and river rafting and hunting out antiques. Nikki was probably swinging on vines through the forest.

Bless their hearts, they really had let her sleep in. Mandy couldn't remember the last time she'd slept till ten.

While she wasn't ready to get out of bed, she did allow herself a luxurious, feline stretch, savoring the glorious isolation of having her very own room. The Mosher family finances were always unbearably tight, but Mandy had decided to allow herself one indulgence on this trip, which might well be her last opportunity to be alone for the next twenty years.

She'd opted for a room of her own at the restored hotel. A room of one's own, she remembered from a college English class, was mandatory for female writers. For young mothers, it was more of an impossible dream, and most of the time Mandy didn't mind. She was gregarious by nature, thriving on the company of others and adoring all children, particularly her own. Just this once, however, she'd wanted to see what solitude might feel like.

So far it felt wonderful.

Mandy's room on the first floor of the Fallon was down the hall from Marianne and Lynne, who also had opted for bargain singles. The shower was down the hall and the room was euphemistically called "Petite," but it was Mandy's own and here she was responsible to nobody: no husband, no toddlers, no cranky high school English teachers.

Susi!

Even as Mandy wondered what had happened last night after she crawled into bed, she noticed a sheet of paper on the floor just inside the doorway of her room. Without raising her head, she was able to retrieve the paper and read Lynne's note:

Mandy,

Susi had an appendectomy last night and is doing fine. We've all gone in different directions, and will check back around noon. Have a great morning!

Lynne

Mandy wasted no time feeling sorry for Susi, who was a real pain in the patootie, and had barely been civil when they'd shared that cabin at Murmuring Pines. Instead, she gazed gratefully around her own tiny little sanctuary. What it lacked in floor space, it made up for with height. The ceilings were tall, and floor-to-ceiling lace curtains hung on a brass rod over double-hung windows. An abundance of dark woodwork gave the room a stern feeling, with thick oaken baseboards rising nine inches from the floor and a commode in the tiny half-bath featuring one of those high, wood-covered water closets with a hanging flush cord.

Slowly she raised herself to a sitting position, waiting for the familiar queasiness to overtake her. When it didn't, she carefully stood and crossed in a couple of short steps to the window. She pulled the shade up to discover sun drenching the charming patio beside the hotel, where a man sat near the fountain consulting a guidebook. He looked vaguely familiar, and it took her a moment to remember where she'd seen him before.

Yesterday, while she'd been dozing fitfully in Nikki's Expedition, he'd come by and looked in the windows at them. Just checking out the car, she figured, and he'd jumped back when he realized there were people in there, hurrying on his way. Mandy had observed him through nearly closed eyes, and Susi, who'd been facing the other direction, wouldn't have seen him at all. Today he seemed to have some kind of sling or cast on his arm, and she didn't remember that from yesterday. Maybe it was somebody else, and it didn't matter anyway. They kept running into the same folks along Highway 49, other modern-day Argonauts.

Mandy caught herself yawning, decided to rest just a little bit longer, and slipped back into bed. The next thing she knew, somebody was tapping on her door and it was twelve-thirty.

Chapter 20

When she reached the hospital, bearing a grocery store bouquet of daisies, Lynne was not surprised to find that Susi Braun had managed to snag a private room. Lynne allowed herself a brief uncharitable moment to wonder if Susi had already alienated a roommate in order to obtain the accommodation. Not that any kind of hospital room was pleasant, certainly, but Susi as a bona fide patient with a legitimate medical complaint would exacerbate the problems of anyone not totally comatose.

"You came," Susi murmured, leaning back on her pillows. Two large and elaborate floral displays already crowded her bedside table. Susi was hooked up to an IV and wore a faded print hospital-issue gown, but somehow she'd managed to apply just enough makeup to avoid looking like a middle-aged woman twelve hours out of major surgery. In fact, she looked almost smug. *I told you I was sick,* she seemed to be saying, *and nobody believed me until I was knocking at death's door.*

Beside Susi's bed sat a tanned and handsome fellow who jumped to his feet and extended an eager hand. "Rick Braun," the man said, offering a toothy grin.

"Lynne Montgomery. I'm sorry we have to meet this way."

His handshake was hearty and his smile engaging. By rights the philandering Mr. Braun should have looked guilty and haggard, but it had been Lynne's experience that those unburdened by conscience rarely did. Sports memorabilia was his business, Marianne had said, a line of work that brought him into regular contact with famous athletes, past and present. The kind of guys who attracted good-looking young women. It was difficult to picture Susi making small talk with aging Heisman Trophy winners or rising NBA centers, but no reach at all to picture Rick Braun in a bar with a bunch of healthy young studs and an array of silicone-enhanced bimbos.

"Can't thank you enough for taking care of my little girl here," Rick Braun said. "It's a heck of a thing, getting sick out in the middle of nowhere like this."

"I'm just glad that we were able to help," Lynne told him. Two could play the insincerity game. She placed the flowers on the windowsill.

"I was moments away from rupture," Susi said with a wan smile. She didn't mention the flowers — in fact, she didn't even seem to notice them. "You saved my life by bringing me in when you did."

Moments away from rupture would probably

turn into *at death's doorstep* by the time Susi made it back to Floritas, but with Rick Braun on the scene, that transportation detail was no longer Lynne's responsibility. Nor was Susi, thank goodness, though Lynne had to concede that she'd put together a comprehensive and challenging crossword puzzle. Maybe by Christmas things would calm down enough so that Lynne could finish it.

"Did your son leave already?" Lynne asked, pulling a chair over to the bed. The others were waiting in the lobby, visitors being limited to two per patient. Nobody had fought for the privilege of going up first.

Rick nodded. "Had to get back to Santa Cruz. He's working as a lifeguard this summer." The chuckle that accompanied this statement suggested that Rick had a bit of lifeguard experience himself, the kind involving girls in string bikinis and boozy bonfires on the beach. The guy had "Ladies Man" written all over him. No wonder Susi was insecure, though if she was as rich as Marianne claimed, her marriage was probably safe.

"Can I get you anything while we're out?" Lynne asked. "We're going down to Jamestown and Sonora today."

Susi waved a weak, dismissive hand. "I'll be all right. Rick's here now."

For just a moment, Lynne saw a flicker of dismay pass over Rick's well-chiseled features.

Somehow it made her like him more.

Marianne felt an enormous sense of peace and well-being as she walked the South Grove Trail at Calaveras Big Trees State Park with Nikki. All of the cares and unpleasantness that had punctuated the past few days seemed to drop away in the cool green tranquillity of this hidden treasure. *Sequoiadendron giganteum,* these massive marvels were called. Like their coastal cousins, the redwoods, many of the giant sequoias were thousands of years old, but these trees were shorter and thicker than the redwoods. Short, of course, was a relative term. Marianne had to bend her head back at an impossible angle to see the tops of any of them.

"You know," Nikki noted without breaking stride, "these trees really shouldn't be here. They belong in Texas."

By now Marianne was accustomed to Nikki setting the pace on their hikes, a speed somewhat swifter than what Marianne might have chosen, either on her own or with the kids. But though she moved like a Roadrunner cartoon, Nikki didn't mind stopping to look at things, and Marianne rather enjoyed the invigorating pace. They'd automatically stopped in the North Grove shortly after entering the park, their teacherly instincts requiring that they take the Three Senses Trail to see, hear, and smell the forest. Then they'd explored the more heavily visited North Grove area, with its Discovery Tree Stump, twenty-five feet in diameter, once used as a dance floor. They'd passed through a fire-hollowed sequoia, then headed to the more isolated South Grove, where a healthy hike was required to reach any sequoias at all.

Consequently, they were all by themselves now. It was quite wonderful.

"They belong right here," Marianne answered. "You Texans always feel like you have a monopoly on size. But big doesn't automatically mean Texan, you know."

Nikki turned and grinned. "Not automatically, perhaps. But usually." She stopped to rub her hand along the bark of a massive tree. "I was surprised to find out how basically useless they are — apart from being amazing specimens, of course," she added hastily. "But you know what I mean. The wood's too brittle to make useful lumber, and the bark's a couple feet thick. I suppose that's a good thing, though, the uselessness. Otherwise people would've cut them all down a long time ago. The way they blew up trees in the Petrified Forest to make sandpaper before the place was made into a national park."

The sequoias would have been cut down, useful or not, Marianne thought, if they actually had been in Texas, a state not noted for its environmental fervor. There'd've been versions of that dance floor all over the state. But she kept her mouth shut. No need to bait Nikki, whom she genuinely enjoyed.

When they reached a clearing, Nikki stopped and brought the satellite phone out of her backpack. "Time to call the kiddos," she announced. "And you can do the same if you'd like."

Marianne walked far enough away to give Nikki some privacy while she made her call, then returned and punched in Briana's cell phone number.

"I *hate* this stupid fair," her daughter announced, wasting no time on pleasantries. Screams in the background identified her location once again as the Midway. A horrid thought suddenly struck Marianne. Was Briana hanging out with carneys? Flirting with itinerant men twice her age in her too-tight, too-skimpy tank top and booty shorts? Mark would never notice, never be even remotely aware.

"I shouldn't have to be here at all," Briana went on. "I'm old enough to stay home by myself."

Marianne took a cleansing breath and examined the intricate leaf patterns of the fern at her side. For this she'd interrupted the serenity of a millennia-old sequoia grove?

"And it isn't very responsible of you to go off and risk your life this way," Briana continued.

Come again? "What on earth are you talking about?"

"You know exactly what I mean. Dad says if you got stung by a wasp or something, it could kill you."

What was Mark thinking, to force-feed Briana's anxiety this way? "That's not going to happen, Bree. And I carry medicine in case I do get stung. There's nothing for you to worry about."

"Whatever. But if you're home, I wouldn't have to be here. I've seen everything a hundred times and I'm sick of the rides. Even Curt is sick of the rides, almost."

"I thought you told me he was sick *on* the rides."

This brought a little laugh. "Well, yeah. So. Have you done that stupid cave thing yet?"

"You mean Moaning Cavern? That's tomorrow morning. I'm sorry you can't be here to go down there with me."

"Mom, I *don't* care about the stupid cave. It's just that Dad keeps asking if you've done it, and if I can tell him yes, then maybe he'll shut up about it."

"I can't imagine why he'd care," Marianne said. "Why don't you tell him that I've already done it if you want?"

Even over the racket of the Del Mar Fair midway, Briana's sigh came through clear and hard as gold-flecked quartz. "Are you telling me to lie to my father?"

Give it up, Marianne thought. "Of course not, darling. I was just thinking that might make it easier on you."

"As if anything could," Briana told her.

Lynne stepped contentedly out into the midafternoon heat of the Main Street boardwalk in Jamestown, one of the most charming of the restored gold country communities that she'd seen yet, and site of a satisfying collection of antique shops. Sonora, named by Mexican miners who were later run off by xenophobic, lynch-happy American forty-niners, had been their first stop today. The town probably had more legitimate nineteenth-century buildings than Jamestown, but because it also served as the Tuolumne County seat, it was far more modern and bustling. Lynne had been quite content to visit Sonora only briefly.

But here, in the place the natives called Jimtown, she felt oddly connected to her late husband, a phenomenon that struck occasionally without warning and was generally — though not always — pleasurable. Monty had adored Westerns and they'd watched zillions of them over nearly a third of a century together. Jimtown claimed to have been used as a set for lots of Westerns, actually, including Monty's beloved *Butch Cassidy and the Sundance Kid*. Though he never came right out and said it, Lynne had always believed

Monty identified strongly with Sundance. The connection was an easy one to make, since Monty, with his blue-eyed blond California surf bum good looks, had borne more than a passing resemblance to Robert Redford.

While Lynne couldn't specifically identify any of the Jamestown buildings as sets from *Butch Cassidy*, the feel of the place was certainly right. Monty, she realized, blinking back a sudden tear, would have loved it here. He'd probably also have insisted on going to the Railtown Museum, which featured sets from *Petticoat Junction*. But none of the Argonauts had been very enthusiastic about going to Railtown and Lynne didn't care enough to do it on her own.

The town's unusually strong preoccupation with gold — evidenced by a plethora of gold nugget jewelry stores and multiple gold-panning tourist operations — had firm roots in history. A seventy-five-pound nugget had been found nearby in Woods Creek in 1848. When she first heard this, Lynne had thought that seventy-five pounds seemed like a mighty big nugget, more on the order of a brick. Then she had realized with a moment of horror that Betsy's faux nugget, the one used to kill Connie Caravaci, was probably comparable in size, albeit lighter in weight. It was the first time she'd thought about Connie in hours, and she wasn't sure whether it was good that she was putting the death behind her or insensitive that she wasn't paying more attention to it.

In any case, these days the town's biggest gold mine was its antique shops, and Lynne had spent an enjoyable few hours exploring them with Betsy. Lisa and Judith had joined them to tour Sonora and stayed through lunch at the Jamestown Hotel, then returned on their own to Columbia. Judith claimed to need extra time for her costume, but Lynne suspected she was actually going to sneak in another nap. Lynne was sorely tempted to do the same thing herself.

Betsy came out of the antique shop now, lugging a bulky hanging display unit with which she was inexplicably smitten. The piece had three shelves, two shallow drawers, and enough dust-catching whorls and curlicues to assure that keeping it clean would be next to impossible. Though by the time Betsy realized that, she'd probably already be tired of it and ready to move it on to its next owner. Betsy had begun talking about starting to sell some of her stuff on eBay, rather than at her own garage sales. Bigger profit margin, she said, and Lynne didn't doubt it, though the logistics sounded like a royal pain.

Lynne opened the back doors of the van so they could stow the shelving unit in the cargo area, wrapping it in a blanket brought along for just that exigency. Betsy had been a den mother once, on various naval bases, and was always Prepared.

"What a great deal!" Betsy said delightedly, wrapping the blanket around her shelf and casting an occasional glance over her shoulder to determine that the shopkeeper wasn't skulking about, looking to renege. She had bargained down the price because the finish was badly marred. Lynne had listened admiringly through the negotiation, a pot that Betsy sweetened at strategic intervals by adding a collection of sixties jelly glasses featuring cartoon characters and a threadbare satin shawl.

"Well, it wouldn't appeal to just anyone," Lynne noted diplomatically.

Lynne thought the shelf was butt-ugly and that Betsy's plan to spray-paint it eggshell white wasn't going to help nearly enough. This was something that *should* have been burned in one of those insidious fires that even today occasionally swept through these Gold Rush towns. In fact, the shelf was nearly as unattractive as the lamp she'd shipped home at the beginning of the week.

While Lynne wasn't opposed to antiques on principle and she enjoyed prowling around shops with friends, her own preference was almost always for clean, modern lines. Monty had hated fussy, old-fashioned furniture, and over their years together, his preferences had become Lynne's own.

Betsy's lamp. Lynne hadn't thought about it for days. By now it was safely at the Danforth residence in Floritas, and Lynne wondered if Betsy's husband had opened it. Jim Danforth's retirement after thirty years in the Navy hadn't done anything to ease or mellow his compulsive tidiness.

And then it hit her.

Whoever had come to Murmuring Pines seemed to have been *looking* for something. The first burglary, when Connie was injured and thrown down the hill, had featured what would have been petty theft but for the disappearance of Nikki's expensive shotgun. The rest of what had been stolen wasn't much: Betsy's funky earrings and CD player, and Susi's sixty bucks.

But somebody had come *back* then, and really torn the place apart, in a display that was childishly destructive. Or maybe angry? And why would anybody be angry enough to trash the possessions of a bunch of middle-aged schoolteachers, anyway?

Because something wasn't there?

"The lamp," Lynne told Betsy. "Your lamp that you shipped home. How carefully did you look at it before you sent it off?"

Betsy turned and frowned. "Not very. I packed it at the shipping place, wrapped it in bubble wrap, and put the shade in a second box so it wouldn't get smushed. But I was in kind of a hurry because we'd seen a place where we could rent some mountain bikes."

"Was there anything unusual about the lamp that you remember?"

The frown turned to a grin. "You mean other than that it was extremely unattractive?"

"Well, yeah," Lynne admitted.

"It was pretty heavy," Betsy said. "And it wasn't working, so it needed to be rewired. But I didn't examine it all that carefully. Once I realized it was like Grandma's lamp, I knew I'd get it no matter what. And the next morning, when everybody was so sick after eating Susi's brownies, I just wanted to get it boxed up and out of the way. Why?"

"Because I'm wondering if that lamp is what somebody was looking for. When Connie was hurt."

"The lamp?" Betsy's tone was incredulous. "Why on earth would anyone care about that lamp?"

"I don't know," Lynne admitted. "But think about this. Gold is really heavy, as we know from all these museums. That's why panning was such an efficient way to do placer mining, because the gold was heavier and everything else washed away. What if the lamp was actually made out of gold? Painted that kind of green-y bronze tone?"

"Oh, please," Betsy said. But she seemed to be thinking about it. "Although I suppose you could say that all the problems started after I shipped the lamp off, except that they really started when everybody ate the brownies Sunday night."

"But the brownies had nothing to do with anything," Lynne said, "other than Susi's students not liking her very much. Why don't you call Jim and have him take a look at it?"

"Sounds silly to me," Betsy said, "but I'll call when we get back to Columbia. Now, how about an ice cream cone?"

Chapter 21

Up until the very moment when she viewed herself in the freestanding full-length mirror in the corner of her hotel room, Judith wasn't sure whether her costume had been worth the effort.

Lisa had been fiddling with her wig and makeup for over half an hour and they had the air-conditioning in the room set to "Antarctica," but Judith was still hot and sweaty. The moustache was itchy and the pants on the borrowed suit were a little snug, but once she saw the results, Judith didn't care.

When she looked into the mirror, Mark Twain looked back at her.

Not the youthful Samuel Clemens who'd come west, arriving long after the Gold Rush had fizzled out, the young man who'd been fourteen years old in 1849 when the action all began. Clemens hadn't shown up in Nevada's Virginia City until 1862, when he started writing for the *Enterprise* and first used the pseudonym "Mark Twain." It was 1864, a full fifteen years after the Gold Rush began, before he made it to the remains of once-bustling Angels Camp and heard the jumping frog story that made his reputation.

No, Judith was the older, lecture-circuit

Mark Twain, the snowy-haired gent with the bushy white moustache and the impeccable white suit. Lisa, who'd dabbled intermittently with community theater as a kid and now assisted the junior high drama teacher with wardrobe and makeup, had done herself proud. As far as Judith could tell, she looked just like Hal Holbrook, and that was plenty good enough for her.

Lisa was waiting until the last minute to dress herself, in a provocatively torn dress with a long black wig and a noose dangling around her neck. She was coming as Juanita, the ill-fated Mexican girl who'd dared defy an American drunk in Downieville, assuring her place in history. Judith loved it that Lisa, who had a nice touch for the ironic detail, had actually researched effective knots for human execution in putting her costume together.

A knock on the door startled Judith. Lisa, still in denim shorts and a tank top, let in Mandy Mosher. They'd run into Mandy when they returned, and she'd confessed with no guilt whatsoever to having slept most of the day.

Now she looked refreshed for the first time in months, wearing blue denim overalls over her Argonauts T-shirt.

"I'm Levi Strauss," Mandy announced, "and one day just about everybody in the civilized world will want to get into my pants."

★ ★ ★

Amos was pretty sure he'd figured it out by now.

He'd spent most of the day hovering in the general vicinity of the Fallon, which was open to the public during the daytime hours when the ice cream parlor was open for business. He'd lingered over a butterscotch sundae, then spent some time sitting in the lobby reading, watching to see where the weaknesses were in hotel security. But it wasn't a lobby where you could blend in, just a cozy Victorian sitting room.

He'd been stopped when he started to go upstairs by a young woman who seemed to be a combination desk clerk/housekeeper, and at his statement that he wondered what the rooms were like up there, she'd broken out a key ring and shown him several in different price ranges. Since she showed him only unoccupied rooms, he had an excellent guide to which rooms he needed to check later. And he'd figured out which room belonged to the mother-daughter duo he'd seen on the balcony.

During the tour he'd also noticed a curtained-off linen area on the first floor where he could hide when they locked the building up.

He'd brought along a cordless keyhole saw that he intended to use to cut holes in the doors. Then he could reach through, open the locks, and let himself into the various rooms. His chatty friend at the desk had told him there were seven rooms occupied by a tour group, which required more holes than he'd hoped to drill. He wasn't sure how long the charge would last on the saw, and he certainly couldn't stop to recharge it for a few hours in the middle of his quest, so he'd brought along a manual version as well.

But maybe he'd get lucky on his first try, let himself into some room, and find the lamp sitting there in all its glory.

Yeah, sure. And there'd be a world champion figure skater leaning against his car when he slipped back out into the night.

But it could happen.

It *had* to happen.

He knew from the itinerary that the women were scheduled to be over in a private room having a fancy dinner at the City Hotel tonight, which meant they'd probably be gone for a couple of hours. That should be long enough for him to get into all their rooms if he had to.

And he'd better find the wretched lamp tonight, because if this failed, he had no idea what to do next.

As Lynne looked around the Argonauts assembled in the Fallon lobby, she felt the same charge of excitement that she had when she'd first begun researching possibilities for this trip. The Floritas teachers had done themselves proud, and the Gold Rush Characters Dinner was off to a smashing start.

Betsy had taken charge of the Characters Reception and was the official hostess. Betsy, who'd faced down Floritas rattlesnakes and Guamanian rat snakes and harbored no fear whatsoever of spiders, was dressed as Lola Montez, the mining camp entertainer whose specialty was a provocative "spider dance." She wore a flesh-colored bodysuit and a lot of diaphanous black webbing, with big black rubber Halloween spiders hanging all over her. She wore a curly dark wig and her makeup was definitely on the tarty side, with bright lipstick and rouge.

Betsy, pouring champagne at a small table near the door to the ice cream parlor, had mercifully not made good on her threat to serve Hangtown Fry for hors d'oeuvres. She'd set out brie and crackers instead. Lynne was relieved to have avoided Hangtown Fry, one of the nastiest-sounding native foods, though this was admittedly not an area noted for its cuisine. Hangtown Fry, named for Placerville during its heavy capital punishment phase, was made of eggs, tinned oysters, and bacon — items originally combined only because they were the most expensive ingredients available when a hungry miner struck it rich.

"If Susi wasn't already in the hospital,

seeing you covered in all those spiders would have sent her there with nervous prostration," Lynne told Betsy, accepting a glass of champagne. She looked Betsy up and down, noticing that her friend was downright foxy in this getup. "You're a knockout, my dear. Has Jim seen this outfit?"

"Oh yeah," Betsy said, grinning. "He liked it a *whole* lot. Hey, can you tell us now what Susi's costume was?"

Lynne nodded. "Lotta Crabtree. Your protégée, Lola. I packed up Susi's stuff to give to her husband and I found a cute little girlie costume in red, white, and blue hanging in her bathroom. Apparently Lotta did a lot of patriotic numbers when she visited mining camps."

"The precursor of the USO," Betsy said. "How perfect. Have you heard anything more about how Susi's doing?"

"Marianne just called the hospital a little while ago. She said they expect to release her in another day or two. When I had my appendix out, I was eleven, and they kept me in the hospital for a week. But times have changed. I guess they don't keep you in the hospital very long for an appendectomy these days."

"They don't like to keep you in the hospital very long for *anything* these days," Judith noted. She furrowed her brow, bringing her two bushy white Mark Twain eyebrows together. "I read not long ago about some places in the South where they were sending women home the same day they had radical mastectomies. I fully expect them to start doing drive-by bypass surgery before much longer. They'll send you home with an IV and a third-copy carbon of what to watch out for."

Marianne had been standing nearby, wearing jeans, boots, a long-sleeved shirt, and a leather vest. With a battered hat and a patch over one eye, she was Charley Parkhurst, the cross-dressing stagecoach driver. And she didn't look like somebody you'd want to mess with. "Rick told me that they'll actually keep her a little longer than usual, because she has such a long ride home."

"She's going to drive back?" Judith asked, furrowing her eyebrows again. "I'd think that would be extremely uncomfortable."

"For everybody in the car," Nikki added, joining the group.

Nikki had removed her mask, the flour sack with cut eyeholes that Black Bart had used to hide his identity from his victims, but the rest of her costume was impeccable: a long linen duster over an authentic nineteenth-century gentleman's suit. For the moment, she'd stashed the bedroll holding the axe used to break into stagecoach strong boxes over in a corner with the flour sack mask. The stolen shotgun would have made a more complete picture, perhaps, but this one was plenty good enough.

"Where'd you find that costume?" Lisa asked. She looked quite exotic as the luckless Juanita, in a long black wig and torn dress, with a disconcerting noose looped around her neck.

"A Western wear place up near Knott's Berry Farm," Nikki said. "I was actually thinking of having a costume made, because I'm a little smaller than most of the guys who wear this kind of thing, but I was able to find what I wanted without much trouble in children's sizes. Larry and I have been getting involved in Cowboy Action Shooting, and I figured I might as well get something I could keep wearing."

"Cowboy Action Shooting?" Lisa asked, frowning.

Nikki smiled. "Cross a Renaissance Faire with a Civil War reenactment and put it in the Old West. Cowboy Action Shooting's been around for maybe twenty-five years. It's basically just a shooting competition that uses guns from the second half of the nineteenth century. But folks get all dressed up in period costumes for the competition and it's a lot of fun."

"You take your kids?" Judith asked. Lynne could hear a faint echo of disapproval in her voice.

Nikki's eyes narrowed slightly. "Of course

345

we take our kids. It's a family type thing, Judith." She sighed. "This is exactly why I never mentioned anything about it before. I didn't want to have to try to explain and justify our private family activities."

"Whoa!" Now Judith looked and sounded angry. "I have to admit I was surprised and maybe a little taken aback when I realized that you'd brought a shotgun along on this trip, even without ammunition. And I also confess that I was initially startled when you were arrested. But I honestly don't think any of us are trying to pass judgment on you, Nikki. In fact, I suspect that the others are just as curious as I am about this Cowboy Action business."

"I know I am," Marianne told her. "In fact, I think it'd be kinda fun to join you sometime. My daughter wouldn't want anything to do with it, but I bet my son would love the whole idea. My boyfriend would probably find it a real turn-on" — she paused a moment and grinned — "though he finds just about anything a turn-on, actually. That's part of the problem with him. But I know it would thoroughly piss off my ex, who hates all guns. That alone would make it worthwhile for me."

Nikki smiled and the tense moment seemed to float away. "I'll hold you to that."

As Dame Shirley, Lynne wore a long royal blue mid-Victorian Era dress, borrowed from the community theater costume collection, which a friend coordinated. She wasn't accustomed to the flowing lengths of fabric, which even in this air-conditioned lobby were extremely warm, but she liked the sense of long ago and far away that the dress created. What she didn't have, however, was a wristwatch.

"Anybody know what time it is?" she asked.

Marianne reached into her vest pocket and pulled out a pocket watch. "Six forty-five."

"Then I think we ought to head over to the City Hotel," Lynne told everyone. "Our dinner reservation's at seven."

Amos had managed to slip into the back of the Fallon Hotel, where he had done everything possible to make himself comfortable in the corner of a curtained linen closet. He'd been squatting on the floor for hours now, waiting for the women to leave. Their cocktail hour seemed interminable, though he was fascinated by the notion of dressing up in cowboy clothes to shoot guns. Repellant as he found firearms in general, this seemed an intriguing idea and an appealing scenario. All that kept it from being genuinely exciting was his experience with Jed and Musk Man and the others, who were probably blowing up bunnies with that nutty woman's shotgun at this very minute.

When he finally heard the door close on the last of them, Amos waited a couple of minutes to be safe, then cautiously rose to his feet. He had a crick in his thigh and his foot had fallen asleep, so he took a moment to stretch and regain his balance. He tried to ignore the broken arm, which was starting to throb alarmingly. He'd deliberately avoided the Vicodin tonight so he could stay sharp, but he'd forgotten just how much a broken arm could hurt.

He'd given a lot of thought to where he ought to look first. He had a pretty good idea which rooms were occupied, based on the unoccupied ones the desk clerk had shown him earlier in the day. He hadn't, however, been able to determine which room belonged to the Danforth woman, the one who'd bought the lamp. And he still wasn't entirely sure which one she was.

Three of them had come out of rooms on the ground floor here, including one of the possible blondes, who'd been wearing a voluminous dress when she swept past his hiding place earlier. The younger woman in the bib overalls had been right across the hall from him, and she didn't seem to have a roommate, so he could probably skip that room or at least leave it till later. This meant the blonde was in one of the two farther down the hall.

When he'd finally gotten sensation back

into all his extremities, Amos crossed the hall and looked at the two possible doors. *Eeny meeny minie mo* seemed as good a method as any to pick his target, and when he'd settled on a door, he brought out the portable cordless keyhole saw and set to work.

Lynne looked around the City Hotel's private dining room at her fellow travelers, sipping at their French onion soup. There'd been some pretty talented chefs in some of the mining camps, according to Marianne, and they'd hauled in some extraordinarily expensive and exotic ingredients for the cost-is-no-object guys who struck it rich. But she doubted any of them had ever prepared a meal comparable to the one under way now. They almost certainly hadn't ever combined portabello, porcini, and shiitake mushrooms as a modern-day counterpart had done for tonight's vegetarian entrée. Though far from vegetarian, Lynne had ordered the mushroom dish herself without hesitation.

"You know," Lynne said, "everybody here picked fascinating characters, real people who were important at the time. But only Mark Twain and Levi Strauss are really known at all today."

"And the most famous folklore about me," Mandy/Levi said, "is just that. I always heard that Levi Strauss put the rivets in his pants so that they wouldn't rip when miners had heavy tools and gold nuggets and stuff in the pockets. But it turns out the rivets came a whole lot later."

"No matter," Marianne said. "Levi's are Levi's and the world is a better place for 'em. Though I wonder what Mr. Strauss would have had to say about the fad the kids have of wearing those huge baggy pants."

"He probably wouldn't have liked wasting the fabric," Betsy said. "Yards of it in every pair. And particularly not for what has to be one of the ugliest styles in all of history."

"Style?" Judith asked rather imperiously. "There are times when fashion has nothing whatsoever to do with style. And I'd include in that category any time underwear shows intentionally."

"Hear! hear!" Betsy raised a glass high.

Judith shuddered. "I always *really* hate it when girls show their bra straps. Particularly the younger ones, who don't have any business wearing bras in the first place. And I can't believe it when I get mothers in my office saying I should let their daughters dress that way. In elementary school."

"That's not as bad as the boys," Marianne said. "I've seen more boys' boxer shorts over the last few years than anyone should *ever* have to. Crotches hanging down around their knees and a big puddle of pantleg bunched up above their sneakers, reaching back and yanking their drawers up now and then just when they were about to fall off altogether. A perennial battle with gravity."

"I reckon they believed those pants were held in place by their massive genitalia," Nikki suggested.

"Yeah, right," Marianne answered. "When it was actually just the grace of God. And excuse me, but boxers are *not* that good looking."

Judith said, "I remember when my own daughter was a high school student, wearing boxers as outerwear."

"Mom, it was just like wearing lightweight cotton shorts," Lisa said, with no hint of rancor, even though it was immediately obvious that this was a disagreement that had never been satisfactorily resolved. "No big deal. Half the fun of it was that you hated it so much. But you know, as far as I'm concerned, the *real* tragedy of the elephant pants era is that high school boys have incredibly cute little butts. And in those pants, you couldn't even admire them."

"Lisa Jean!" Judith told her. "You're a teacher now. You're not allowed to admire student butts. It's sexual harassment."

"Nonsense. It's a job perk," Marianne said. "But I always think I'm the one being harassed, by people whose rear ends I *really* don't want to know anything about."

As everyone laughed, Lynne reached for her camera, then realized she'd left it back at the Fallon. She remembered setting it on a table in the lobby after shooting various group "portraits" in the serious old style of the nineteenth century.

"I think I forgot my camera at the hotel," she told them. "I'm going to run back and grab it. Don't any of you all eat my dinner. But don't wait for me if they bring more food before I get back."

As Lynne unlocked the door to the Fallon lobby, she was startled by a buzzing noise that abruptly ceased as she pushed open the door. Looking down the corridor toward her room, she saw a figure jump back and dart into a doorway.

"Hello?" Was this the night watchman, who hadn't revealed himself at all the previous night? And if so, what the devil was he doing? "Who's there?"

She walked down the hall and was startled to see a hole in the door to Marianne's room, with a little pile of sawdust and an oval piece of wood lying on the hall floor. She looked around, confused, then took another step to check on her own room, just beyond Marianne's.

Her door had the beginnings of a similar hole, right beside the knob, but the cut hadn't been completed.

Lynne had a sudden image of Connie Caravaci lying pale and unconscious at the bottom of the ravine at Murmuring Pines. Best to just get out of here fast and go for help. She turned, her long skirts swishing as she moved, and came face-to-face with a strange man. Without thinking, she let out a scream, just as he rushed toward her, his hand upraised, holding something she couldn't identify.

She sidestepped as he reached for her, and she realized as she moved that his left arm was in a sling. She had a fleeting memory of Marianne flipping the escaped convict onto the asphalt and wished she'd taken one of those self-defense courses that were always being recommended for women who live alone.

Too late now.

She slipped free of his grip and turned, moving as quickly as she could into the lobby, hampered by all her skirts and petticoats. He was right behind her and she looked around frantically for a weapon.

The empty champagne bottles stood on a table. She picked one up, turned, and smashed it across the man's raised right hand. He moved just in time to keep her from connecting, dropping whatever it was he'd been holding. Go for the vulnerability, she thought, and swung the bottle a second time, aiming at his left arm, held close to his chest in a sling.

She connected with a satisfying *thunk* and

the man let out a bloodcurdling wail of pain, collapsing into the green velveteen courting chair in the middle of the lobby.

Before she could stop to think about what she ought to do next, he raised his right hand and said, "I give up."

Still holding the champagne bottle as menacingly as she could manage, Lynne stepped back. He was a slight man, balding, utterly innocuous in appearance.

Tears were running down his face.

Chapter 22

"Who *are* you?" Lynne asked. "And what on earth were you doing?"

This meek little man didn't say a word. He didn't look like a criminal, either. Not like the young thugs so regularly featured on TV or in the movies, the kind of scary punks they'd encountered just yesterday in the parking lot of the John Marshall Gold Discovery Center. Not like the Cary Grant of *To Catch a Thief*, or the Jersey Mafioso of *The Sopranos*. This timid, seemingly terrified man might have been an accountant responsible for some massive embezzlement, the sort of fellow nobody ever suspects because they can't quite remember what he looks like.

He sat utterly still and said nothing.

"Don't even think about moving," Lynne told him. She glanced around the room, looking for some way to keep him from bolting. It wasn't realistic to expect to keep him in custody indefinitely, armed with nothing but a champagne bottle and dressed in about eighty yards of cotton. To her intense relief, she discovered Nikki had forgotten her rolled-up axe and flour-sack mask. A generous length of rope was tied around the axe bundle.

She offered a silent prayer of thanks that

this fellow hadn't discovered the axe, which would have made much shorter work of hotel room doors than whatever little buzzing thing he'd been using, and which would also have made him a far more dangerous adversary. She stepped over to Nikki's forgotten props and untied the rope.

She considered, then brought over a straight-backed chair with no arms, something almost too plain to be in this fussy little parlor.

"Sit on that chair," she ordered, wielding the champagne bottle menacingly. It made a nice weapon, sturdy enough to do some real damage without breaking. "Don't make me hit your arm again."

Without saying a word, pale eyes wide, the little man stood, walked three steps to the chair, and sat.

Still holding the champagne bottle at the ready, Lynne wrapped the rope around his body a couple of times and tied it behind the chair, then pulled the remaining length to the front and wrapped it tightly around both his feet before securing it to itself and the chair legs. She'd been afraid he might kick or try to get away, but the poor fellow was so scared he actually adjusted his legs to make it easier for her.

Now she backed over to the telephone and called the front desk. "This is Lynne Montgomery in the lobby of the Fallon," she announced, "and I've just caught somebody trying to break into our rooms. Could you call the police, please? . . . No, I don't know who it is . . . No, I don't know where your watchman is . . . Listen, I'm here alone with this guy, could you please stop talking and send me some help?" She hung up.

The man was watching her with an almost detached curiosity, and he no longer seemed to be crying.

"Is it the lamp?" she asked now, and his widened eyes gave her the answer. "You've been following us around, haven't you, trying to get it back?"

Nobody'd read him his rights, but he seemed aware that he could remain silent, and he did so.

"Well, I can't imagine why you'd want it," Lynne went on, "but it isn't even here anymore. And a really wonderful woman is dead up in Nevada City because you hit her over the head and threw her down the hill."

He gave a strangled sound, then spoke softly, with his chin tucked down into his chest, not making eye contact. "I never touched her."

"Yeah, right." Lynne was starting to get angry now. "She smacked herself in the head with that gold-painted rock and then decided to roll down and see what was in the bottom of the ravine. She's dead, you know. And you're responsible. I'm not a lawyer or anything, but my son's a cop and I seem to remember him saying that if you commit a murder in the course of another felony, like robbery, that makes it a capital case."

"I never touched her," he repeated. "I never even saw her."

"Oh, please. Do you expect me to believe that?"

He hesitated, seemed ready to say something, and was interrupted when the door swung open. A park ranger entered with weapon drawn, and close on his heels came Betsy Danforth, dressed as Lola Montez, dangling spiders.

"What on earth?" Betsy said as she pushed herself into the room. "I realized I'd brought your camera, Lynne. But what —"

"Please step out of the way, ma'am," the ranger told Betsy. He seemed unfazed by their costumes as he surveyed the room and spoke briefly into a radio. Then he turned to Lynne. "Now what's going on here?"

"I found this man trying to break into my room here," Lynne said, "and I know he's looking for an old lamp that my friend here" — she indicated Betsy — "bought at an antique shop on our way up here last Sunday." She briefly explained about the broken fan belt and Connie Caravaci and Murmuring Pines. The ranger radioed, listened, then radioed again, asking that Nevada County sheriffs be notified immediately.

"So you've been trying to find my lamp?" Betsy told the man. "Well, I hate to tell you, but I shipped it home Monday morning."

He closed his eyes and said nothing.

Betsy turned to Lynne. "I left a message for Jim last night after we talked about this. Maybe it's time to call him again."

"I could call David," Lynne suggested, "and he could pick it up from your house and bring it to the police station. They could look at it there and figure out whether it's full of gold bullion or what."

"Before you ladies do anything more," the ranger told them, looking at the trussed figure in the middle of the parlor, "let's figure out what we have going on here, all right?"

The door opened again and the rest of the Argonauts rushed into the room, all in full costume. "They told us you'd called for police," Judith explained, "so we knew we had to come help."

"What the —" The ranger was starting to look nervous. "People, I'm going to have to ask you all to leave."

Judith Limone drew herself to her full height. "We are residents in this hotel," she told him, "and I believe we're entitled to an explanation." She seemed to have forgotten she was dressed as Mark Twain.

The ranger noticed however. "Ma'am, sir, whoever you are, whatever you're doing, you need to step outside right now."

"We're in the middle of dinner, actually," Lynne told him. She turned to the group. "Guys, I'd love to tell you more, but this fellow doesn't have much to say. He's the one who's been following us, trying to get that lamp that Betsy bought on the way up here when the van broke down."

"But how would he even know I had it?" Betsy asked. "I've never seen him before in my life."

"I'm guessing it was his shop," Lynne said. "And that was probably his daughter who waited on us that day."

"No!" The involuntary exclamation from the formerly silent man startled everyone, including him.

Lynne looked at him curiously. "But it *was* your shop, wasn't it?"

He closed his eyes, and the period of communication seemed over.

"Right now, we don't even know what his name is," Lynne said, "and it's going to take a while for anyone to get down here from Nevada County. So maybe we ought to just go back and finish dinner. But I *am* going to call my son David and have him go get that fool lamp out of Betsy's house and take it into custody, so to speak."

"I told them at the restaurant to hold everything till we got back," Judith said. "But I do believe you're right, Lynne." She turned to the ranger. "We'll be over at the City Hotel when you need us."

From the look on the ranger's face, he hoped that would be never. But he nodded. "I'll keep that in mind. Mrs. Montgomery, you'll need to stay until the sheriff arrives. Enjoy your dinner, ladies." He glanced at Judith and Marianne. "And gentlemen."

Lynne's son David called four hours later, on Nikki's super satellite cell phone. By then the man in the parlor had been identified as Amos Ledbetter and taken away, evidence technicians had examined the damage to the doors, and the hotel had been cleared for the Argonauts to reenter. Mandy had gone to bed and most of the rest of them had been drinking a lot of wine. Dinner had more than lived up to its advance billing, even with the unforeseen delays.

But everybody was too wired to go to bed just yet.

"I have permission to tell you this," David said, "from Detective McMasters. He said you've earned the right to know. *Earned the right to know.* Mom, just what have you been up to, anyway?"

"Oh, nothing," Lynne answered, giving David's own favorite response to the same question, asked hundreds of times during his youth and adolescence.

"Well, that's not exactly what he told me,

but we'll talk about that later, okay?"

Lynne laughed. She was one of the ones who'd been drinking a lot of wine, a benefit of having the fancy dinner two blocks away in a town with no vehicular traffic. She realized in a moment of wine-fueled revelation that something about her son being a cop, a legitimate authority figure, had shifted the mother-son axis. David now considered it his obligation and responsibility to keep his poor addled mother out of trouble.

If he only knew.

"David, don't keep us in suspense here. What was in the lamp?"

"Well, it was a very deadly little lamp, Mom. The thing had been entirely gutted and it was packed solid with armor-piercing nine-millimeter handgun bullets."

"With *what?*" The little man hadn't said another word once the ranger arrived. But nothing about him suggested somebody who'd be trafficking in armaments.

"The kind of bullets that are illegal, Mom, because they can go through body armor. They're made out of hardened brass and coated with Teflon. These particular ones were hand-loaded, probably because it hasn't been legal for private citizens to possess them since 1986. Only law enforcement officers are allowed to have them. And you'd better tell Betsy she isn't likely to see that lamp again for a long time."

"Hold on a minute," Lynne told him. "Let me tell the others."

She passed on the information, watching the faces of her old and new friends. Most intrigued by the information was Nikki, which wasn't surprising when you considered that she had pretty effectively outed herself in the past couple of days as a modern-day Annie Oakley.

"Bad, bad stuff," Nikki said. "Who was it for?"

"I don't know," Lynne said. "I'll ask."

But David didn't know, or if he did, he wasn't saying. Cops were like that.

Amos Ledbetter kept an attorney on retainer, to review contracts and answer the occasional oddball question arising out of the provenance of various acquisitions. That attorney made it immediately clear that Amos needed somebody else to navigate the legal morass he had wandered into via the well-trod path of rationalization. The attorney suggested several names, hedging on a recommendation until Amos asked him irritably whom he'd hire if his own wife or son got into trouble. Then he named a name, cautioning that the criminal lawyer was likely to be expensive.

"Cost is no object," Amos told him, noting dispassionately that he'd waited nearly an entire lifetime to make that statement. And that when he did get to make it, it wasn't for some splendid rarity, but rather in hopes of getting out of jail. So far Amos's jail experience had nothing to recommend it. "Would you call him for me? And tell him to hurry up, because I've been trying to explain myself here, and I'm having trouble getting anybody to believe me."

"Amos, listen very carefully," his attorney said. "Keep your mouth shut. No matter what you may have already said, *do not say another word* until you have a lawyer at your side. Officer Friendly is not there to help you. Do you understand?"

With a sinking heart, Amos agreed to be silent. He filled that silence trying to remember just what he had already told the police, who had actually been quite nice to him once he got out of Columbia and was transported up to Nevada City. He'd been interviewed by the detective he'd seen on TV, a fellow named McMasters, and had pretty much spilled his guts trying to talk his way out of everything.

Well, none of it *was* his fault. And he couldn't have stopped what happened to that poor woman because he wasn't there when it happened.

He'd explained that he'd been searching another cabin altogether, using the pass key Musk Man had picked up from behind the counter in the Murmuring Pines office, when he heard a loud crash outdoors, went to the window, and saw the unconscious body of Connie Caravaci rolling down the hillside below him. Horrified, he'd run to join Musk Man, finding his companion wiping the floor in an open cabin, whistling cheerfully after finding a shotgun in the closet.

"Not a substitute for the lamp," Musk Man had told him, "but a nice little party favor anyway."

Amos didn't want to think what kind of party. By then he knew that the lamp wasn't in any of the cabins or tents the women were using. Musk Man insisted, however, that he go back into the cabins anyway, and pilfer a few small items to enhance the appearance of a burglary. Musk Man had nothing to say about what had happened in the cabin before Amos saw the woman rolling down the hill, and Amos hadn't dared to push the subject.

Surely the police would understand that Amos had nothing to do with hurting that woman. And he was also out of the gunrunning business, since he obviously wasn't going to be very effective as a courier anymore.

The down side of this, he was starting to realize, was that he wouldn't be able to safely return to his shop, either, not until all of the smugglers were in jail. Since Amos had no idea who they were, this could take a good long while.

He decided that the very first subject he'd bring up with his new lawyer would be the Witness Protection Program.

Chapter 23

In the morning, Lynne woke with a bit of a hangover and a partially drilled hole in her hotel room door.

The events of the previous night came rushing back and she thought of that odd, pathetic-looking little man, and of armor-piercing handgun ammo, and of Connie Caravaci. She'd thought of Connie a lot last night, every time she looked at Marianne's Charley Parkhurst costume and remembered Connie saying that was who she would have been at the Notable Characters Dinner.

Marianne had also confessed a certain sadness for the same reason, and they'd both wondered about Connie's children, and what would become of Murmuring Pines. Lynne had noticed a tone of wistfulness, and she wondered if Marianne might actually take the plunge, cash out her Southern California real estate, and bring her kids up here to start a new life. She could see Marianne running Murmuring Pines quite easily, though that difficult, custody-seeking ex-husband of hers would probably fight the move.

Lynne took her time showering and getting dressed. She passed through the Fallon parlor, which held no signs of the previous night's activities. Even the straight-backed chair she'd tied Amos Ledbetter to was gone, along with the champagne bottle weapons and Nikki's prop axe.

She arrived in the ice cream parlor for the tail end of breakfast. Nikki had been out running, and sat straddle-legged on a chair drinking out of a water bottle, discussing the upcoming cave expedition with Marianne. Most of the Argonauts were planning a late morning visit to the nearby Moaning Cavern, which offered the opportunity to rappel 180 feet in darkness, down to the cave floor. For some reason, Marianne and Nikki found this prospect appealing, and had even brought along their own rock-climbing equipment.

"I'm almost afraid to ask, but does anybody have any news?" Lynne asked as she brought a slice of quiche and a blueberry muffin to one of the small tables, where Judith sat under a black-and-white photograph of a typical mining town, with rows of ramshackle huts and tents and a few scragglylooking fellows posing with pickaxes. Judith's hair was back in its trademark braid, but there was a red streak across her upper lip where her moustache had been applied.

"I don't think so," Judith answered.

"That looks sore," Lynne told her, running her finger across her own upper lip.

"It is. I should have tried it before the actual night. But if I had, I might have been tempted not to do it again last night. So it worked out okay. I did it once and it was at the right time. How often in life do you get to say that?" Judith smiled. "Not nearly often enough. And I did love wearing that costume."

"You should do it again for the Halloween Carnival," Betsy suggested from a nearby table.

Judith laughed. "I can't do that. First of all, very few of the kids would have any idea who I was supposed to be. Probably more of them would guess Colonel Sanders than Mark Twain. But more important, I have to maintain my image. There's only one Halloween costume for me, I'm afraid."

They all laughed appreciatively. Principal Judith Limone invariably attended the Pettigrew Elementary Halloween Carnival as a splendidly regal witch.

"So, who's going caving?" Lynne asked.

As of yesterday, Mandy and Betsy had both announced their intention of staying behind today and exploring Columbia, maybe going up to the schoolhouse on the north end of town that all of them had so far managed to avoid. Had Susi still been part of the group, she most likely would have remained behind with them, but arranging Susi's activities was no longer Lynne's job. She allowed herself a small private smile.

"I was thinking I'd go by the hospital and see Susi before Mandy and I take in the sights," said Betsy, who'd always possessed an uncanny knack for reading Lynne's mind. "No dark underground spaces for me, thank you very much."

"She'll want the whole story," Marianne warned, "and she'll be mad as a hornet that she missed all the excitement."

"You make it sound so appealing," Betsy told her, and everyone laughed.

Moaning Cavern was out in the middle of nowhere, which probably made sense, Lynne thought. Caves in the movies always featured photogenic entryways behind bushes on hillsides, but she'd taken geology a long time ago and knew that anywhere you had the right combination of minerals and dripping water, you could have a cavern below the surface of the earth.

Archaeologists and spelunkers had, in fact, found a fair amount of ancient human remains, mostly children, down in Moaning Cavern, a fact she'd learned researching area caves before the trip. That wasn't something this group of dedicated elementary teachers would want to hear about, even though there was no evidence to suggest ritual sacrifices, just childish carelessness. Kids exploring a hole in the ground wouldn't stop to think that the earth might fall away into nothingness just ahead, after all. And with semi-nomadic native tribes moving through the area, the opportunity for repeated catastrophe increased.

Inside the frame building that sat atop the cave opening, they learned that a tour would be starting in about fifteen minutes. The rappelers had a choice: go down at the beginning of the tour or wait until the rest of the Argonauts had walked down the 238 steps. Nikki and Marianne signed waivers allowing them to use their own rock-climbing equipment that they'd brought along, while Lisa planned to use the equipment available on site. All decided they'd rather wait to go down until Lynne and Judith could be there to provide an appreciative audience.

Lynne and Judith finally set off down the stairs, leaving the rappelers to peruse the gift shop.

Lynne hadn't expected to be so challenged by what was, after all, just a stairwell. But it was a difficult stairwell, barely eighteen inches wide, starting off with long straight stretches of steep wooden steps. These stairs reminded Lynne of the Anne Frank House and a canal-front hotel where she'd once stayed in Amsterdam. Except, of course, that the steep stairways in Amsterdam didn't have damp limestone formations jutting out into them.

Betsy had been right to skip this tour, Lynne thought. This was not an experience for the claustrophobic.

When they reached the bottom of the wooden steps, they entered a spiral staircase. The guide had told them before they started out that this was the first example of arc welding on the West Coast and that the stairway was essentially one single piece of metal because of the welds. Lynne chose not to think about metal fatigue.

It was no longer accurate, however, to call this Moaning Cavern. The guide had also explained that the characteristic whistling moans which had given Moaning Cavern its name were gone forever. The installation of the staircase had altered the acoustics, silencing the cavern. In addition, plugging the top by sticking a gift shop over the entrance had pretty effectively ended any occasional random whistling. Even without the "moaning" however, the cave was still impressive.

The cave was made from calcite water dripping, and its formations were mostly calcium carbonate. Though touted as colorful, this cavern was limited to Southwestern earth tones, browns and golds and terra cottas. Iron in the dripping water had formed certain darker formations, such as the Chocolate Waterfall cascading in stone down one enormous wall. For the most part, though, the formations Lynne could see on her downward trek were almost fabric-like, and indeed were called "ribbons" and "draperies." Nearly all were in light shades. Not until they neared the bottom could she see any of the more traditional stalagmites and stalactites.

It was interesting enough, but overall Lynne didn't enjoy the experience much, and she half wished she'd stayed back in Columbia with Betsy.

Marianne was ready.

She'd put on her rock-climbing harness, adjusting the straps just a trifle, then donned her hard hat and leather-palmed gloves. She probably should have worn long pants, she thought too late, because she was likely to bump into the rock walls during the first narrow dark section of the underground chimney. Oh well.

The guide who was helping them was a friendly young man. "It'll be totally dark in the first part," he cautioned them, "so don't panic. As soon as you get past the narrow chimney, the cavern opens out and there'll be lights down there where your friends are waiting on the platforms."

"We land on a platform?" Nikki asked.

The guide shook his head. "You land out beyond the platform, and George down below will haul your ropes over to the platform. Couldn't be simpler."

Nikki went first, swinging out over the opening with tremendous grace, then dropping abruptly out of sight. When she was reported safely at the bottom, Lisa positioned herself and clamped her gear onto the ropes.

Lisa screamed as she went down, a good-natured, amusement park thrill ride kind of scream. That enthusiasm boded well for Marianne's own ride, and now, finally it was her turn. She swung out over the opening, braced herself, and pushed off, beginning her descent.

She moved first into sheer darkness.

Then, moments into her descent, Marianne felt her chest tightening, closing up, constricting as if she were being squeezed by a giant anaconda. No air was entering her lungs. Nothing. She fought panic, was vaguely aware of passing through the narrow chimney, then coming out into light just as she realized she was about to lose consciousness. She tried to cry for help but couldn't get a sound out. She tried to wrap her arms around the rope.

By the time she swung free in the lighted cavern, everything had gone fuzzy on her.

Lynne watched Nikki come down first, waving one arm like a hard-hatted rodeo bronco rider. She jumped onto the platform where they all waited anxiously.

"Dynamite!" she announced with a glorious grin. "I may just have to do that a couple more times." At almost fifty bucks a trip — and a mighty short trip at that — this was an indulgence that only Nikki could really afford.

Lisa followed, shrieking all the way down. Lynne glanced at Judith, who clenched the railing as she watched her only child descend by rope into a central cavern large enough to hold the Statue of Liberty. At the bottom, Lisa had a bit of trouble swinging over onto the platform, but once there looked absolutely delighted with herself. "That was better than Magic Mountain," she announced.

The rope started to move again. Lynne turned to watch Marianne, then gasped in horror as the woman swung from side to side, her head lolling back, her hands falling away from the rope and dangling at her sides.

The guide was over the fence instantly, reaching out and grabbing the ropes, hauling her toward the platform. Nikki scrambled over behind him, leaning toward the semiconscious woman, grabbing her shoulders.

"What is it, Marianne?" Nikki asked urgently. "What happened?"

"C-c-c-c-a-a-n-t-t b-r-e-e-e-e —" The effort seemed to be exhausting her. She moved her head slowly, looking for something. "B-e-e-e-e-s-s-s-t-t-t —"

"Beast?" Judith said in confusion.

But Lynne was already reaching for Marianne's fanny pack, which she'd strapped around her own waist so Marianne would be less encumbered on her descent. "She wants the bee sting kit, I think." She turned to Marianne, forcing herself to remain calm. "Is that it? Did you get stung somehow? Are you in anaphylactic shock again?"

Marianne managed a weak nod, then lapsed out of consciousness as the guide and Nikki helped lift her over the chain link fence onto the platform into Judith and Lisa's waiting arms. Lynne dug frantically in the fanny pack, pulling out the bright red bee sting kit.

Lynne snapped open the plastic case. Inside were a small loaded syringe, four antihistamine pills in a sealed plastic pouch, a green string, and an alcohol prep pad. She fumbled to get the direction sheet opened, then took a deep breath to calm herself before proceeding. The syringe held enough epinephrine for two injections, it seemed.

Lynne removed the guard from the needle, wiped Marianne's thigh with the alcohol pad, hesitated a moment, then jabbed in the needle and depressed the plunger.

She realized, when nothing happened at first, that she'd been expecting an immediate miracle. Judith reached for the pack and Lynne passed it to her, watching out of the corner of her eye as the principal read the instructions and looked at Marianne, frowning.

"We can give her a second injection if there's no improvement," Judith said.

By now the guide had called back upstairs and another limber young employee had appeared, not even winded from the mad dash down all those steep stairs. "What's happening? Can we get her upstairs?"

George, the guide who'd walked down with Lynne and Judith, shook his head. "Not until she's stabilized. She'd never be able to manage the stairs." Unspoken was the fact that Marianne Gordon was not a small woman. Moving her without her assistance would be a serious challenge.

Lynne was watching Marianne closely, waiting for some sign of recovery.

Nothing.

"Y'all must have some kind of rescue plan," Nikki said. "What would you do if somebody had a heart attack down here?"

The guides looked at one another. "There's a basket," George said after a moment. "Kind of a cross between a chair and a gurney. If we have to, we can haul her up on the ropes that way. The stairway's too narrow."

Marianne's breathing was so shallow it almost wasn't happening at all. She'd lost color and her hands were cold.

"She's not better," Lynne said. "In fact, she looks worse to me."

Judith looked at her watch. "I'd say she

needs the second shot. I'll do it if you'd rather not, Lynne."

Lynne shook her head. "That's all right." She adjusted the syringe for the second shot, held it in front of her, and sniffed. Something was odd.

The syringe smelled like peanuts.

Lynne had no idea what epinephrine was supposed to smell like, but she was fairly sure that it wouldn't be peanuts. Peanuts were, in fact, one of the things that Marianne was deadly allergic to.

Lynne turned to George. "There's something wrong with this bee sting kit. We need another one. Like instantly."

George started to argue.

Judith turned to him. "Right now," she told him crisply. "Don't you have a first aid kit down here?"

He nodded. "But not with a bee sting kit. We're two hundred feet below ground here. There aren't any bees down here."

"But you've got one upstairs?"

He nodded.

"Then get it down here, *now.*"

Lynne looked at Marianne. The light in the cave was odd to begin with, but the unconscious woman's color seemed to be worsening and she barely seemed to breathe.

George was on his walkie-talkie again. "We need the bee sting kit down here, right away. Yeah, I know. She already — listen, just do it!"

Lynne turned toward the stairway, waiting to hear footfalls as somebody raced down to them, but she got a major surprise. With a minor whoop from above, a young woman rappelled down the ropes. She was at their side, swinging over the fence, in less than a minute. She pulled the kit out of a pocket and held it uncertainly.

Lynne snatched it away from her. There wasn't any time to worry about manners. Marianne was dying.

She ripped open the pack, identical to the one she'd just used, repeated the same procedures. This time she didn't bother with the alcohol pad, just jabbed the needle into the woman's thigh and held her breath, readying the syringe to administer the second dose.

Marianne moaned.

"Give her the second shot," Judith ordered. "I know it says to wait ten minutes, but I don't think we have ten minutes, particularly if . . ." The possibility that the other bee sting kit had been tampered with hung over them. Judith was right. Time was crucial.

Lynne got the syringe ready, held it over Marianne's thigh, took a deep breath, and plunged the needle in.

They stood around her unconscious form, holding a collecting breath. Nikki had her hand on Marianne's shoulder, rubbing and massaging without even noticing what she was doing.

Then Marianne moaned again, and stirred. A few moments later, she opened her eyes.

"Wha—"

"Don't try to talk," Nikki told her as the others let out a cheer that reverberated through the cavern.

It might not moan anymore, but under the proper circumstances, this cavern still knew how to holler.

Getting Marianne back above ground proved a serious challenge, and eventually they strapped her into the basket and hauled it up. By then she was feeling better enough to protest, but only mildly.

"I'm not going to let you try to walk up those stairs," Judith told her. Judith seemed to have forgotten that she wasn't Marianne's principal, but nobody was going to remind her otherwise.

"Guess not," Marianne conceded, and the fact that she did it without a fuss was significant all by itself.

Before loading her into the gurney/basket, Nikki had undone Marianne's rock-climbing harness and set it aside. As Lynne gathered it to carry back upstairs, she watched Marianne climbing into the basket.

"What's that?" Lynne leaned forward and pointed to a reddish smear on Marianne's shorts. "Is that blood?"

Everyone leaned in.

"She probably just scraped herself," Lisa said.

"Look under the fabric," Lynne told Nikki.

Nikki looked at Lynne, frowning, then pushed the loose khaki leg of Marianne's shorts upward. Just about where the tiny blood smear had been was a round raised welt the size of a golf ball.

"Give me the harness," Nikki said, her voice like flint.

Lynne handed it over and Nikki stepped into the best light, turning it over and inspecting the webbing. "Aha!"

"What?" Judith moved in for a better view.

"There's a . . . it looks like some kind of a tack," Nikki said. "It's worked into the webbing so you can't see it easily. And it's located where it would poke through somebody's skin when they pushed off and dropped all their weight into the harness." She pulled it close to her nose and sniffed. "It smells like peanuts."

"Why, that son of a bitch!" Marianne's voice was low and weak, but there was no mistaking the anger in her tone. "Mark tried to kill me."

Epilogue

Labor Day Weekend, Sunday, 4 p.m.

Lynne looked contentedly around her patio. It was barely two months since the Highway 49 Revisited tour, but she felt as if she'd known all these women forever.

She'd gotten up before sunrise to start the coals to smoke a small turkey, a bird that was now reduced to brittle bones and its smoke-blackened skin. The cats had eaten their own turkey scraps, reward for vigilance in guarding the smoking bird against predators. They now lay sprawled in the sunny part of the yard, in front of a vibrant bed of dahlias, zinnias, and white marigolds, backed by pale creamy sunflowers. The yard was looking mighty nice this summer.

"You won't believe what UPS brought me the other day," Betsy announced, pushing back her plate.

She got up and moved to a back corner of the patio where a pale green bed sheet covered something about three feet tall on a rolling cart. A neat little sign was pinned to the bed sheet: NO PEEKING. THIS MEANS YOU. While everyone had noticed and remarked upon the covered object, Lynne didn't think that anybody had actually peeked. Teachers tended to play by the rules, or at least by most of them.

Now Betsy positioned the cart so everyone could see it. She whipped off the sheet with a flourish. "Ta da!"

There stood an ugly Victorian lamp with a large bronze metal base and a complicated fringe shade.

"Is that 'the lamp'?" Lisa Limone asked. She'd just returned from a ten-day rafting trip down the Colorado River, with a deep tan and a new boyfriend who worked for Heal the Bay up in Los Angeles. "You know, I never did get to see the darn thing. Betsy shipped it off too quickly."

"Well, this isn't *the* lamp," Betsy said. "That one's in federal custody and I'm told I'll probably never see it again. But it's exactly the same, except of course that it isn't full of armor-piercing ammunition. Which means it's also exactly the same as the one my grandparents owned, which is the only reason I wanted the fool thing in the first place."

Judith frowned. She looked totally relaxed, despite an earlier statement that she'd already been contacted by two-dozen parents unhappy with their children's classroom assignments. This included the parents of the notorious Tarantino twins, who were distressed that neither of their darlings was in Mrs. Betsy Danforth's class.

"Then where did you get it?" Judith asked.

Betsy grinned. "It was shipped to me by a dealer on eBay, along with a note saying that it was offered as an apology. When I got in touch with the dealer, he wouldn't tell me any more. But since the government isn't big on apologies, I assume it came from Amos Ledbetter. Who also credited my Visa account about a month ago with the full price I paid for the first lamp. So in a sense, it was absolutely free."

Nikki Mason cocked her head in appraisal. "And worth every penny, I'd say. Dang if that thing isn't ugly!"

The others laughed. In two more days they'd be back at work. All had returned last week to their various Floritas classrooms, getting ready for the new school year that started Tuesday.

Judith turned serious. "What's going to happen to him? The antiques dealer?"

"I asked my son David," Lynne said, "and he got in touch with somebody at the Bureau of Alcohol, Tobacco and Firearms, the folks who ended up handling the arms-smuggling case. David has a bit of an 'in' with them because he was the one who picked up the lamp from Betsy's husband and found the bullets in the first place. Since Amos Ledbetter cooperated with the government in setting up a sting with the original lamp, they've dropped most of the charges against him. Contingent, of course, on his testimony against the other men who've been arrested for arms smuggling, and against the man who killed Connie Caravaci. David said the federal agents were so vague that he figures once Ledbetter finishes testifying in the Nevada City murder trial, he'll just quietly disappear."

"Oh?" Nikki said. "What, are they turning him over to the Corleones and the Sopranos?"

Everybody laughed.

"No, not disappear the mob way," Lynne hastily clarified. "The government way. They'll get him a new identity somewhere."

"I can't say I'm altogether sorry to hear that," Betsy said. "He certainly messed up our tour, but there was something so forlorn about him that I think being arrested and publicly humiliated is probably punishment enough. He looked so pathetic, sitting all trussed up in the Fallon lobby with that broken arm."

"Well, I have no sympathy whatsoever," Susi Braun put in.

Susi had lost fifteen pounds and had confided earlier (in a public announcement) that she was having Botox injections to get rid of her wrinkles. She wore a cute little sundress that Lynne had seen at Nordstrom last week, marked down to $250. Nobody had heard another word about the philandering Mr.

Braun's indiscretions.

"That man knew the difference between right and wrong," Susi went on. "When he made his bed, he knew he might have to lie in it. If you can't do the time, you shouldn't do the crime."

Lynne wondered briefly how Susi would grade a student English assignment as riddled with clichés as this speech.

Marianne said, "I think it's a question of intent, Susi. He didn't actively intend to harm anybody. Which is more than you can say for whoever gave you those laxative brownies, and certainly a lot more than you can say about my wretched ex-husband."

"Are they going to be able to make the attempted murder charges stick?" Mandy Mosher asked. *Her* little sundress had probably come from Target, was cuter than Susi's, and fell in graceful folds across her gently bulging tummy. "I was afraid to bring it up before now, since it's kind of a touchy subject."

Marianne laughed. "Touchy doesn't begin to cover it. But Mark actually left a ridiculous amount of evidence, once we knew to look for it. Once he knew I was going on our trip, he started pumping the kids for details about the plans, so he could figure out how to do it. The object was to get me into anaphylactic shock any way possible, knowing that then I'd use the bee sting kit, which he'd altered by replacing the epinephrine with peanut extract. They were both clear liquids, and I think he figured that the bee sting kit would just be thrown away as my lifeless body was rushed off in an ambulance."

"How could he be so sure you'd use the rock-climbing harness?" Mandy asked.

"He couldn't," Marianne said. "He couldn't be sure of anything, really, but that's just the sort of gamble that would appeal to him. And I guess he figured the stakes were high enough to justify the risk. We always carried insurance that would pay off the mortgage if either of us died. With me gone, he'd have clear title to a house he could un-load for twice what we paid for it originally."

"Not to mention no child support pay-ments," Nikki added.

"Indeed," Marianne agreed. "What's scary is how close it came to working if Lynne hadn't smelled the peanuts in the fake epi-nephrine. And he'd hedged his bets by also replacing the oil in my Vitamin E oil gelcaps with peanut oil. He sucked out the vitamin oil with a syringe and then injected the peanut oil."

"Which is why that oil was absolutely worthless for preventing scarring when I rubbed it into my toes," Susi said. Trust her to work the conversation back to her favorite topic, *The Susi Braun Story.*

Lynne stole a glance at Susi's toes,

showcased in a pair of flimsy sandals that were probably even more expensive than her dress. There were no visible scars. Maybe she'd had her toes Botoxed too. "If Marianne had taken one of those pills instead of giving them all to you, Susi, she'd also have gone into anaphylactic shock and used the syringe."

"It didn't matter to Mark how it happened," Marianne said. "Just that it would happen. And that it would happen while he was five hundred miles away, hawking hot tubs at the San Diego County fair."

"And of course you might actually have been stung on the trip," Betsy said. "You were outdoors almost all the time."

"Quite true," Marianne said. "And if I had been stung, I'd have reached right for the bee sting kit. He was even laying the groundwork by telling Curt and Briana how irresponsible I was to go off into the wilderness where I might get stung and die."

"The slime," Betsy muttered.

"Oh yeah. I think he was counting on me being outside far away from help, or alone taking my vitamins, or down in the cave — which his computer history showed he'd researched, by the way. That's how he got the idea to boobytrap my rock-climbing gear. And why he kept asking the kids if I'd been to the cave yet."

"How are your kids doing with all this?"

Mandy asked. "I think it'd be really horrible to learn that your father tried to kill your mother."

"It'd be a lot worse to learn that your father actually *did* kill your mother," Nikki pointed out. She and Marianne had arrived together, talking about a Western fair with cowboy action shooting that was coming up in October.

Marianne nodded. "Quite true. And I think they'll be just fine." She turned to Lisa. "Briana's in your village, Lisa, so you'll have the full brunt of her adolescent charm. I hate puberty."

"Funny, the rest of us think it's really great," Judith said. "And I'll keep a close eye on Curt for you, too. I put him in Bob McCormick's class so he'd have a good male role model while all this is going on."

"And I thank you," Marianne said. "The thing that makes me a little nervous is that Mark and I still own the house in joint tenancy, and it's still worth a ridiculous amount of money, and the insurance policy that pays off the mortgage if one of us dies is still in effect. I can't believe that he'd try anything more, but he *is* out on bail —"

"If he harms one little red curl on your head," Nikki vowed, "I promise you that I'll hunt him down like a dog."

Marianne grinned. "I feel better already."

"Oops, I almost forgot." Susi reached down

into her Kate Spade bag and pulled out a little box wrapped in gold foil. "I was rushed into surgery before I could give the award for solving the gold country crossword puzzle, and after that I never did get any more completed puzzles from anyone."

"I don't think we were deliberately being slackers," Lynne said mildly. "We were kind of busy there for a while."

"Whatever." Susi handed the box to Betsy. "Congratulations. You were the first to finish and had all the answers correct."

Betsy took the box. "Geeze, first the lamp and now this. I'm having quite a week here." She opened the box, peeked in, and smiled in delight. "This is absolutely perfect, Susi. Thanks so much!"

Betsy turned the open box so everyone could see its contents.

It held a pair of small gold nugget earrings.

As Lynne looked around the circle of women who had become her friends under such stressful circumstances, she realized just how much she'd enjoyed the trip. What was that bumper sticker the Minnesotans had on their RV? She smiled as she remembered: TEACHERS DO IT WITH CLASS.

Gold Country Crossword Solution

Across

1. Country of origin for most 49ers (US)
4. River where first gold was found (American)
9. Dame Shirley's husband's occupation (MD)
12. Seeing the __ (elephant)
15. *By the Great Horned Spoon* author, first name (Sid)
16. __ Pacific Railroad (Union)
17. __ Hopkins, merchant turned hotelier (Mark)
18. What Jenny Wimmer boiled in lye (gold)
19. __ Rock, site of first English graffiti (Independence)
23. At center of vigilante seal (eye)
24. Transcontinental one finished 1869 (RR)
25. Copper bit used in Strauss's canvas pants (rivet)
26. Assayman in Nevada City (Ott)
27. Lola's stage makeup (rouge)
29. Judge who ruled against hydraulic mining, 1884 (Sawyer)
30. Major strike (bonanza)
32. Tri-branched mining river (Yuba)
34. Bar in cradle, etc. to catch gold (riffle)

35. First gold found in fish "soup" (Downieville)
39. __ Valley, site of Empire Mine (Grass)
41. Killer stretch in Nevada on overland route (Humboldt)
43. Visitor to Roaring Camp (baby)
45. Periodic table name for gold (Au)
46. Sixty __, potent liquor (rod)
47. Fort and mill owner (Sutter)
48. Rock containing minerals (ore)
49. Tom __, doctor turned gambler turned robber (Bell)
50. Loose rough dirt (grit)
52. Nickname for goldseekers (Argonauts)
54. __ Camp, site of formal battles (Chinese)
55. Mining method using water (placer)
56. Long __, 12-foot mining trough (tom)
57. Disease on overland trail (cholera)
58. __ Angeles (Los)
60. Business partner to Wells (Fargo)
61. Leland __, grocer (Stanford)
64. Group fighting in 54-Across (tong)
66. Dugout canoe used to cross isthmus (bungo)
68. Hydraulic mining diggins (Malakoff)
70. Heavenly camp (Angels)
72. Town started by Irish brothers (Murphys)
75. Periodic table iron name (Fe)
77. Dire straits for sailors (Magellan)
80. First miner in Quartz, married

a Donner (App)
81. Donner __, snowbound site (Pass)
83. Rich __, Dame Shirley's home (Bar)
84. Chinese Golden Mountain (Gum Shan)
87. Gem of the Southern Mines
    (Columbia)
88. Type of weight for gold (troy)
89. Nickname for Jamestown (Jimtown)
90. Spider Dance performer (Lola)
91. Scratches out a living (ekes)
93. __ Dorado (El)
94. Rock found with gold (quartz)
96. Most common mining town meat
    (pork)
102. Used to fight bulls (grizzly bear)
103. Charley Parkhurst's pronoun (she)
104. Odd Fellows abbr. (IOOF)
105. Type of gold (flake)
106. Dandy mining camp reporter (Bret)
107. Inclined water trough (flume)
108. Black Bart's specialty (robbery)

Down
2. Search for (seek)
3. Placerville wheelbarrow maker
   (Studebaker)
5. "Nozzle" in hydraulic mining (monitor)
6. Rare formal pathway (road)
7. Less glamorous mineral (copper)
8. Hottest hour for mining (noon)
9. Common animal transport (mule)

10. Forty-__ (niner)
11. Bandit Murietta (Joaquin)
13. Used to lead 9-Down (halter)
14. General mining lifestyle (misery)
20. Name for mining town (Diggins)
21. Rock the __, mining tool (cradle)
22. Original name of North Bloomfield (Humbug)
28. Rough __ Ready (and)
31. Enticement to go west (ad)
32. Original name of San Francisco (Yerba Buena)
33. __ Trees Calaveras Park (Big)
36. Condition of placer miner (wet)
37. Honorific for Louise Clappe (Dame)
38. Filled Marysville Streets before 1884 ruling (mud)
40. Forty-niners' expectations (nuggets)
41. Typical miner abode (hovel)
42. Author of first report of finding gold (Bigler)
43. Spread word of gold through SF newspaper, *The Star* (Brannan)
44. Revolutionized trousers (Levi Strauss)
48. Tinned ingredient in 74-Down (oyster)
51. __ Grande (Oro)
52. SF theater (American)
53. Mining town milk source (goat)
55. Lucy Whipple's specialty (pie)
57. Shopkeeper turned railroad tycoon (Crocker)
58. __ tom, mining tool (long)

59. Staging town for northern mines (Sacramento)
61. Series of attached riffle boxes with continuous water flow (sluice)
62. Shortcut country for sailing Argonauts (Panama)
63. Yan __, Chinese Camp tong (Wo)
65. Emigrant __ (Gap)
67. Fellows in IOOF (Odd)
69. Scourge of mining towns (fire)
71. Assent in Sonora (si)
72. Disease contracted crossing 62-Down (malaria)
73. Jewelry formed from gold (ring)
74. Luxury dish cooked in Placerville, 2 words (Hangtown Fry)
75. Avian river (Feather)
76. Preferred over alcohol by Chinese (opium)
78. Ran Placerville meat market (Armour)
79. __ Toy, Cantonese prostitute in SF (Ah)
82. Mining town dame (Shirley)
85. Indian tribe (Miwok)
86. First woman hanged in California (Juanita)
92. Mindset of 49ers on arrival (eager)
94. Chinese pigtail (queue)
95. __ Mountain overlooks Jamestown (Table)
97. Formerly Spanish Corral (Ophir)
98. Turns ore into coins (mint)

99. Unit of gold measurement, abbr. (oz)
100. __ Hill, site of Chilean and French wars (Mok)
101. Mother __ (lode)

Gold Country Crossword Puzzle

created by Susi Braun
with some help from Emily Toll

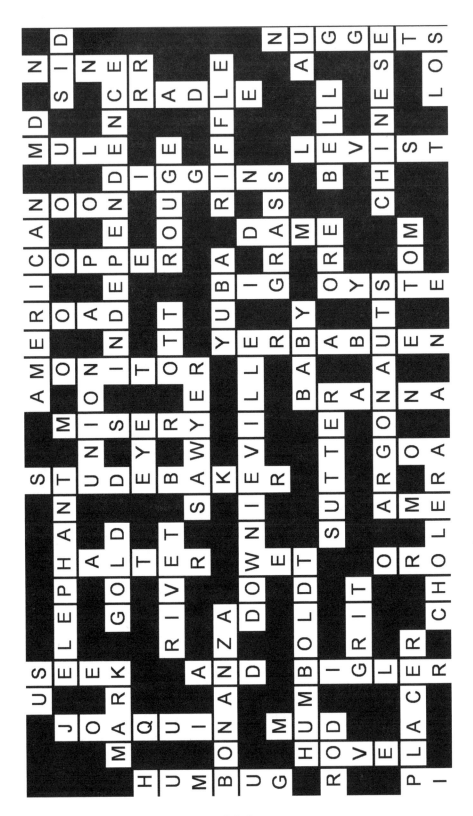

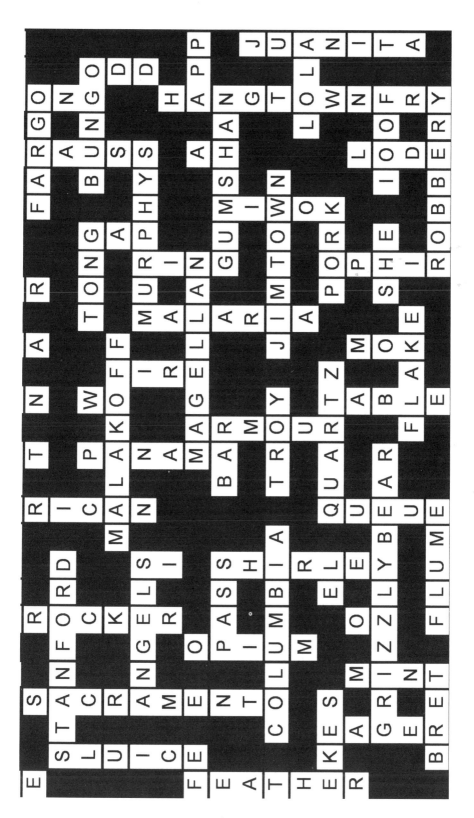